Praise for the
Award Winning

THE ALIEN SKILL SERIES

Readers' Favorite Book Awards 2021
GOLD MEDAL WINNER - Category Preteen

Wishing Shelf Book Awards 2019-2020
SILVER MEDAL WINNER - Category
Teenagers

Feathered Quill Book Awards 2021
FINALIST - Category Young Readers.

IAN Book of the Year Awards 2020
FINALIST - Category Juvenile.

Reviews:

"An extremely timely message for today's readers."

"Solid aliens-crash-to-earth tale."

"One of the best series I have read."

BOOKS BY RAE KNIGHTLY

Prequel
The Great War of the Kins
Subscribe at: www.raeknightly.com

THE ALIEN SKILL SERIES

Ben Archer and the Cosmic Fall, Book 1
https://www.amazon.com/dp/1989605192

Ben Archer and the Alien Skill, Book 2
https://www.amazon.com/dp/1989605095

Ben Archer and the Moon Paradox, Book 3
https://www.amazon.com/dp/1989605141

Ben Archer and the World Beyond, Book 4
https://www.amazon.com/dp/1989605044

Ben Archer and the Star Rider, Book 5
https://www.amazon.com/dp/1989605176

Ben Archer and the Toreq Son, Book 6
https://www.amazon.com/dp/1989605214

The Knowledge Seeker
https://www.amazon.com/dp/1989605311

THE
KNOWLEDGE
SEEKER

"Knowledge must belong to all, or to none."
Eodain Atheneumson

Rae Knightly

THE KNOWLEDGE SEEKER
Copyright © 2021 by Rae Knightly.

For information, go to:
www.raeknightly.com

Cover design by PINTADO
Book Formatting by Derek Murphy @Creativindie
Published by PoCo Publishers
ISBN Paperback: 978-1-989605-31-8

First Edition: November 2021

For the Enlightened People.

CONTENTS

PROLOGUE

The woman hums as she cradles the infant in her arms. The young child sighs contentedly, closing his lids over big, grey eyes as the song lulls him to sleep.

> *"Twinkle, twinkle little star,*
> *How I wonder what you are.*
> *Up above the world so high,*
> *Like a diamond in the sky.*
> *Twinkle, twinkle little star,*
> *How I wonder what you are."*

(Lullaby from the Enlightened Era, circa, 1850)

CHAPTER 1 *The Coming of Dust*

My heart sinks as I watch the enemy approach. Tens of thousands of marching boots raise thick clouds of dust, obscuring the afternoon sun, which scorches the desert plains. Already, the advance troops are hammering away at our defensive wall, which is all that separates this vengeful invader from the hill on which I stand. Once the Roarim breach the wall and take over the City of Eliadys, there will be little hope for us up on the hill.

A sharp pain shoots from my left hand up my arm. I stifle a wince and rub the place where, six years ago, the Roarim cut off my ring finger. The ghostly jab is like a warning of the suffering to come: the enemy will be upon us within a few hours, sowing death and destruction in their path. And all we can do for now is wait and watch from up high as the bulk of our troops try to keep the enemy out for as long as they can.

The faint sound of creaking leather makes me glance sideways. Uncle Denesius's hand is clenched so hard around his leather scabbard that his knuckles have turned white. His tall frame towers beside me—stoic and commanding—and his gaze is set on the horizon. A gust of hot wind lifts his burgundy cape, the edge of it brushing against the back of my throbbing hand. The woolen fabric feels rough and used against my skin.

Poor Uncle Denesius! Did he really think the Roarim would lie low after he defeated the head of their army six years ago? Did he not foresee that a new leader would take his place? Unless the rumors are true...

I hesitate, but need to know. "Uncle," I say in a low voice, so the soldiers positioned along the fortifications before us do not overhear. "Do you think the Wraith Lord is out there?"

A vein in Uncle Denesius's temple throbs, and I instinctively know I should not have asked that question.

"There are no such things as wraiths, Termite!" he snaps, turning hard eyes toward me. "I already told you that!"

My cheeks burn. His harsh words bother me because I suspect his anger is hiding fear. It is not good for a leader to go into battle like this. But the Grand Protector of the Atheneum fears nothing, or does he?

There are no such things as wraiths...

A troop of Knowledge Seekers rushes to join their companions, lining up along the fortifications that surround the hill and the Atheneum. Their burgundy capes flow, and their greatswords gleam in the sharp sunlight. I take comfort in the sight of them. These men will fight to the death to protect the Atheneum and what lies within.

I do not have such a cape, so I close my right hand over the pommel of my curved sword, which is smaller and thinner than the traditional Seeker blade. It is all I have to offer. "We will defeat them again, Uncle," I venture, deciding to ignore his anger. "You led us to victory before, and you will do so again."

Uncle Denesius does not answer right away, but when he does, his words chill me to the bone. "No, boy," he says, his voice cold. "Not this time."

One of the Seekers turns to glance at us, his eyes wide. He is only two years younger than me. I know this because he was Anointed yesterday when he turned fourteen. He received his official name—Odwin Atheneumson—, his own Talisman, his greatsword, and a brand new Seeker cape, which hangs down his stiff back. Its burgundy color is rich and full.

The young orphan glances at Uncle Denesius, perhaps waiting for a comforting gesture or a reassuring word. When he receives none, he pulls the cape closer around his shoulders and turns to face the army swarming beyond the wall.

A torrid wind picks up, bringing with it the sounds of thumping feet, grinding carts, and sharp metal. Battering rams thud against the defensive wall, the violent sound reverberating through the air all the way up the hill, and, each time, I feel as though I am being punched in the gut. Hundreds of our archers fight bravely from atop the defensive wall, sending volleys of arrows at the enemy, but, really, they look like tiny ants facing a storm.

Frantic screams from fleeing citizens rise from the jumble of low structures and narrow, dusty roads of Eliadys. Families and elderly people hurry out of their clay homes—homes that had to be rebuilt after the last attack—and their disorganized escape jams the messy streets.

I rub my hand. Is this it, then? Will the City of Eliadys fall? Will the Roarim steal the Knowledge contained in the Atheneum tonight? Silently, I calculate the date according to the calendar of the Enlightened People: today is June 7th, 2613.

Will this be a day of triumph or disaster?

The afternoon sun beats down on my neck. It is the type of heat that prickles your skin when you sweat because it mingles with the incoming dust and sand.

"It is no accident that they have chosen this day to attack," Uncle Denesius says. "They know that we held the Anointing yesterday and that the Knowledge Seekers are home from their travels. They have us all in one place, like sitting ducks."

I stare at him.

He rubs his thick, trimmed beard, then looks down at me. "I must speak to you in the Council Room," he says. Without waiting for an answer, he turns and strides towards the Atheneum with a couple of guards in tow, leaving a familiar smell of tobacco behind him.

My heart leaps. So he has not given up after all. And he has summoned me to the Council Room, even though I am not yet a Knowledge Seeker. It is an honor and a privilege to serve the one who has saved us multiple times from the attacks of the Roarim.

I gather my senses, wondering what Uncle Denesius will request of me. He has a plan, no doubt—a plan to save the City of Eliadys, the Atheneum, and its priceless contents.

I adjust the strap of my scabbard that holds my sword and head off to follow my uncle.

"Psst! Termite!"

The whispering voice makes me halt.

Odwin Atheneumson glances at me. Sweat covers his brow. "Is it true, what Uncle Denesius said? That we have no hope?"

I catch my breath. The youth is searching for the reassurance he did not get from our uncle. "There is always hope, Odwin," I say. "You know Uncle Denesius. He will find a way to defeat the Roarim. He always does."

Odwin blinks rapidly.

Clearly, I did not convince him. "Just... stay close to the other Seekers and do what they do," I add. "You will be fine."

He takes a deep breath, nods, and takes his position again.

I bite my lip, realizing I was of little comfort.

Uncle Denesius has almost reached a side entrance to the Atheneum. He never runs, yet his entourage is always sprinting after him. He stops and barks orders at some Senior Seekers running along the fortifications nearby.

I walk rapidly, spurred on by a sense of extreme urgency. Yet, I do not run. It might look like I am panicking.

I shield my eyes against the falling dust and lift my head to take in the massive Atheneum. The solid structure has survived the harsh passage of time, providing unquestionable proof as to the might of the Enlightened People. The Atheneum is said to be a smaller replica of an important building up north, called the Capitol, but it was destroyed in the Final Wars.

My throat constricts. Will the Atheneum still stand tomorrow, at sunrise?

The veil of dust reaches the dome, which crowns the Atheneum building, and hazes out its four superimposed layers of narrow windows and solar panels. It is said that the original dome, made from ironwork bolted together, collapsed a century ago, crushing many priceless Books under its weight. Lacking the knowledge to rebuild the dome with the same techniques, a group of Knowledge Seekers turned to ceramic tiles, and their craftsmanship can still be appreciated today.

A sudden heaviness grasps me. The Library sits under that dome, and the Books contained in it are more precious than a thousand of our lifetimes. They transcend my lifespan and must survive at all costs. I understand the consequences. Each and every Knowledge Seeker will give their life to protect it. And so will I, even if I am not yet one of them.

Uncle Denesius has already disappeared through the door.

I rush after him, but something catches my boot. I trip and fall flat on my stomach. The wind is knocked out of me.

"Ready to scamper, bookbug?"

The mocking voice makes me tense. I glance up at the Seeker, who is peering down at me, head half-turned.

Roddrick!

Roddrick pulls in the leg that tripped me. He always double-checks that the Grand Protector is absent before striking.

I pick myself from the ground, rubbing my scraped chin.

"Let him scamper, Roddrick," another Seeker says. "Perhaps he will hide under our uncle's cape. In any case, his flimsy dagger will be of no use to us here."

My blood boils. "It is *not* a dagger!"

Roddrick sneers.

It takes all my willpower to ignore them and continue. I focus on the door that Uncle Denesius used a moment ago and raise my maimed hand to shove it open.

"Watch those fingers!" Roddrick yells after me,

sending a brief snicker among the Seekers nearest to him.

I enter the coolness of the corridor; the heavy door sliding closed behind me. I shut my eyes and breathe too fast. It is not my fault if I am not yet a Seeker. It is not my fault if I have not yet received a greatsword.

Before I can stop myself, I slam the wall with my open hand, welcoming the sharp blow that travels up my arm to my shoulder.

Roddrick's words have hit their mark. My left hand stings. All these years and the missing digit still hurts.

A ghost pain...

A ghost pain inflicted by a ghost lord.

I shudder and push the thought out of my mind. The missing finger will not define me. I will not let it. I try to focus through my anger, and a realization makes me open my eyes. It is me the Grand Protector has summoned. Not Roddrick.

Roddrick does not know.

A puff of air escapes through my mouth. I may not be a Seeker yet, but whatever it is that Uncle Denesius wants me to do, Roddrick is not part of it.

A troop of soldiers rushes past me, forcing me to flatten myself against the wall. The fresh marble calms the throbbing in my hand. I focus on the smooth surface as I advance deeper down the corridor, letting the usual thoughts push out the troubling ones. These walls speak to me. They tell me of ancient times: when men and women lived in opulence among green forests and rich soils, when tables were laden with food, when technology was readily available, and Knowledge was shared as if it were as abundant as the dust outside.

Proof of the might of the Enlightened People is all around me. It is in the bones of the architecture of the Atheneum from the delicate stone decorations ornamenting the ceilings in the great halls to the faded solar panels on the rooftops that still provide us with electricity after five centuries of use.

The corridor leads into a massive, square hall behind the main entrance, where my boots sound hollow on the light pink and beige mosaics. I avoid looking at the Library doors at the end of the hall, which soldiers are barricading with heavy logs. This is not a time to be mulling over what happened there, the last time the Roarim came.

I clamber up a wide, marble staircase that leads to the Council Room. I find the door half-open, and I see Uncle Denesius standing upright behind his antique XXIst century desk, giving orders to some Senior Seekers who almost knock me over as they rush out.

"Come in, Termite," he says, waving me in impatiently.

I hurry inside.

"Close the door," he instructs two guards. "Do not interrupt me under any circumstance!"

The guards bow and head out of the Council Room at once.

I swallow. Is this meeting more important than the battle outside, then?

A movement to my right makes me aware of two other figures within the room. It is Thoron, Uncle Denesius's guardsman, and the giant, Draxis, with his huge hammer nestled in his hands. I eye Thoron, never knowing what to expect of the silent, devoted man. But Draxis? Well, Draxis is Draxis, and his presence calms me somewhat.

Still, this is an unusual assembly.

A sudden, dull explosion rattles the floor on which I stand. Great, rumbling sounds follow, and the light coming from the towering window at the end of the office dims. I turn towards it to find thick, orange dust swirling outside.

"The defensive wall!" I breathe.

"Eodain!" Uncle Denesius calls, snapping me to attention. He has used my real name, not the one I hate: *Termite...*

"Yes, Grand Protector," I reply at once.

"Do you trust me?"

"Of course, Uncle." *Does he need to ask?*

Uncle Denesius's brown eyes are penetrating. "You will do my bidding," he says.

"Yes, Grand Protector."

He pauses, and a horrible doubt creeps into my mind.

"Eodain," he says. "You will flee the Atheneum."

CHAPTER 2 *The Knowledge Seeker*

I must look like a fish. I have never seen a fish, except in the Books. But like the fish, my mouth opens, closes, and opens again. I stare at Uncle Denesius, at Thoron, at Draxis, then back toward Uncle Denesius.

I must have misunderstood.

The door swings open behind me. "Grand Protector," a nervous guard blurts out. "The defensive w—"

"I KNOW!" Uncle Denesius bellows. "GET OUT!"

The door shuts.

My heart beats loudly in my chest. "Uncle?" I breathe. My head is spinning. What is happening? Shouldn't we be rushing outside to assess the situation?

Uncle Denesius takes in a deep breath, never taking his eyes off me. "You heard me, boy." He says, restraining his voice. "You will flee the Atheneum. Thoron and Draxis will accompany you. You will use the tunnels below us—you know which ones I mean. You will escape into the mountains and get as far away as possible from this place. You will not turn back. You will not falter. You will do this for me, your Grand Protector."

My arms drop to my sides. *Ready to scamper, bookbug?* Roddrick's words tumble around in my mind. Did Roddrick know about this after all?

This was not the kind of mission I was expecting. I was expecting something heroic, something worthy of mention in the Books.

I shake my head. "No, Uncle. You cannot send me away with Thoron like last time. I am sixteen. I can fight now." I stop, briefly thinking about the Roarim soldiers who must be barging through the broken fortified wall right now, then add boldly, "Wraith Lord or not; I am not afraid."

Uncle Denesius's fist smashes into the desk so hard that it sends his pipe spinning in the air. It shatters into pieces on the ground. "Enough! You, of all people, should know better! There *is* no Wraith Lord! People do not come back from the dead! You saw me slay Lord Erawan,"—he jabs his index finger at me, then at Thoron—"and you. He is dead and buried. Get this foolish superstition out of your heads. I will not hear of it again."

Uncle Denesius leans his hands against the side of the desk and lowers his head between his arms.

I want to kick myself for bringing up the Wraith Lord again, but I cannot help it. Why will he not even discuss the rumor? There must be a logical explanation.

"Uncle," I venture. "Please do not send me away. I am not leaving you. There is no question in my mind. You know I would never abandon you, or the Atheneum, or the Books. I want to stand and fight!"

Slowly, Uncle Denesius lifts his head again. I can tell he is struggling to contain himself. "You do not understand yet, little Termite. The Atheneum will fall. The Roarim will steal the Books. The Knowledge of the Enlightened Era is at risk. The Roarim cannot be allowed to be the sole masters of such power. I cannot let that happen." He straightens, an inner fire lighting his eyes with determination. "Come forth, Termite."

I glance questioningly at Thoron and Draxis, but they have not moved an inch. I step around the desk and stand before Uncle Denesius with the usual awe and careful respect that his presence evokes.

He looks at me—really looks at me—then reaches up and lifts an object from his neck. He passes a light chain over his head and presents the object dangling at the end of it to me.

"My Talisman," he says, as if I did not know. "It is yours now." He slips the chain over my head. The small technetium memory device drops down to my chest, feeling heavier than it actually is.

I frown as I look at it, then at Uncle Denesius. A heavy silence passes between us as I come to realize the implications of this gesture. I shake my head. "No," I whisper. "I cannot accept this. It is not mine..."

"It is yours," Uncle Denesius interrupts me. "I have added your fingerprint from our database to it. It answers only to you now."

"But..." I stammer. "I am not yet a Knowledge Seeker! I have no right to a Talisman—least of all yours!"

A strange smile creeps onto Uncle Denesius's face. "Ah, but you are. Did you not speak the words of Anointing below the Great Dome?"

My face goes blank for an instant; then, I grasp what he means. "Are you referring to the time you caught me sneaking into the Library? But I was only eight! That was just pretense—a child's game."

"Still," Uncle Denesius says in a low voice. "You spoke the words of Anointing. You even made the Sacred Pledge: if a Talisman falls into enemy hands, the Knowledge Seeker must take his own life so that the Talisman cannot be accessed. Lose one, and the other is forfeit. The Pledge ensures that the Seeker understands the burden of his nomination, and remains true to it above all else. You have always been a Knowledge Seeker. It is what you were born to be. There is no need for peer approval. You have mine, and that should be enough."

Uncle Denesius rests a firm hand on my shoulder. "You are a Knowledge Seeker. From now on, you shall be known as Eodain Atheneumson, son of the Library, protector of the Books, wielder of the Talisman."

I am stunned. He speaks of fleeing when I should be fighting; he speaks of making me a Knowledge Seeker, when he could have made me one yesterday, at the Anointing, along with Odwin Atheneumson... And he gives me his own Talisman!

For Spirit's sake! No one will ever believe me!

"But... Uncle..."

I break off at the sound of running feet outside the office. I hear distant war cries and horns blowing.

Uncle Denesius bends down and closes his arms around me in a hug. The smell of tobacco caught in his Seeker cape fills my nostrils. I think he is saying goodbye, but now, he whispers in my ear, "I want you to take the Talisman to the place of which only you and I know."

I freeze in his embrace.

He waits.

My mind whirls. I know exactly what he is referring to. Now I understand. But the task is mind-boggling. I wanted a heroic quest, but I may have gotten more than I bargained for.

"I am counting on you," Uncle Denesius whispers. He waits until I nod into his shoulder, then straightens and looks at me intensely.

All my life, Uncle Denesius has been my rock and my mentor. He is the father I never had. I will do anything to make him proud. "I understand, Uncle," I say, because one does not say 'no' to the Grand Protector, even if the request is insane. "But you must come with me. Together, we have a greater chance of succeeding."

He shakes his head. "I cannot abandon my men. I must stay and lead the fight. I will hold the Roarim off for as long as I can."

My stomach squeezes. *He is buying me time to escape...*

Uncle Denesius's voice is gentle. "All these years, I did not make you a Seeker because I was afraid of losing you. But of all the Seekers, you are the one who best understands the value of the contents of the Talisman. That is why I am giving it to you. I believe in you, Eodain Atheneumson. I know you will succeed."

My heart bulges. I would do anything for him. Roddrick always said I was the favorite of all the orphans, that the Grand Protector treated me like his son, hence Roddrick's hatred for me. Now I think he may have been right.

Ready to scamper, bookbug?

I lift the Talisman and glance at the small, rectangular shape. This tiny, harmless-looking thing— an advanced memory storage device from the past—is used to keep all the Knowledge contained in the Library. It contains Knowledge from the Enlightened People, with precise instructions on how they lived, how they made electricity, how they communicated with one another through satellites, how they traveled long distances with the help of machines... It is all in there. Knowledge worth fighting for, worth killing for. Knowledge that has brought a blood-thirsty army to our doorstep.

A shallow boom shakes the floor. The window rattles.

"Go on, then," Uncle Denesius says without emotion.

I realize that this is goodbye.

I am not ready!

"Uncle..." I breathe. I feel an urge to say something profound but am unable to say more. Saying goodbye would mean accepting that we may never see each other again.

But Uncle Denesius is focused on something happening behind me. I turn and catch Thoron giving him a small nod, as if an unspoken conversation had just taken place between them, and I understand that Thoron must have received his own set of instructions before I arrived.

More booming noises.

Draxis lifts his mighty hammer to rest it on one shoulder and approaches me.

I do not want to say goodbye to Uncle Denesius! How can we be parting? There are so many things left unsaid between us. I have so many questions. There is so much Knowledge to discuss.

Draxis pulls at my arm.

"Wait," I say weakly, torn between staying and obeying my orders.

I keep my eyes on my uncle as I back away.

He stands before his desk, tall and powerful. His eyes are closed as he prepares for what he knows must come.

Thoron opens a secret passage hidden in the wall. He turns and bows at his master, even though the Grand Protector is not looking at us.

"Wai—"

Another blast, and this time the huge office window crashes inward, thrusting glass in all directions.

"Uncle!" I scream as Thoron shoves me into the passage.

Then, the door shuts, and Uncle Denesius is gone forever.

CHAPTER 3 *The Library*

My mind is in turmoil.

Thoron lights a torch, and the flame illuminates the corridor. At the end of it are winding stairs that go deep into the hill under the Atheneum.

"Wait!" I repeat. "We need to help him! He might be hurt!"

"No time," Thoron replies, heading down, as the shaft shakes from a distant explosion.

Draxis is so big he barely fits into the narrow stairs, making any attempt to return nearly impossible. All it takes is for his gigantic hand to wrap around my arm, and he is half-carrying, half-shoving me down the steps.

After a long descent, we find ourselves in an underground vault with columns connected by arches made of brown bricks. Rows of wooden tables and chairs are laden with ancient electronic devices—leftovers from the past. Lights on some of the computers flicker as they are fed by the electricity from the solar panels, but they are fragile and few. I know this because I have spent countless hours studying them, trying to figure out how they work, while marveling at the ingenuity of the Enlightened People. It is said that each person owned multiple devices with access to all the knowledge available to humanity, right there, at arm's-reach.

And now, all this could be lost to the Roarim.

We rush to the left, away from the electronic devices and towards four gaping tunnels in the far wall. I know each and every tunnel like the back of my hand. I have traveled them many times with Uncle Denesius and other times on my own, breaking several rules in the process. *Rules are only broken if one gets caught.* That was my motto.

The tunnel on the left would take me up to the Library itself, while the two in the middle lead to dead ends after many exhausting and confusing twists and turns. Thoron is entering the last one to the right, which I know leads to a terrible maze of tunnels, only one of which takes the daring adventurer outside. One wrong turn and the tunnel will become our grave.

I haven't had a minute to process anything. I am fleeing when I should be fighting. I have the Grand Protector's Talisman when I should have earned my own. I am heading down dark tunnels like a rat when I should be up on the fortifications, protecting the Atheneum.

But Uncle Denesius has given me a direct order, one that supersedes any mixed thoughts I may have.

Take the Talisman to the place only you and I know of.

I fend off a shudder. No one has ever attempted what he asked of me. "Hold on!" I yell, freezing in my tracks. Draxis almost topples me over as he bumps into me.

Thoron reappears from the tunnel, holding a burning torch as he looks at me. His eyes narrow. "We need to go," he says.

"Just—hold on a minute." I whirl to face Draxis, daring him to hurry me on. I need to feel I have some sort of control. My giant friend is an easier target than Thoron, simply because he is my friend.

Draxis lowers his gaze.

I am being unfair. I should be focusing on Thoron, but if I glared at the guardsman like this, he would simply shrug and move on. Uncle Denesius has chosen my companions well. I realize that arguing with them will get me nowhere. I need to be smarter about this.

Dull bangs and shouts echo down into the vault from the distant battle.

"Eodain," Thoron urges, and I know my window of action is closing fast. It strikes me that he is using my real name. Just this morning, he was still calling me *Termite*.

"Wait," I insist. "We cannot just leave like this. The way through the tunnel is long. It could take us a full night to reach the other side. We need more torches. We need water, provisions, knives, and…"

Thoron waves the torch inside the tunnel, and I notice bulks on the ground.

Satchels and backpacks!

The escape was planned! Someone prepared the items beforehand and left them here for us to find. Goosebumps rise on my arms.

Uncle Denesius!

Since when had he foreseen this? How long had he been planning this escape?

"Good," I utter because Thoron is looking at me impatiently. "Then that leaves us with one more thing."

Thoron does not move, but a glint in his eyes tells

me he is curious.

Uncle Denesius made me a Knowledge Seeker. Now we will see if my companions respect my new position. I hold my breath, then plunge headlong: "I must go to the Library," I say.

Thoron snorts and turns around. He has had enough.

My pulse quickens. "Just wait, would you?"

Thoron glances back at me and growls, "What now?"

"There is a Book..." I say, as calmly as possible. "...in the Library. I must take it with me. It must not fall into the hands of the Roarim."

Thoron looks at me without conviction.

I only have one chance at this... I stay eye-level with him, then add, "It is a Book about the Sky Spirits."

I hit the nail on the head.

Thoron raises an eyebrow. He is stronger than me and by far a better swordsman. He isn't Uncle Denesius's guardsman for nothing. But what he has in strength, he lacks in Knowledge. Contrary to the Knowledge Seekers, Thoron is from the city. He is illiterate, like the rest of the people there. He still believes in folktales and legends about the Enlightened Ones. He believes in Sky Spirits. *Heck, he probably believes in the Wraith Lord himself.*

"This Book cannot fall into the hands of the Roarim," I repeat. "The Grand Protector has said it over and over: the Roarim may take over the Atheneum, but they must not be allowed to control the Sky Spirits. You know this as well as I do."

Thoron glances at Draxis, probably to give himself a moment to think rather than to look for approval from the giant. I have caught him in a dilemma. Clearly, his orders are to get me out of here, but he also knows about the power of the Sky Spirits.

He sets his jaw and gives the tiniest of nods. "We must not delay," he says.

I nod back. So, it would seem I am in charge, even if he does not like it. It would make sense since I am now supposed to be a Knowledge Seeker, but I will need some time to get used to it. I fear saying more will make him backtrack, so I remain silent.

Thoron lifts the torch in front of himself and heads for the first tunnel. Before long, we are climbing a new set of stairs, similar to the other one, but this time my heart beats so fast I think it may burst out of my chest. I am going to the Library—maybe for the last time. The muscles of my legs hurt from so many stairs, but I press along, pushed on by the violent sounds of war and a terrible urgency that I might be too late to see that sacred place again.

We finally reach a narrow landing and come face-to-face with a white-washed wall. A rectangular slit indicates the location of a hidden door.

Thoron unsheathes his sword and signals for us to be quiet. Slowly, he lifts the latch, and the secret door sways outward. Thoron sticks his head through it to check the room. Then he pulls back, nods at us, and we slip through the door after him.

By now, my legs are shaking, not only from the climb but also because the fear of losing this place is too overwhelming.

Beyond the closed door is a bookshelf, making the secret exit invisible to the untrained eye. The familiar smell of musty air fills my nostrils, and I welcome it. It is the smell of the Books: thousands and thousands of ancient Books, gathered over the past centuries by the Knowledge Seekers, who searched the ruins of the cities of the Enlightened People. They are stacked on endless bookshelves after having been meticulously restored, bound, and classified according to a theme. The walls are filled with them. Some Books are thick and complete; others are in rags, carefully pasted together and placed in new protective jackets. I have spent hours watching and helping the Seekers repair them. Many have images, though the colors have faded. Still, they have provided my knowledge-hungry brain with endless hours of wonder. *How could it be that such an enlightened era could have come to an end?*

A brief darkness passes over the massive Library, set under the jaw-dropping dome. The darkness comes from a particularly thick cloud of dust that billows before the long, narrow windows that circle the top. Then the wind shoves the dust away, and the dim light turns a dirty yellow. There are howls on the wind that make my skin crawl. I do not know if the sound comes from dying men or if the wind itself is toying with my senses.

The Roarim truly must have come in the tens of thousands to have caused such a dust-storm from the plains.

"Hurry up, boy," Thoron growls behind me, making me jump.

I glance at him and then at the torch in his hand.

A torch. In the Library. Filled with parchment-dry Books...

I open my mouth in contempt, but Thoron has noticed his error before I can say anything. His nostrils flare. "You have five minutes," he warns, before retreating towards the main library doors to keep the flame away from the precious knowledge.

I turn to face the Library. I need to find the Book on Sky Spirits, but I also need to say goodbye.

I could not leave without bidding farewell to this

grand old lady within the Atheneum. This Library nourished my intelligence and lulled me in its silence when I sought refuge from tormentors; it took me on thrilling adventures through the words printed on the pages of its Books. It awakened many questions that I yearned to share with other Knowledge Seekers but never had the chance to ask.

What my companions do not know, is that I learned many of the Books by heart. But that is part of a secret I have kept to myself for years.

With dread filling my gut, I step towards the central vessel where the Anointing takes place. The water contained in it ripples from the center outward, disturbed by the explosions outside.

I stretch my maimed hand out over the surface and speak the customary words of Anointing.

A sharp piece of silex sticks out of the center of the basin, and I prick my finger on it. A few drops of blood drip into the basin, turning the water dark, and I think of the Seekers who will lose their lives outside.

There. It is done.

Uncle Denesius may consider me a Seeker, but it is the Library I seek approval from. I know the Anointment is just part of a ritual and that the Library is not a living being, but somehow this gesture has always seemed crucial to me. And suddenly, I understand why.

It is not the Atheneum I seek recognition from. It isn't even the Library within it or the other Knowledge Seekers. It isn't even the Books. No. I seek recognition from those who *wrote* the Books, from the ingenious minds that invented so many things that they would seem magical were we to see them today. I seek recognition from the Enlightened People.

I pledge myself to them. I will honor their Knowledge and wield it in a respectful way. *I swear to do so.*

Ferocious sounds come from outside the walls of the Atheneum. The Roarim! Have they reached the fortifications already? If so, they will be at the door of the Atheneum soon.

How could they have breached the city wall so fast? How could they have made it through the city and up the hill already?

"Eodain!" Thoron bellows, his voice echoing across the Library.

I glance at him, knowing it is time to go. I start heading back to the secret passage when I remember why I am here. I told Thoron and Draxis I would get the Book about the Sky Spirits. I rush to the opposite side of the Library. A large entrance leads to another room containing the forbidden section. I glance up out of habit and read the sign in gold letters:

VISITOR CENTER
2097

It has always struck me that the Atheneum was built exactly five hundred years before my birth and a few years before the Final Wars began. But the entrance is blocked by double doors made out of metal bars. A chain locks both doors together, and I do not have a key.

"Draxis!" I yell, pulling at the bars in the faint hope the doors will open.

The giant lumbers to my side, knocking into tables and chairs along the way.

"Give me a hand, will you?" I say. The Seekers will have to forgive my intrusion into this forbidden space.

Draxis swings his hammer and slams it onto the chain, which snaps and clatters to the floor. The metal doors swing open.

I rush inside and run along the bookshelves, my eyes scanning the themes as I go: World War I, World War II, the XXIInd century, The Final Wars, nuclear warfare... It strikes me that Uncle Denesius did not want to make this dark and dangerous Knowledge available to the Seekers.

I stop before *Satellites* and pull a ladder to clamber up to the fifth ledge. I reach out, and my fingers run over the book spines. They stop at a yellowed cover which I pull out. I glance at the faded letters on the front cover:

NATIONAL GEOGRAPHIC MAGAZINE
May 2087

Satellites: A Vision From Above

"Are you done yet?" Thoron's voice carries from the main doors of the Library.

My eyes fall on the other titles. There are so many! Valuable, irreplaceable titles. I wish I could take them all with me.

Everything is in the Talisman, I remind myself. *And in my head...*

"Coming!" I yell back. I clamber down the ladder and head for the main Library room.

A thundering crash from above sends tiles and glass flying. Something massive sails through the dome and smashes into the bookshelves. The force knocks over several other bookshelves, which start collapsing on each other, like a row of dominoes. I barely have time to throw myself on the ground before the nearest bookshelf topples over me, pelting me with heavy books. I wrap my arms over my head and am only saved from being crushed when the heavy piece of furniture leans into the next bookshelf, creating a triangular nook underneath.

"Eodain!" Thoron yells.

I gasp and scan my body. Aside from multiple bumps from the fallen books, I am intact. But I am also stuck. "Here!" I shout, my nose filling with the smell of old, varnished wood.

"Draxis! Get him out of there!" Thoron's voice is above me. "Are you all right?" he shouts at me.

There is loud screeching, and I feel books and wood moving above me, squashing me.

"Argh! Stop!" I say.

"It's Draxis!" Thoron says. "He's freeing himself from under the bookshelves."

Shouts erupt into the halls outside, and my blood turns cold.

"DRAXIS!" Thoron yells. "Get over here—NOW!"

There are sounds of thudding footsteps outside, followed by hammering against the Library doors.

Thoron says, "Brace yourself, Eodain!"

At once, the weight lifts, and books slide off my back. Dust from outside seeps through the gaping hole into the Library, sending me into a coughing fit as Thoron helps me up.

I have lost the magazine!

Draxis looms over me, his arms trembling from holding up the bookshelf, but I fall back to my knees, sifting frantically through the Books on the ground.

"There is no time!" Thoron yells. "We have to get out of here!"

The magazine is trapped under a bookshelf. I tug at it, but some pages rip. "Draxis! Lift the bookshelf higher! Quickly!"

Draxis groans under the effort. The bookshelf lifts,

releasing the rest of the magazine.

Something smashes through the Library doors. I turn and catch a glimpse of gleaming swords through a broken slit in the wood. The Roarim are pressing against the barricaded doors to get through.

Just as my hand closes around the magazine, Thoron yanks my arm so hard I think it will rip out of its socket.

Draxis lets go of the bookshelf, which comes crashing to the ground in a cloud of dust.

"GO!" Thoron yells as we leap over books and furniture. As Thoron dives into the secret passage, the Roarim burst into the Library in a jumble of blood-chilling shouts, scraping metal, and black boots. Their bodies, covered in solid armor and fearsome helmets, send chills up my spine.

I push against Draxis, who is struggling to get through the hidden door. His large frame pops through, and I stumble after him. An arrow zips above my head and snaps against the wall beyond me. I turn and pull the door shut, then seal the latch. I fall back, panting, but loud thuds tell me the Roarim are already piling up against the door. Their proximity makes my hand throb so hard I can barely breathe.

I leap to my feet, rushing after Thoron and Draxis as we descend into the vault. I grip the National Geographic and its ripped pages tighter under my arm, tears of despair spilling down my face.

I will not let the Roarim touch me ever again.

CHAPTER 4 *Tunnels*

There is no hesitation this time.

We plunge into the fourth tunnel. Thoron flings a satchel at me and picks up a bulging backpack and crossbow for himself. Draxis drops his head to fit into the tunnel and lifts the remaining backpack onto his shoulder. I stuff the magazine and ripped pages into a side pocket of the satchel and stumble in the semi-darkness, using the light from Thoron's torch to guide me. I am spurred on by the sounds of angry shouting coming from high above the vault.

After a while, Thoron stops, and I bump into him. The tunnel is wider here, and we are able to stand next to each other. We have reached the first split in the tunnel.

Thoron grabs three new torches from the ground and lights them. He gives one to Draxis and one to me. He keeps the third one and throws the fourth, almost-used-up one, far down the left tunnel. "That should distract them for a while," he says, then he heads down the tunnel to the right.

Wordlessly, we follow him, our footsteps sounding hollow and our breath coming hard. I let my feet take me deeper and deeper into the hill, but my mind is still above ground, my imagination running wild as to what might be occurring up there.

Is Uncle Denesius alive? What about the Knowledge Seekers? Are they still fighting? Will some be able to go into hiding? Or have their Talismans fallen into Roarim hands? If so, that can only mean one thing...

I dare not finish the thought as the Sacred Pledge hovers in my mind.

The Roarim may get their hands on the Books, but the Seekers would never give them access to the Talismans. I can picture the invaders cheering at their victory, marveling at the contents of the Library. They have the power now—the power over Knowledge. They can become rulers of the living, masters of the creations of the Enlightened People, owners of indescribable wealth as they barter with the Knowledge. Knowledge in the hands of one oppressor, is dangerous; it can be used to submit humanity to darkness and servitude.

Uncle Denesius and I have always understood this. The only way to prevent a tyrant from taking control of the Knowledge is to spread it as vastly and freely as possible.

A tyrant... the likes of the Wraith Lord...

I shudder.

The memory of Lord Erawan's death still haunts me. I will never forget the terrible sadness at the loss of life, mixed with the overpowering elation of the Seekers at their victory over the Roarim. The Atheneum was safe. The Books were safe. There would be lasting peace. Or so we had thought.

If the Lord of the Roarim survived somehow, or if

rumors of his unnatural resurrection were real, then he would seek vengeance till the end of his days. He would not rest until he had Uncle Denesius and the Knowledge Seekers in his grasp.

"The Wraith Lord rides a mighty dragon," traders from distant lands alleged. "He creates dust-storms to hide in, then attacks unsuspecting victims from above, from the back of a terrible beast with teeth as long as a man's arm."

I set my jaw. Fables spread by town-folk, no doubt, but the image is difficult to get rid of in the darkness of the tunnels.

Thoron and Draxis do not show any signs of slowing down, even after hours of running. I am out of breath, and a painful stitch nags at my side, yet I do not want to show weakness. Thoron has already made it clear that I am a burden. I know he would rather defend Uncle Denesius in battle since he was appointed that role when my uncle hired him a decade ago. He is only here because of his loyalty to the Grand Protector. He obeys Uncle Denesius blindly, no matter what instructions he may receive. That leads me to wonder what his final orders might include.

I admire that in Thoron. I have sometimes questioned Uncle Denesius's wisdom, though rarely out loud. Thoron did not have to question anything, he only follows orders. Perhaps that is the blessing of the illiterate. The more I read the Books, the more questions formed in my mind, sometimes to the point where I thought they would drive me crazy.

Innocence is bliss, I read once. How wise was the one who had written that!

"Whoa!" Thoron bursts out, coming to a halt.

"What?" I blurt out, panic surging through me as I try to peek over his shoulder.

Thoron stands aside and lights the passage ahead. Boulders larger than a man's head are piled up to the ceiling of the tunnel.

I gasp and rush forward, pushing against the rocks that have tumbled into the tunnel. They will not budge. "How can this be? Did we take a wrong turn?" My mind whirls. I go over the twists and turns behind us. *One wrong turn, and we are dead...*

"No," I answer my own question. I know without a doubt that this is the right way. That is how my mind works, how I can pull up memories in the smallest details, how I can remember every page of the Books...

Thoron approaches the collapsed tunnel. "This is recent," he says. "Perhaps the explosions earlier destabilized the ground."

Thoron has a good point. But that would mean the only way out is back the way we came. Hours and hours of travel, only to fall right into the hands of the Roarim.

Draxis harrumphs behind me.

I already know what he is trying to say. Draxis and I have a connection that way. His mind works in simple ways, and I have known him long enough to decipher his grunts and groans.

"Do you think you can do it?" I ask him, checking the expression on his moon-shaped face.

His pebble eyes twinkle down at me over his big nose. He waves a hand at the fallen rocks as if they mean nothing to him.

I puff through my cheeks. "All right, give it a go. But do not turn me into flatbread when you pass by me."

Draxis shrugs at my weak joke.

I hold my breath and press my torch flat against the rocky wall, so I do not burn him. He squeezes past me, and for a second, it feels like he will crush my spine.

The end of a sharp piece of old plastic string used to sew his shorts together scratches against my upper arm, leaving a long mark as he goes. Then he is past me, and I can breathe again.

Now he is pushing his way around Thoron, who yells when the giant steps on his foot. A lot of swearing ensues, but Draxis ignores the guardsman's vile words and begins moving big rocks aside. I step back to give him enough space to maneuver.

Before long, I slide into a sitting position, allowing myself some rest. The tunnel, carved into the hill under the Atheneum long ago, is cold and humid, and the ground is hard and uneven. I wrap my arms around my legs, then realize I have not checked the contents of the leather satchel yet. I open it and find something that sends a new wave of emotion through my tired body. It is a burgundy-colored cape. A Seeker cape.

I also find a round, leather flask containing water, and a bag of dried fruit and dried meat. After drinking from the flask and tearing at a piece of meat, I consider the cape.

My hand trembles as I take it out. The texture is thick and warm. My heart bulges. I bet Uncle Denesius left this for me! It is one of the last pieces that define me as a true Knowledge Seeker. I have the Anointment, I have the blessing of a peer (Uncle Denesius), I have a Talisman, and here is the cape. It is all there, except for the traditional greatsword. My shorter curved sword will have to do for now. But there is no doubt in my mind. I am truly a Knowledge Seeker.

I should be thankful. I should be proud. But I am not. This wasn't how it was meant to be. I did not earn this title like the others: with dignity, recognition, and honor.

On the one hand, if I had stayed and fought among

the other Knowledge Seekers, I would have insulted the Grand Protector by not abiding by his order. On the other hand, by fleeing, I will be branded a traitor and a coward by my Seeker companions. There is no right way about this.

But there is... The voice at the back of my mind is tiny but insistent. *This is not about you....*

I try to settle my thoughts. This is not about what others will think of me. This is about the Knowledge. It always has been about the Knowledge. The Atheneum has been taken. The Books have fallen into filthy Roarim hands. The Seekers and their Talismans are doomed in one way or another. But not this Talisman.

I pull out the object that hangs from the thin chain around my neck and squeeze it.

The Books may be held hostage by the Roarim and used to enrich their greedy aristocrats. They may seal up the Knowledge and sell it in small quantities for great profit, but as long as this Talisman remains out of the oppressor's hands, there is still hope for humanity.

I know exactly what Uncle Denesius wants me to do with the Talisman: he wants me to spread the Knowledge contained in it among men and women again, in a free and equal manner, thereby releasing them from the Roarim's grasp.

Years of constant battles to defend the Atheneum left the Seekers with little time and resources to think about spreading Knowledge. I have always believed this to be a mistake. The Seekers should have split their efforts between training to defend the Atheneum, searching the ruins of the Enlightened Era for Books, and educating people in the Knowledge. There just never seemed to be time for the latter. And, yet, if the Seekers had educated people, I would not be in this predicament.

It is too late now. Other than my new companions, no one except my uncle knows that I am a Seeker. I am his beacon of hope. And with that thought in mind, I fall into a restless sleep rolled up under my new cape.

* * *

I am eleven when Uncle Denesius is gifted a giant.

At first, he is upset about it. Giants are unpredictable, dangerous, and very expensive to feed.

Uncle Denesius and I are tinkering on the computers in the vault under the Atheneum. It is one of those things we both enjoy doing, though our many other obligations mean that we rarely have a chance to be there together. Perhaps I enjoy it even more, considering that Roddrick, does not. Uncle Denesius and I have an understanding of these machines. We take them apart, name each section by comparing them with the few manuals we have and feel awed by their complexity. The few times we are able to direct energy from solar panels into computers are some of the most exciting times of our lives. That is until a major dust storm blows in from the plains two years later and knocks half the solar panels off the roof...

Today, we are working in silence, side-by-side, on something called a satellite router. It is damaged, and we do not believe we can fix it, but its significance is not lost to us: this object was used to connect computers to satellites. We are interrupted when a messenger announces the return of a long-awaited group of Knowledge Seekers.

Uncle Denesius drops everything and says, "Come."

I jump to my feet, thrilled at having been invited along. Interesting things always happen around Uncle

Denesius.

We clamber up the winding shaft from the vault to the main building, then cross the front hall. To our surprise, the messenger tells us that the Knowledge Seekers cannot come inside. They are waiting in the inner courtyard by the main gates of the Atheneum. We hurry outside. The main gates are open, allowing me to view the pathway that leads down the hill to the City of Eliadys. But it is not the view of the city that captures my attention.

"Wow!" I exclaim.

A cage lies at the center of the cobbled courtyard, and inside its thick, metal bars is a giant! A real, live giant! His hands, and nose and feet are gnarled, tufts of messy brown hair lie on top of his head, and his mouth is full of big, square teeth. A heavy chain goes from his neck to a pin on the floor of the cage. The giant sits with his legs bent and his arms resting on his knees, looking forlorn. It is said that this new species of humans have begun to appear in the farthest regions of the north, where snow blankets the ground all year round.

Uncle Denesius is not impressed with this new addition. "What is this?" he barks.

A Senior Seeker detaches himself from a group of onlookers. He is a well-respected Knowledge Seeker and has traveled far and wide in his lifetime. "Grand Protector," he says, bowing deeply. "Forgive the cumbersome gift. I knew you would not be pleased, but bear with me. The Northerners say they can no longer pay their taxes in Books. This was all they had to offer. A dozen of their men died trying to capture this beast. I believe them, Grand Protector. I have seen their land. Their resources dwindle, their forests are all but gone. They have not found any new traces of ancient cities to plunder for Books."

The Senior Seeker stares earnestly at Uncle Denesius. "Grand Protector," he continues. "The Northerners say that this giant will be a great support in our aim to protect the city. This creature can help us rebuild the defensive wall. It is a fighter! We can train it to defend us!"

"Train it?" Uncle Denesius exclaims. "We could never train such an animal! It is madness!"

"No," the Seeker insists. "Not madness. The Northerners have explained to me how this beast can be mastered. I will tell you."

Uncle Denesius looks from the Seeker to the giant. He sighs and nods. "Come," he tells the Seeker, placing an arm around the man's shoulders. "Tell me more."

They head into the Atheneum, followed by the other onlookers, and I am about to follow when I spot something fall out of the cage. The giant grunts and reaches through the bars for it. It is just out of his reach, making him rage. He howls and slams against the bars, and I can tell that he is hurting himself, but still, he continues.

Curiosity gets the better of me, and I head towards the object.

The giant is going wild with fury, probably thinking that I will take the object from him.

I hesitate. My heart is beating wildly, but when I see that the cage bars hold, I continue forward and pick up the object.

I stare at it in wonder. It is a simple hairpin, but it is also more than that. It is the size of my hand. A purple flower made of rough cloth is pasted on one side, with a yellow bead sown in the middle. A single, very thick strand of brown hair protrudes from the hairpin, as would naturally happen after a woman or girl removes it from her head.

I am taken aback by this object. Clearly, it does not belong to the giant. He does not seem like the type that would wear flowers in his hair. Yet, it is obvious that it is not a hairpin made for normal human beings. This one belongs to another giant. His daughter, maybe...

My head snaps up, and I look at the giant, an awful feeling growing in the pit of my stomach.

The giant has his hand outstretched towards me. His eyes are sad and begging.

"Who did this belong to?" I whisper, certain that I know the answer.

The giant rattles the cage and growls.

"Did you leave a family behind?" I ask. My throat constricts. How could anyone have forcefully taken this man from his family? It is one thing not to have parents and grow up alone, but to tear an existing family apart seems like the cruelest thing in the world to me.

And so, I reach out my hand with the hairpin in it. The giant could have killed me with a swat of the finger. But he does not. He picks up the hairpin and hides it within the folds of his shirt, close to his heart.

And that is the start of how Draxis and I became friends.

I could never figure out why he did not try to break free, even after years of cruel treatment to tame him into submission. He could have done it. He could have taken any opportunity to barge through the soldiers who trained him, run down the hill, and crash through the city. He would have left chaos in his wake and would have ended up hurt. But he would have been free to make the long return trip home to his family.

Only, he never did. And in a purely selfish way, I was always glad he stayed.

CHAPTER 5 *Lost*

I wake up when Thoron nudges me with his foot. It takes me a couple of seconds to figure out where I am. As I stretch my cramped legs, a tiny breeze dances through my hair. I leap up. "Is it done?" I ask.

I can barely see Thoron when he nods.

"Why is it so dark?"

Thoron grunts. "You fell asleep and left your torch burning. I put mine out and lit it again when the one Draxis was carrying also died." He lifts the weak flame before me. "It will not last long."

My blood runs cold. I reach out and find the consumed torch next to my satchel. I must have slept the night away. "We have to get out of here!" I lift the strap of the satchel over my head so that it rests on my shoulder.

Thoron does not bother answering. He probably thinks I am dumb for stating the obvious, but when I look at the stump of his torch, I start to suspect he fell asleep, too.

I rush forward and find Draxis sprawled on the ground among a heap of big rocks.

"Draxis!" I gasp, bending down beside him. I open my satchel and pull out the round, leather flask I found in it last night, then hold it up to the giant's lips. Draxis drinks thirstily then grunts as he sits upright. I offer him some dried apricots and dates, then take his massive hand in mine and feel the scales on his skin.

"Are you all right?"

He nods, clearly exhausted.

"You did it, Draxis! You cleared the tunnel!"

He waves me on. He knows we have to leave.

"Come on, big guy," I say gently, munching on a dried piece of fruit. "We will have a feast when we get out." My stomach squeezes as I say this because at the end of the tunnel is an endless landscape of dry, jagged mountains. A good hiding spot, no doubt, but food and water will be scarce.

My mind whirls at the prospect. If I ever fulfill my mission, how am I going to find a way to liberate the Atheneum? Where will I find an army strong enough and willing enough to follow my command? *I am just a termite...*

My place is with the Books: reading them, analyzing them, and remembering every page... My place isn't out in the wilderness, leading troops into war.

I shudder at the thought and hurry after Thoron, just as my torch fizzles.

No one says a word. We press on.

The last torch dies two hours later, and we have to move forward by pressing our hands against the rough surface of the cave walls. We do not speak. We sweat profusely, urged on by a sense of panic. If we miss a split in the tunnel...

My mind is blurred as I frantically try to

remember the route we must take from previous times I explored these tunnels with Uncle Denesius. I am convinced we took the correct turn a while back and that there are no more split tunnels, but I do not remember the way being so long. Time has slowed because we are moving in total darkness. For all I know, we could be heading deeper and deeper into the mountains.

My fear subsides somewhat when we start climbing. I remember this section because the tunnel narrows until I have to bend down ninety degrees, with my back scraping the roof of the tunnel. The air is less humid, and the smell of warm dust fills my nostrils.

"We made it!" Thoron gasps, and I can see a yellowish circle ahead where the tunnel opens into a hazy afternoon.

I crawl forward until, finally, I am breathing the fresh air outside the tunnel again.

My heart leaps. *One obstacle is out of the way. Now on to the next one.*

But then Draxis grunts behind me, and my stomach does a double-flip.

"Draxis!" I burst out, whirling to face the giant.

He is a few paces behind me, struggling to get through the last section of the narrow tunnel. The hard rocky surface presses against his large body, and I realize he cannot get through.

The giant realizes this, too, because he stops struggling and lies there with his head and arms jutting out of the hole.

I grab his scalded hand with both of mine and pull with every muscle in my body. "Thoron! Help me!" I urge, exasperated by the guardsman's inaction.

Thoron drops his backpack and grabs Draxis's other hand, but by his lack of effort, I can already tell he knows Draxis will not get through.

I glance at Draxis and instinctively know the giant is too tired to break his way through like he did earlier. The boulders were easy enough for him to move aside, but this is a long, narrow shaft that would take him days to knock down.

We don't have days...

Adrenaline shoots through my system. "Come on, Draxis!" I cry, rage giving me an energy I did not know I had. I drop to my knees and claw at the dry, hard earth. After fifteen minutes of frantic digging, all I have managed to do is make a dent in the tunnel under Draxis's arm.

Thoron stands back, observing the tragedy unfolding before us.

By now, tears blur my vision. I feel a gentle touch on my shoulder. I force myself to look into Draxis's eyes.

He looks back at me quietly, then takes his arm off my shoulder and wedges his way back into the tunnel. When he turns his back on me, my heart stops.

"No, wait!" I shout, stricken. "Draxis?"

My giant friend does not waver. He heads straight back down the tunnel at a steady jog.

"DRAXIS!" I cry, leaping forward, but Thoron holds me back.

"DRAXIS!" I struggle, but Thoron pushes me back, and I fall heavily onto the ground.

"Smarten up, you fool!" Thoron shouts. "He has no choice! The only way out for him is to head back. The longer he waits here while we fail to get him out, the more he will weaken. He needs to do this while he still can."

"But he has no torch! It is pitch dark in there! He will get lost!"

Thoron looks grimly at me without answering.

I lie down on my back and cover my face with my hands to hide my despair. Draxis will never make it. He has water and food in his backpack, which will keep him alive long enough to lengthen his plight, but he could die in the dark tunnels, alone and lost. The thought is crushing.

"Get up!" Thoron barks.

I lift my hands and glare at him. How can he be so insensitive?

He nudges me with his foot. "Get up!" he repeats. "We need to get deeper into the mountains before nightfall. We cannot be caught out here in the open."

I hate that he is right.

Thoron has already picked up his backpack and is heading away from the tunnel. He does not even turn back for a last glance.

But I do. The sight of the empty, dark tunnel gnaws at my gut. I tear my eyes away and stand up to follow Thoron. I have barely taken a few steps when the guardsman stops in his tracks. He throws himself at me and shoves me to the ground again.

"Wha...?" I burst out angrily.

"Shh!" He thrusts his finger to his mouth, peeking over a boulder.

I pick myself up again and glance over the boulder myself.

At first, I do not see anything: only dry land and rocks as far as the eye can see. We are halfway up a mountain, and visibility would be excellent if it weren't for the hazy dust veiling the horizon. The mark of the enemy is spreading, even here.

Then I spot people running to my right. I frown and focus on the area. The people are wearing armor and helmets. I hold my breath, thinking these Roarim soldiers are after us, but, instead, they pass us by way down the mountainside. I see a head bobbing behind some rocks as a victim flees several paces ahead of the Roarim. One of the soldiers lifts a bow and shoots an arrow at him, but it misses and the soldiers keep up the chase. I let out the breath I had been holding.

"Let's go," Thoron mutters, nudging me in the shoulder.

"What?" I stare at him, wide-eyed.

"Whoever it is they are chasing, there is no hope for him. We must go into hiding."

I glance from the Roarim soldiers to Thoron, then back again. "Are you just going to let them slaughter an innocent person? We can take on those soldiers, you and me!" I jump up and unsheathe my sword.

Thoron pulls me down by the arm. "Our mission precedes all. Think of the Talisman. Think of the Grand Protector who has sacrificed himself so you could live." He glances around the sides of the boulder as if assessing an escape route.

My heart bursts at his words. I grasp my sword until my fingers hurt, and it takes all of my willpower not to throw myself at him. How dare he bring up Uncle Denesius! I wonder if I could take him on. My fighting skills would surprise him because he does not know I have been trained, but still... This is the Grand Protector's private guard and one of the greatest swordsmen in the land. It would be a risk.

I glance down the mountain. The fleeing man appears again, stumbling over the rocky terrain, running for his life. My anger evaporates. "Wait!" I shout. "That is a Seeker!" I recognize the burgundy cape. I bend forward, squinting. Yes, I am certain of it, now. That is a Knowledge Seeker. His life and his Talisman are about to fall into Roarim hands.

I do not give it a second thought. I fling my satchel from my shoulder and rush forward. My foot slips on the loose gravel, and I let the weight of my body carry me down. Dust rises around me as I slide on my backside and scrape my hands.

"Eodain!" Thoron's warning voice is already far behind me.

I ignore him. Thoron turned his back on Draxis. I will not let him turn his back on a Seeker.

The Roarim have surrounded the Seeker, and he is fighting for his life, his sword glinting as he thrusts it around him, trying to keep the soldiers at bay.

I jump over rocks and slide down the escarpment, causing a small avalanche of pebbles in my wake, but the soldiers are too intent on trying to kill their prey to hear my approach.

I have never fought a real battle. I have never shown my fighting skills to anyone besides the one who trained me. I have never killed anyone and would prefer not to have to hurt anyone. But instinct kicks in and I know I can get away with injuring the enemy. Years of training flow through my arms and legs, and I am on top of the Roarim before they know what's coming.

I had always hoped to learn to wield a greatsword, but the one who trained me told me to fight with what I had. And all I ever had, was this curved sword.

I must get close enough to take down these fully armored Roarim, so they do not have room to swing their greatswords at me. I must slash at them with stealth and speed before they know what hit them.

I slide down and slice a soldier's knee as I pass by him, then I place my hands on the ground and swing my legs from under my body to kick another one hard in the shins. He loses his balance and falls backward.

The other soldiers turn around, confused.

I am up at once, narrowly avoiding a stabbing blade from a third soldier. I grab his sword arm to force his blade down and slit his wrist, then swing him around in front of me, just as a fourth Roarim lunges at me. They crash against each other.

Out of the corner of my eye, I see Thoron throwing himself at the first two fallen soldiers and snuffing them out. Thoron does not take prisoners. He goes straight for the soldiers' necks.

I swallow bile and turn around just in time to face the last soldier. He swings his sword at me, and I duck. I lift my leg and kick him in the chest, but the blow backfires on me. The hardness of the armor makes me lose my balance, and I fall on my back.

The soldier catches himself from falling, straightens, and rushes towards me, sword raised for the strike.

Without warning, Thoron's greatsword whizzes through the air and lands through the soldier's neck. The Roarim staggers forward and tumbles in a heap beside me.

A wave of nausea washes over me, and I have to shut my eyes. When I open them again, Thoron has removed his greatsword from his victim and is finishing off the last injured soldiers.

I stagger to my feet.

To the side, by a boulder, the Knowledge Seeker hunkers down, hiding under his cape.

I approach the shivering form, who lifts his arm from his head and peers at me. The face is pale, and the eyes are wide with terror.

I gasp.

It is Roddrick.

CHAPTER 6 *The End*

We stare, not sure what to make of each other.

Roddrick, of all people!

I have never seen him look so fearful and lost. I can tell he loathes me for catching him in this undignified position. Not to mention I just saved his life, and that only makes things worse. Now he will think he owes me. I do not believe the great Roddrick Atheneumson ever expected to have to bow to the little Termite. Not that I want him to bow before me, or make him feel like he owes me anything, but our already difficult relationship has just taken a new dip.

He tries to regain his composure and stares at me with hard eyes. "Who trained you in sword fighting? Was it not forbidden to you?"

I am in no mood to answer. I do not owe Roddrick any explanation.

Fortunately, Thoron arrives by my side. He hands me my satchel and wipes his bloody sword on his cape. "That was stupid!" he mutters under his breath, and I know he is aiming those words at me. "We need to get out of here. More troops will come when these soldiers do not report back. Get up, Roddrick; we have a long way to go. You can update us on the way. Is your Talisman safe?"

I catch Roddrick tensing. He is still on the ground, brooding. Now he stands, slowly, brushing dust from his cape. His silence makes us stare at him.

"Roddrick?" Thoron insists, laying eyes on the Seeker. "Your Talisman, is it safe?"

Roddrick's hand lifts to his chest where the object would be hanging from the chain around his neck. He pulls aside his collar so we can see his bare neck. There is no chain there.

Thoron and I gawk at him.

"Roddrick!" Thoron gasps. "What happened?"

Roddrick wipes his mouth with the palm of his hand. When he lowers it, his voice is shaky. "They swarmed the city and the Atheneum; thousands and thousands of them. The Seekers did not stand a chance. The last thing I heard them say was that they were going to destroy their Talismans..."

I stare at him in horror. *The Seekers lost the battle?*

Roddrick swallows. "I... I fought my way through and almost made it out of the city unnoticed. But then this squad spotted me, and I have been running ever since."

"Roddrick!" Thoron barks. "Your Talisman. Did they get it?"

Thoron shakes his head. "I destroyed it a few paces back."

I glare at him. He fought his way through the Roarim? Highly unlikely! He fled, more like it. I am used to Roddrick's lies.

Yet, at the same time, my heart squeezes at the

thought of the Knowledge Seekers. Have they been killed? Did they fulfill the Sacred Pledge? My head sways with thoughts of terrifying questions.

Roddrick is eyeing me. His face is dark and tense. I try to deflect the thought that I know is crossing both our minds and say, "How is it you escaped the Atheneum? Were there others?" I feverishly hope others made it out with him.

It is the wrong question. Roddrick's face turns livid. He is so furious I can barely make out his words.

"I hid before the Roarim arrived..." His eyes are like daggers, but he adds. "There were no others."

Great. Now he thinks I wanted him to admit he was fleeing. But his hate towards me goes deeper. And this is because I know that both of us are thinking of the Sacred Pledge, the one that states that a Knowledge Seeker who loses his Talisman must take his own life.

Roddrick has lost his Talisman. He should have taken his own life. He knows it. And he knows that I know it.

We look at each other without saying a word. I could give an order for Thoron to kill him at the snap of my fingers. Of course, I will do no such thing. I am not that cruel; I am in no mood for more bloodshed. Tormentor or not, Talisman or not, I still consider Roddrick to be a Knowledge Seeker. There are too few of us now. War has changed the rules. That we hate each other cannot be part of the equation. We are on the same side: we both swore to protect the Atheneum and its contents.

Still, I want him to know he is walking on eggshells.

When I don't react, his eyes narrow, and he looks me up and down, taking in my brand new cape. "How come—" he begins, when a massive boom rattles the earth beneath our feet.

Roddrick topples back into the boulder, Thoron staggers, and I crouch down to stop myself from falling. Loose rocks and gravel roll down the mountain.

"Watch out!" Thoron yells.

We dart away, barely avoiding the landslide that buries the dead soldiers below.

Ripples of shockwaves travel beneath our feet, and it feels like a long time before the ground settles. We pick ourselves up and turn in the direction of the sound. We know the city of Eliadys and the Atheneum are behind the flank of the mountain. The veil of dust hanging in the air there confirms this. But now, a massive column of black smoke appears from it, leaving me stunned in horror. The hellish smoke reaches for the sky and mixes with the dust.

Blood rushes through my ears—thrust through my veins by a heart that is beating too hard.

No!

My feet carry me forward, slowly at first, then faster and faster. My tired and painful muscles are no longer of importance. I must get there. I must reach that column of smoke. I must stop the impossible from happening.

"Eodain!" Thoron warns, but he, too, is running without trying to hold me back.

We race along the foot of the mountain, oblivious to the fact that we are retracing our steps after struggling so many hours in the tunnels. Heading back is much faster above ground, yet it still takes us two hours at a steady jog—two hours that seem to last forever. The column of black smoke looms ever larger above a small bluff before us. Dusk is falling fast, yet, with the air becoming thicker, it is difficult to tell whether it is night or day.

I clamber up the bluff and freeze when I reach the

top. I hear Thoron and Roddrick coming up beside me. I stare out at the darkening valley.

It is worse—much worse—than I ever imagined.

Before me lies the city of Eliadys and, in its center, the hill topped by the Atheneum.

Except, there is barely anything left of either.

It isn't just the Atheneum that has been obliterated. It is half the city. Everything is burning. Huge, hungry flames lick at the few remaining walls of the Atheneum. Entire streets are aflame with burning homes. Thick clouds of smoke billow upward in a monstrous tornado, creating a hot wind that blows through my hair and cape. The sky above is black with smoke and orange flames, mingled with dust from the plains.

The sight is blood-chilling.

The one, most precious thing that remained on this Earth—the source of Knowledge and wisdom, the legacy of the Enlightened People—is gone forever. Thousands of years of observation and study and ingenuity from the human mind—obliterated. The implication is staggering; irrevocable.

It is as if the memory of an entire planetary civilization has been wiped out in one swipe from a godly hand—an evil, uncaring god with no inkling of compassion.

The inferno ravages the place where the Atheneum once stood, intent on destroying every Book, and every Seeker, so they may join the dust in the plains.

And Uncle Denesius... I sway. *Uncle Denesius is in there!*

A kind of madness takes a hold of me. Blood rushes through my ears. I do not realize that my feet are taking me forward. The flames up on the hill are calling me, inviting me to search among their devastation.

I take another step, but an arm wraps itself around

my chest and is holding me back. I blink, confused. I must hurry. There is little time. I must...

"Eodain!" Thoron's beard is scratching my ear. It is his arm that is holding me back.

I push at it, annoyed that he is delaying me.

His grasp tightens.

"Let go!"

"It is too late!" Thoron yells over the roar of the blaze. "They are gone!"

I shake my head. *No! Not gone. It cannot be!*

His arm is like steel, and I roar in frustration. "LET. ME. GO!" I push, and this time he releases me. I whirl to face him.

They are gone! Thoron's words bounce back and forth in my head, but my mind cannot grasp their meaning. Uncle Denesius, the Books, the Seekers, the Talismans—all gone.

Thoron stands there without moving. The fire reflects in his dark eyes, and his brown hair is almost comical as it sways back and forth on top of his head, moved by the wind.

"Let him go, then," Roddrick mutters at Thoron's side. "Nothing matters anymore."

Thoron raises his hand to silence him without taking his eyes off me.

Roddrick casts him an offended look but says nothing more.

"There is nothing left, Eodain," Thoron says.

"There has to be." My voice is strained. My ears will not stop ringing... "Something... someone..."

"There is nothing!" he snaps. "There is no one! It is only you, now."

His words are heavy with meaning. Crushing. Yet they elude me. In fact, I am facing him because I cannot bear to face the carnage behind me.

A sprinkle of ashes blows over us, and a tiny piece of paper gets stuck in Thoron's beard. My eyes fall on it. A piece of paper... My mind whirls. A piece from one of the Books!

The wail that is deep within me threatens to burst out. The ringing in my ears dies down. I am suddenly aware of the roaring fire, the oppressive heat, and the thick, unbreathable air. It is real. This madness is real!

Thoron speaks every word slowly and clearly, "Eodain Atheneumson! You are the last Knowledge Seeker! Do you understand?"

CHAPTER 7 *Fire in the Sky*

I stare at the charred land, covering my mouth with my cape to try and lessen the intake of dust and ash. The blaze on the hilltop to my right taunts me, but I cannot bear to look at it. It roars like a gargantuan monster intent on destroying everything in its wake.

I am lost in this nightmare. There is no end to it.

The vengefulness of the Roarim stupefies me. They did not even bother to save the Books. Never in a million years would it have occurred to me that they would no longer even care about the Knowledge. Their loathing towards us must run so deep they did not even want to take the Atheneum, only to destroy it. This is not a war for power over Knowledge but a war for annihilation. I am certain they never forgave Uncle Denesius for having killed their Lord. They remained silent for six years, no doubt planning this abomination in great detail. Their wrath is now complete. Lord Erawan is avenged.

Roddrick's alarmed voice breaks through my

thoughts. "Thoron!" he yells. "We've got trouble."

Thoron and I turn away from the devastation and glance back. It takes a while for my eyes to adjust to the dark, but then I notice pinpoints of light to the northwest of where we came. At first, I think new destructive fires are popping up. Are the Roarim burning the crops that are growing outside the city?

"The Roarim!" Thoron exclaims. "They must have gotten cut off from the defensive wall by the fire and retreated." He squints. "It looks like they are setting up camp!"

I shield my eyes and realize he is right. The pinpoints of light are organized into a clear pattern. They must be small campfires.

"More are coming," Roddrick says, pointing in a general north-westerly direction.

If not for the fire behind me, I could barely guess the movement of Roarim troops in the darkness.

"We are cut off now. We cannot go back the way we came," Thoron observes. "The risk is too great that we will run into them." He turns towards the inferno. "We will have to stay one step ahead of them by crossing the City of Eliadys and making it through the defensive wall before the Roarim army marches home."

My stomach squeezes, but I am too distraught to object. I focus on Thoron's brown boots as he searches for a path for us to take through the destruction. We step down from the bluff and make our way down to the City of Eliadys. We walk along charred streets where the houses have burned to the ground. Whether any inhabitants of Eliadys survived is not a thought I dare linger on, but I am painfully aware of the vast number of bodies over which I must step.

The Roarim have destroyed everything. They have crushed civilization to the ground, leaving us nothing to hold on to.

In the darkness, lit by small, scattered fires, white ash begins to fall around us. It is like the snow Draxis used to mention—a memory he pulled up from when he was very young. What falls from the sky now is a cruel version of snow as it is made up of specks of paper. Some charred pieces that land on the front of my cape contain letters.

I reach out my hand and watch the flakes settle into my palm, then dance away as the hot wind tugs at them.

A larger piece lands on my arm and sticks to the textile. I pull it off and stare at it. It is the corner of a page, the size of my thumb, with the number "274" printed on it. 274—that is a page number. This Book had at least 274 pages of information in it. I turn the paper around and catch my breath. A single word is printed there:

hope

The "e" is half chopped off, but that is the word that I am reading. Or maybe my brain is playing tricks on me, for there is no hope here. Hope was lost tonight.

I scrunch up this tiny remnant from the Library and let the hot wind take it away. I place one foot before the other, my surroundings reflecting my emotions.

By now, we are close to the bottom of the hill where the Atheneum once stood. I advance as if in a trance, still unable to process what has happened and exhausted by endless hours of travel. Since last night in the tunnel, I have not rested, and I think I may be becoming delirious. I trip and stumble, but avoid falling. I glance down and see a blackened foot sticking out from under the rubble. I turn away but then stop and look again. The foot belongs to a smaller person. The face is hidden behind a dark-red cape. A Seeker cape.

I lift a corner with the tip of my sword, and my stomach heaves.

It is Odwin, the young Knowledge Seeker I saw on the fortifications yesterday before the massacre began.

Thoron bends down and closes the youth's eyes. "Odwin Atheneumson," he whispers. "May the Enlightened Ones embrace your spirit."

I want to say something meaningful, but instead, I scamper to a piece of wall that once held a house and a family, and retch.

When I am done, I turn and find Thoron and Roddrick standing there, solemn and unmoving. My throat burns and aches for water. I taste vomit and bits of ash crunch between my teeth. Yet, I do not take my flask of water out of my satchel. Odwin did not get any relief; why should I? I step forward to continue our journey, but my ears pick up a sound.

"Do you hear that?" I ask, turning my head towards the sky. At first, I only hear the raging fire on the hilltop and the wind that pushes in all directions, but then I hear it again.

A kind of growl. It is coming from the plains beyond the defensive wall.

Thoron, Roddrick, and I stay rooted to the spot, listening. The sound is unnatural. It rises and falls, depending on where the wind is coming from, and it is approaching.

We glance at each other with blank expressions. I have never heard such a sound before, but it is making goosebumps rise on my skin. It sounds like one of those giant hornets that flew around the gardens of the Atheneum. Only, this hornet sounds a hundred times louder. And it is coming from high in the sky.

Something clicks in my mind.

"A DRAGON!" I yell.

Roddrick and Thoron throw themselves to the ground.

I jump back, slamming into the wall behind me, just as a dark form dips through the smoke right above us. Hideous, sharp teeth glint in the dark from the monster's mouth.

Roddrick yells, clamping his arms over his head.

The angry-looking beast shatters the night as it soars over us, its wings making so much noise I have to block my ears with my hands. It hurtles past us and disappears into a swirling cloud of dust and smoke.

I follow the sound, terrified that it will come back.

Words spoken by traders come back to me, "The Wraith Lord rides a mighty dragon. He creates dust-storms to hide in, then attacks unsuspecting victims from above, from the back of a terrible beast with teeth as long as a man's arm."

The three of us glance at each other, faces haggard, cheeks drawn, and I have no doubt we are thinking the same thing.

The Wraith Lord!

My thoughts scramble. *There are no such things as wraiths*, I tell myself. *No such thing...*

As if acting on a signal, we all jump to our feet and race along the bottom of the hill. I listen for the sound of the fanged beast. I think I hear it. I run faster, but then the sound fades.

The Wraith Lord! That was the Wraith Lord!

I stumble on in terror, the words bouncing around in my mind, and I know I want to be as far away from here as possible.

* * *

"What is it, Uncle?" I stare in wonder at the image he unfolds before me. It is about the length of my outstretched arms and full of detail, though the colors are faded. Still, I can read the title at the top center of it:

GROUND STATION

Uncle Denesius bends over beside me and follows the details of the central image with his index finger.

The structure depicted reminds me of a common daisy that bends its petals as it follows the sun. Only, this structure is artificial, and I am impatient to find out its purpose.

Each section of the Ground Station has a name printed on it: the round object is called a parabolic dish, *the odd box at the end of the arms is called an* antenna feed, *the parabolic dish is connected to the oval base by a* tracking positioner...

I glance at the top of the unfolded paper and spot a machine that seems to float in the night sky. I know what this is!

A satellite!

My eyes roam to the printed word for confirmation. I am right! This depicted machine is an active, functional satellite launched into space by the Enlightened People!

So, this Ground Station has something to do with satellites!

"Listen carefully," Uncle Denesius says, pointing at the Ground Station. He speaks in a low voice as if the Enlightened Ones were secretly listening to us. "This Ground Station is how the Ancient Ones communicated with the satellites. Look, see these people in a room full

of computers?" He points to a small image in the right corner. "This is the Ground Station's command center. Instructions were given to the computers here. The computers sent the orders to the satellite dish, and the dish sent a signal to the satellites orbiting around Earth. From there, the signal bounced back to one or several determined locations, somewhere else on the planet. That is one of the ways the Enlightened People communicated and sent information between each other over vast distances."

I stare at the image in wonder, once again dumbfounded by the ingenuity of the Enlightened People. It is accompanied by a pang of longing for those better times, when it seemed the world was filled with magic.

Uncle Denesius pulls up an old map and places it on top of the image of the Ground Station. He points at a location on the map, which I know is the current position of the Atheneum. It sits at the northernmost section of a protruding stretch of land once known as Florida.

"It is strange," Uncle Denesius says, "that the Enlightened People focused only on the danger of rising sea levels when they should also have focused on droughts. Rising sea levels destroyed many ancient coastal cities, but they were followed by rising temperatures and deadly heat waves that dried up entire bodies of water and destroyed thousands of acres of arable land. Did you know that the hill the Atheneum is built on was once surrounded by rising waters? But the centuries of heat waves that followed made the water retreat, leaving us with the topography we have today. Clean water is life, Termite. The Final Wars were not only caused by populations displaced by rising waters, but also by the lack thereof."

We stare at the map and its large patches of blue.

"It looks nothing like it, now," I observe, thinking of the desert plains south of Eliadys and the barren, rocky mountains that surround us. "Indeed," Uncle Denesius agrees. "The weapons used during the Final Wars were so powerful that they changed the face of the Earth. Some caused earthquakes that cracked the land and sent shockwaves that made mountains rise where there were none before."

Uncle Denesius slides his finger south of the Atheneum. "It is one of the reasons it has become so difficult to travel here." He stabs at a place I know well.

"Roarim City!" I say.

Uncle Denesius nods. "Yes, that is Roarim City. But it is also much more than that."

I look up at him.

"Roarim City is also where the Ground Station is located," he says.

My eyes widen. Could it be true? I squint to read the original name of Roarim City: NASA, Cape Canaveral, Florida.

I frown. "Are you sure?"

Uncle Denesius removes the map and points to a name printed under the Ground Station: Cape Canaveral, Florida.

I gasp.

I am twelve years old, then, but Uncle Denesius's words imprint themselves in my brain.

"This NASA Ground Station still exists," he says. "One of my spies has seen it from afar and lived to tell the tale. But to get there, one has to cross the unforgiving desert, then weave one's way between cutthroat pirates living in the mangrove marshlands to the southwest, and swarms of Roarim soldiers to the southeast." He stares at me with meaningful eyes. "The

trip is too perilous." He sighs.

"And, yet, if we could reach the NASA Ground Station one day, then perhaps we could reactivate some of the satellites. And if we could do that, perhaps we could send a signal to the rest of the world to say that we are still alive. Perhaps there are others out there with access to technology. And if we could do that..." he pauses, eyes lost in thought, "...perhaps we could connect the Talisman to the computers in the command center..."

My eyes almost pop out of my head. "...and spread Knowledge back to the people of the Earth!" I finish for him.

CHAPTER 8 *The West Tower*

As I walk through the rain of ash, I ponder upon Uncle Denesius's words: *The NASA Ground Station, located in the heart of Roarim City, 200 miles south of Eliadys....*

That is where he wants me to go.

"Keep your eyes peeled," Thoron says, pulling me out of my dark thoughts. "We are approaching the defensive wall."

I glance up, and through the dusty ash, see the dark outline of the wall ahead of us. It runs east to west, connecting two mountain ranges, thus protecting the northern lands from Roarim attacks coming from the south.

The defensive wall has crumbled at its center, revealing a V-shaped hole where the Roarim burst through. I cannot see the far end of the wall, but to my right, it fuses with the rising flank of the mountain where Thoron and I initially fled. *And where I lost Draxis.* I choke up.

"Not a living soul in sight," Roddrick notes.

I shudder and glance up at the mountain again. "Oh!"

"What is it?" Thoron freezes, weapon in hand.

"The West Tower!" I say. "It still stands."

Thoron lowers his sword and grimaces.

I ignore his frustration. "Wait a minute," I say. "Roddrick finished my water supply an hour ago. There are provisions at the West Tower. We cannot continue without them."

Thoron swears. He knows I am right.

Roddrick jumps in, "The Roarim must have plundered those provisions by now. We will not find anything there. We will just put ourselves at risk."

Thoron looks from Roddrick to me, then answers, "We do what the Seeker says."

I stare at Thoron. I am still not used to having him defend my position, especially before another Seeker.

Thoron turns and changes course. I follow, but Roddrick pulls me back. "Hey!" he shouts at Thoron, his nostrils flaring. "Since when do we do what *he* says?" He turns to me. "And you? Are you going to tell me now why you are wearing a Seeker's cape?"

Thoron backtracks. "Let him be, Roddrick."

Looking me up and down, Roddrick frowns. "Look at you!" he says, shoving me away with his hand. "All dressed up like a proper Seeker, with a cape and all. Who did you steal it from, Termite?"

The tip of Thoron's blade appears under Roddrick's throat. "Are you done yet?" the guardsman growls.

I stare at both men without moving an inch.

Thoron lowers his sword. "There is no Termite here. You will address him as Eodain Atheneumson, son of the Library, protector of the Books, wielder of the Talisman."

Roddrick's face goes through several transformations: from anger to surprise, to disbelief, to disgust. He spits at the ground in front of me. "I do not believe you. The last time I saw this scum, he was fleeing the fortifications like a frightened rat."

Thoron's sword is at his throat again. "That is enough, Roddrick. He was not fleeing. The Grand Protector made him a Knowledge Seeker before the attack. I am witness to this nomination and have sworn to protect the Seeker and the Talisman with my life. I do not pretend to understand every decision made by the Grand Protector, but that is the way of things now. And..." he turns to me, "...that is the Grand Protector's own Talisman that hangs around Eodain's neck, so I will ask you to honor it."

Roddrick's face turns as pale as a ghost's. The news has rendered him speechless.

"One last thing," Thoron says as he sheaths his sword. "The Talisman answers to Eodain only. The Grand Protector has made it so. Keep that in mind, *Hyena*!"

I stare after Thoron in amazement. He has called Roddrick Atheneumson by his nickname. Just as I earned the nickname *Termite*, Roddrick's nickname is *Hyena*. I haven't heard anyone call Roddrick that in years. No one would dare.

I follow Thoron as we begin to climb a sharp path up the mountain. I am dumbfounded by the show of power between the two of them. Had our situation been different, I might even have enjoyed this little showdown. Yet, there is something twisted about it.

Thoron has made it clear that the Talisman only answers to me. It is only after I put myself in Roddrick's shoes that I understand why Thoron felt the need to say that. It was Thoron's way of warning Roddrick not to try and steal the Talisman from me.

I shudder at this realization. Had Uncle Denesius not put this safety net in place, I would be dead by now. My connection to the Talisman is the only thing keeping me alive.

I am overwhelmed at Uncle Denesius's power over others, even after his death.

Narrow stairs that cut into the rock wind up the mountain to the base of the West Tower, which tops the end of the defensive wall. There is an East Tower at the other end of the wall, but I cannot tell if it is still standing in the darkness.

We reach the entrance and find the heavy, wooden door of the Tower half torn and standing ajar. Dead archers from Eliadys are scattered along the defensive wall, and I can see they also lie within the Tower. Perhaps they had sought refuge here, but the Roarim managed to burst through their line and finish them off.

We move forward with caution, our weapons raised, our eyes adjusting to the gloom.

Thoron finds some torches and lights them. "Avoid the windows," he says, handing one to me. "Once this dust settles, any light coming from within the Tower could be seen for miles."

I gulp and nod. In any case, if any provisions remain, they will be kept locked in the cellars below.

We head down winding stairs, stepping over bodies, and my stomach heaves again. I fear what we will find below.

To my surprise, the door to the provisions room is still closed. Some soldiers lie slain before it. The Roarim did a good job ridding the Tower of the living but did not bother to loot the place.

Thoron and Roddrick move three of our slain

soldiers, and we enter a room filled with bags of corn, dried meat, apples, a couple of loaves of bread and cheese wrapped in cloth. I lift the lid on an ancient plastic vat and find it filled with clean water. Every two days, people from Eliadys would bring up pails of water from our deep wells and fill the vat for the sentinels standing guard in the tower.

I fill my leather flask and drink thirstily. The cool liquid slides down my throat, washing away some of the ash and dust. I finish my flask and fill it up again.

Roddrick finds another flask on a shelf and does the same.

Thoron has gone to the end of the room, where he has spotted flasks of wine. He uncorks one and gulps it down.

I grab one of each food item and fill my satchel, then watch the others do the same while simultaneously stuffing themselves. Thoron splits one of the loaves of bread and throws me a piece. I slide down into a sitting position against the wall. I know I should eat, but I am overwhelmed by the events of the day, and my stomach is still queasy.

I fall asleep in this uncomfortable position. When my eyes flutter open, it is several hours later. Dawn must be near because faint light comes through the narrow windows. The others are still sleeping, and I know this is the time for me to act.

Getting provisions was a crucial reason to come to the Tower, but I had another reason to come here: one Thoron and Roddrick would not understand.

Feeling cramped and numb, I stand and slip out of the room. I climb the stairs, but go all the way to the top of the Tower this time. I listen for distant sounds of marching soldiers or flying dragons as I go, but hear only the wind whooshing through the stairway.

I reach the top, which is open to the elements. The sun tries but fails to break through an eerie curtain of dust and ash that still hangs around the tower. I cannot see further than a portion of the defensive wall, on one side, and the dark lump of the hill where the Atheneum stood, on the other. There is no sign of the Roarim army, who must still be camping north from here.

The fabric roof that protected those who used the Tower lies crumpled on the ground. I lift the textile, one corner after another, and find the spyglass used for observation. I pick it up, admiring its golden color, and my heart constricts because it belonged to Uncle Denesius.

CHAPTER 9 *The Sky Spirit*

Uncle Denesius turns to me as I reach the top of the Tower. He is sitting on a bench placed before the spyglass, which rests on a tripod. The only source of light comes from a couple of lanterns. He smiles at me.

Warmth fills my chest. I expect other boys my age to be here, but the only other person present is the Atheneum Scribe. The white-haired man adjusts the spyglass; then, he opens the thickest book I have ever seen. The book rests on a wooden stand placed next to the spyglass.

Uncle Denesius gestures for me to sit beside him, and I hurry to obey. His eyes raise to the man standing behind me. "Thank you for bringing Termite from the Atheneum this night, Thoron."

I turn to watch my uncle's guardsman bow.

"You may retire now," Uncle Denesius tells him, and Thoron leaves without a word.

"You, too, Scribe. You may retire. Termite and I will manage the Logbook tonight."

The Scribe's eyes widen as if he has never been given time off work in his long life. He bows profusely, repeating, "Thank you, my lord. Thank you!" With that, he hurries away.

I look up at Uncle Denesius, and we exchange a secret smile. I sit up straight with pride. The Grand Protector has invited me to perform a special task. No wonder the other orphans are jealous. No wonder Roddrick accuses me of being the Grand Protector's favorite.

I am only nine, then. Roddrick is ten. We still hunger for attention from the adults, even if it is just a smile, a tap on the shoulder, a word of encouragement. We cannot wish for more; there are no comforting hugs or words of love because we have no parents. Our parents abandoned us as babies at the foot of the Atheneum, no doubt, because they could not care for us and could not handle an extra mouth to feed. If the one we affectionately call Uncle *had not taken us in, we would have died of hunger in the streets.*

Uncle Denesius stands and carefully turns the pages of the Logbook. "Do you know what we do here, Termite?" he asks.

I shake my head, eager to find out.

"Come," he says.

I slide off the bench and hurry to Uncle Denesius's side. I stand on tip-toe to peer at the pages of the Logbook and see three columns there.

"See here, the first column?" Uncle Denesius says, pointing at the one on the left. "That is where we write today's date." He points to the second column. "This is where we put the hour. The hour is crucial, Termite. See the sand clock? It is half full. That means it is half past the hour. It is currently thirty minutes past nine o'clock. And here, in the third column, is the direction;

usually west to east."

I see many rows of similar-looking information.

"Listen, Termite," Uncle Denesius says. "Every single row in this book logs the passage of a Sky Spirit over the Tower."

My eyes widen, and I stare at him.

He looks down at me and nods. "That is right, Termite. This book was started many generations ago and has been maintained ever since. Every night, without fault, the passage of a satellite has been noted down for posterity." He flips through the left side of the book, and it is all the same thing; row upon row of information: a date, a time, a direction.

I frown. "Uncle, why are the rows so squished together at the beginning of the book?"

Uncle Denesius smiles. "That is a good observation, Termite. The reason is simple. As time passes, the satellites weaken. Year after year, they fall from the sky and perish on the ground. The smallest ones fell first, hundreds of years ago, because their low-orbit trajectory made them vulnerable to friction from the Earth's atmosphere. Only the bigger, high-orbit ones remain. They run on small thermonuclear cells, making their source of power practically eternal. There used to be thousands of them, Termite. Thousands, that connected every person on the planet." He trails off, and I stand in silence, awestruck by this fact.

"Why are we logging the passage of the satellites, Uncle?" I continue to ask questions because thinking about the dying Sky Spirits makes me sad.

"Another good question, Termite..."

I beam.

"Even though we have lost touch with the Sky Spirits, I maintain the hope that this will change one day. That is one of the reasons I send the Knowledge

Seekers out into the land, searching for Knowledge. Perhaps, one day, we will find the information that will allow us to communicate with the satellites again. Perhaps you will live to see that day, Termite."

My chest swells up. Yes! I will find a way to communicate with the satellites again.

Uncle Denesius sits back on the bench, and I join him, awed by this man's depth of wisdom.

He continues, "After many years of observation, the Scribe has come to notice a pattern in the passage of the satellites. It has become possible to predict the passage of some of them. This is important, Termite. Once we have a machine that will allow us to communicate with the satellites, we must do so at the exact time of their passage above the Tower. Once the satellite has gone behind the horizon, the contact-point is lost, and we must wait for the next satellite."

I nod, absorbing every piece of information he gives me.

Uncle Denesius bends back and lifts his head towards the sky. "So, Termite. Who will spot the first satellite tonight?"

I grin. "Me, Uncle!"

He laughs. "We will see, Termite. We will see."

We gaze at the night sky in silence. At first, I open my eyes as wide as possible, trying to take in the whole firmament. But when they start to water, I realize this is going to take some practice. In fact, Uncle Denesius is the one who spots the first satellite. He points it out to me: a spot of light moving on the horizon, just above the distant mountain range. I follow it in amazement. That is a man-made object, one that emerged from generations of research and combined human effort. I cannot imagine the people of Eliadys attempting to construct anything of the sort today. I wish it were otherwise.

We are three hours into our observation, and Uncle Denesius has spotted two more satellites. I spot only one, but I am mighty proud of it.

Uncle Denesius stands and writes down the information in the Logbook.

I stifle a yawn. It has been a long day since I was up at dawn doing chores. But I will not let sleep get the better of me. I swing my legs back and forth under the bench and start humming, enjoying Uncle Denesius's presence and the excitement of the quest to find Sky Spirits. There isn't much opportunity for humming or singing in my life, but at this moment, the song slips out of my mouth before I realize it:

"Twinkle, twinkle little star,
How I wonder what you a— "

Without warning, Uncle Denesius strides towards me and slaps me so hard on the cheek my head snaps back. Blood spurts out of my nose. I can feel the outline of every finger of his hand branded on my skin.

"Who taught you that song?" he yells. "I will have their head on a stick! Who was it? Answer me!"

I think his blow may have ejected my voice out of my body because I cannot find it.

He stabs his index finger at my face. "That is a Roarim song. A song of the enemy. It is forbidden, do you hear me? Never, ever will you sing that song again. Is that understood?"

I nod. Say yes, just say yes to everything he says...

"So, who was it? Tell me, now!"

My mind is blank. I have no idea where that song came from. It popped into my head out of the blue. "I don' know, I..." His hand balls into a fist. "The Ol' 'anny!"

I splutter. "It wa' the Ol' Nanny!" The whole left side of my face is burning so hard that I am having difficulty pronouncing the words. His hand unfurls, and he steps back.

It is a lie, but I had to say something. The Old Nanny, one of the women who raised the orphans of the Atheneum, died a couple of years ago, so he cannot verify my accusation.

Uncle Denesius stands, unmoving before me. I dare not raise my head or twitch, even though blood drops from my nose. The companionship between us has evaporated.

"You will take over from here," he orders me. "I expect to see the completed Logbook on my breakfast table, tomorrow."

It is when he turns and walks away from me that tears spill out of my eyes. I want to call after him. I want to apologize. I open my mouth, but that is when I see it: the falling satellite.

I blink hurriedly to clear my vision, certain that I am imagining things. But I am not. A spot of light that looks like a star falls from the sky towards the Earth.

"Uncle..." I breathe, turning to Uncle Denesius, who is about to disappear down the stairs. It is a split second of indecision that could determine my future. If the remnants of the fallen satellite are discovered, and it comes to light that I did not report it in the Logbook, I could be banished. But the numb shock and disappointment at Uncle Denesius keep me silent, and I end up never telling a soul about it.

I stare at the falling star, which hits the ground beyond the mountain range. The pointed top of a mountain flares up in white light, then goes dark again.

It turns into one of the worst nights of my life. I am exhausted from trying to stay awake watching for passing satellites, terrified of my unconscious wrong-doing and anguished at having lost Uncle Denesius's approval. I am tormented by his violent reaction to a simple song and that I neglected to tell him about the fallen satellite. What if he finds out?

Never again does he accompany me when I am appointed to assist the Scribe looking for Sky Spirits.

* * *

I find the Logbook in a corner, with the spine open and the pages facing down. Gently, I pick it up, blowing away the accumulated dust as I turn it upright in my hands. Several pages are bent, and I flatten them until I come to the last page. It holds the last entries from the Scribe, his handwriting having become wobbly with age.

The Logbook is too heavy to carry. Right now, the expectation is to travel lightly. Yet, I hesitate before grabbing the final three pages and ripping them out. I cannot save generations of work contained in the Logbook, but these last months of observations will have to do.

I sit cross-legged and comb through the pages which I have laid out in front of me. The scarcity of data is depressing, but two things stand out. One, there will be a satellite in twenty days, and two, if I miss that one, it will be ten days before the next one travels through the sky.

"Twenty days," I mutter. That is the number of days I have to reach Roarim City and understand how to activate the Ground Station. I make a mental calculation. Roarim City is two hundred miles away. It will take me around eleven days to get there—if I am lucky enough not to run into marauding pirates or vile enemy soldiers along the way. That will leave me around nine days to figure out a way to enter Roarim City, undetected.

I will have one shot at connecting the Talisman to the satellite and transmitting the Knowledge contained in it. If I am late, I will have to wait another ten days for the next satellite. I highly doubt the Wraith Lord would let me stay that long at the heart of his city.

I fold the last three pages and stuff them, along with the spyglass, in my satchel. If the Wraith Lord gets his hands on the Talisman, he alone will have access to Knowledge that could crush the remainder of humanity. The only way to deflect this danger is by making the Knowledge available to all.

I stand solidly and look out over the desert plains, as far as the dust will allow. Uncle Denesius was right to entrust this quest to me. He knew that, above all other Knowledge Seekers, he could count on me.

"I will not let you down, Uncle," I whisper.

I turn, and as I head out of the building, something bright catches my eye. It comes from the base of the tower. As I lean over, I am struck by fear.

Roarim scouts are winding their way up the mountain. They will reach the West Tower within minutes. Are they the advance team for the Roarim army? Are the troops preparing to march home? If so, this is the last place we want to be!

I dash down the stairs with my satchel thumping against my side and my sword in hand, shouting at the top of my lungs, "The Roarim! Thoron, Roddrick, get out of there!"

By the time I reach the bottom, soldiers have erupted through the door. Thoron leaps up before them, roaring and crashing into them.

Some soldiers make it through, and one of them

rushes towards me. I see him blink under his steel helmet. "A Seeker!" he yells, noticing my burgundy cape. "We have a Seek—" He crashes to the ground, lifeless.

Thoron's maddened gaze falls on me, then he turns and charges at the other soldiers.

But it is too late; the news is spreading down the mountain. "There is a Seeker in there! Get the Seeker!"

My heart leaps, and I rush to Thoron's aid. We must get out of the Tower, or we will be trapped. Swords clash as we are swarmed through the only exit out of the Tower.

"Where is Roddrick?" I shout, but Thoron does not have time to answer.

Just when I think we are lost, a Roarim soldier outside the door screams and is flung to the side. Another one follows. The battle within the Tower lessens and focuses on something happening outside. Roarim soldiers are being flicked away like flies until only a couple remain, and these flee down the mountain.

A shadow blocks the doorway, and I leap in joy. "Draxis!" I rush to hug the big giant.

He grunts, his left hand covering my back. He moves aside, and I realize he is not alone. A bald man with a thick blonde beard, and in his early forties, looks at me in astonishment. "Eodain!" he exclaims.

"Pedregal!" I greet him, a huge wave of relief washing over me.

He hurries over and squeezes me in his arms. "I was looking for survivors at the Atheneum when I found Draxis. He made it clear to me you had survived and that he was looking for you. We spotted the Roarim soldiers heading this way and decided to follow them." He glances over my shoulder. "Who else have you got?"

I stand aside to let Thoron out. Roddrick stumbles after him, his face pale. I notice that he is not wearing his Seeker cape.

Thoron nods at the newcomer, still breathing hard from the fight. "Your timing is appreciated, swordmaster," he says.

"So it would seem," the bald man agrees. "Unfortunately, we do not have time for further chitchat." He glances down the mountain. "Those soldiers will be back with reinforcements."

Thoron nods, but he glances my way. "I recognize your fighting style now, Eodain. It would seem you were trained by Eliadys's very best."

Pedregal and I exchange a knowing glance, and the bald man shrugs. There is no point in keeping the secret anymore. "Yes," I say. "Pedregal has done me that honor."

Roddrick snorts. His eyes are dark with jealousy. "What makes you so special, then, *Eodain*?" He stresses my name to show he is only using it because the others are around. I will always be Termite to him.

My stomach squeezes at his vehemence. I glance at Pedregal, but this time I stay silent. The reason why the swordmaster trained me is something I swore never to reveal.

"We do not have time for that," Thoron jumps in, annoyed, and I am once again surprised by his timely interference.

I am about to point out Roddrick's missing cape when a dozen arrows whizz above our heads. Shouts rise up the mountain.

"What did I say?" Pedregal shouts. "No time for chitchat. RUN!"

We sprint across the defensive wall, Roarim soldiers in hot pursuit.

CHAPTER 10 *Over the Plains*

Arrows fly by us as we scramble over the dead soldiers on the defensive wall. Shouts below and behind me warn me of the approaching Roarim.

We reach the edge of the breached wall and begin a hair-raising descent down the V-shaped hole cut through the stone blocks. We have to reach the ground before the Roarim do.

I make my way down, fighting an urge to leap from one slab of crumbled stone to the next at the risk of breaking my neck. Instead, I climb down, making sure I have a good foothold on a stone before moving on to the next one. An arrow hisses by my ear and snaps on a stone right beside Pedregal's hand. He swears and almost loses his balance. I grab on to his wrist until he stabilizes. We glance at each other and continue our descent without a word.

The base of the wall is littered with stones and boulders, but we are able to make our way around to the other side. We jump onto the hard, barren ground and race along the base of the wall, towards the East Tower, this time. Roarim soldiers above us make good use of their bows and arrows, and it is a miracle that none of us are hit.

We reach the end of the defensive wall that clings to the face of the mountain, then freeze because a deep gash in the ground, caused by an ancient earthquake, hampers our passage. The gash stretches to the right of us, across the desert plains.

Thoron heads into the mountains instead, which are rugged and jagged, with many nooks and crannies. These all make for excellent hiding places, but I realize this treacherous terrain will hamper our progress. One slip on these knife-like rocks could lead to serious injuries.

Thoron heads right into this maze, no doubt thinking of losing the Roarim in there.

I hesitate to follow and consider the root-like rift. It crosses the plains southward. Roarim City lies southward.

"Thoron!" I call out. He turns, and I point below my feet. "Down there," I say hurriedly. "They will not expect us to head into the plains."

An annoyed look passes across his face, then vanishes as he considers the option.

"Eodain is right," Pedregal says. "We will never make it out alive from this jagged mountainside. It will take us too long to navigate it."

Thoron does not look happy at having been outvoted by Pedregal, but he says, "Fine. You go on ahead, all of you. I will lead the Roarim into the mountain. Follow the rift. I will catch up with you as soon as I can."

"But, Thoron..." I object.

"Go!" he says and turns to head into the mountain.

I stand there, my stomach tight. Uncle Denesius sacrificed himself so I could escape. Now Thoron is doing the same thing.

And we are barely out of Eliadys.

Pedregal does not wait. He crouches down to find a safe passage into the rift, and the rest of us follow hastily.

The bottom of the rift is smooth enough for us to make good headway, and the walls of the fissure cast a welcome shadow as the sun chases away the morning. We jog on for many hours. My feet thud on the ground in time with my heartbeat, and I feel my steps taking me further and further away from my home. *I have no home*, I remind myself. *The Atheneum is gone.*

By noon, I am drenched in sweat. The sun beats down into the rift, and my throat is burning for water. The Seeker cape is a heavy weight on my shoulders, and my back is soaked.

"Wait!" I gasp, slowing to a stop and bending down with my hands on my knees to catch my breath. "I need a break."

The others stop. They turn towards me, their faces haggard, and I suddenly realize they have been waiting for me to signal a resting time. *Me—the last Knowledge Seeker.*

I shudder, despite the heat, and sag to the ground. Draxis, Pedregal and Roddrick do the same. Roddrick and I take out our few supplies from the Tower and share them with Draxis and Pedregal, who only made it out of Eliadys with their weapons. I know Draxis holds himself back when I hand him my flask of water but realize that with two extra people—one being a giant— our supplies will not last long. I share a loaf of bread and cheese, but keep the dried meat and apples for later.

The sun beats down on the land, and the stifling heat makes me nod off.

* * *

I am eleven years old when I catch Pedregal stealing from the Library. By then, the Library is a usual refuge for me. As soon as dinner is over, I hurry out of the mess hall and creep into the Library through a loose window only I know about. I crouch in a nook amongst the bookshelves, studying the Books well into the night, before heading back to the dormitory and slipping into my bunk without waking the other young orphans.

At night, the great Library doors are shut and locked, and many would find the cavernous room intimidating—filled with ghosts of the past. But not me. I find comfort among the Books written by the Enlightened People. They are my ancestors, after all. They are the ancestors of the survivors who remain on the Earth today. Why should I fear them?

But that night, I almost second-guess myself when I hear footsteps on the marble floor. They are slow and silent, not the regular footsteps of someone confident, who is authorized to be here. The footsteps head my way and stop close to where I am sitting. I freeze, my heart thumping in my chest, imagining a vengeful ghost with empty eye-sockets.

Then the footsteps pass by me, and I catch a glimpse of the dusty leather boots belonging to someone who spends his time outside, in the city, or riding horses. In other words, it is not a ghost. Nor is it a Knowledge Seeker.

I leave my hiding spot and crawl to the end of the bookshelf, where I peek down the main corridor of the Library. There, I see a man stopping before a stack of books. His hand hesitates over them as if he does not really know what he is looking for. He glances around as moonlight comes through the high windows of the dome, illuminating his face.

I gasp. It is Pedregal, the Atheneum's swordmaster. He teaches the Knowledge Seekers in the art of sword-fighting. I know him to be a quiet, respectable man—something which I have heard the cleaning ladies of the Atheneum say they find charming. Though Pedregal is dedicated to his work and to the Atheneum, he has always struck me as a bit of an outsider.

Yet, here he is, grabbing a couple of minor volumes and slipping them under his cape, all the while glancing around. I duck back so he will not spot me.

I cannot believe that this noble man would steal from the Library. He knows full well that stealing Books is punishable by death. Why would he risk everything to do so?

The concept of right and wrong has grown strong within me, even more so after the failed attempt by the Roarim to take the Atheneum last year. The attack lost me, my innocence. Men can do evil, and I vowed to stand up against any wrongdoings from that moment on.

And now this swordmaster is doing wrong: he is stealing the Books. Anger wells up within me, and before I can think, I leap into the middle of the corridor just as Pedregal makes his way out again. I stand firmly, with my legs slightly apart and my arms crossed over my chest.

It is a stupid move. This is one of the best—if not the best—swordsman in the country, aside from Thoron, that is. He could slice me into pieces before I have a chance to open my mouth. "Where do you think you are going with that?" I burst out.

Pedregal stops in his tracks. His eyes dart left and right as if he is expecting soldiers to leap at him. But when he realizes I am alone, he looks at me in surprise and—curiously—with worry. "Eodain!" he says. "What are you doing here?"

That is one of the things I have always liked about him. He uses my real name, not the other one.

"I might ask you the same thing," I say, trying to sound confident but realizing I may have gotten myself into a life-threatening situation. I assumed Pedregal would have drawn his sword on me by now, but instead, he bends down on one knee to be at eye-level with me.

"You should not be in here, lad. You should be fast asleep in your bunk by now."

I cut him short. "And so should you." I glare at him. "Why did you take the Books?"

He is taken off guard. He stands and now, seems hesitant. He knows I saw him steal. Now, I am a witness.

He surprises me again by speaking gently, "Eodain..." he looks at the floor, then takes out the books from under his cape and shows them to me. "Yes," he admits. "I was stealing these Books." He looks at me, maybe to judge my reaction.

"Why?" I ask.

His hand holding the Books drops to his side, then he lowers to the ground and leans against a bookshelf. He taps the floor, indicating I should sit next to him, but I prefer to stand. Just in case.

He sighs. "It is for my parents," he says.

I stare at him.

"You do not go out much, Eodain. You do not know what it is like out there, in the City. Often, my parents and I go without food." He looks at the ground again. "I steal small Books that the Knowledge Seekers have not paid much attention to and will not miss. Yet,

even small Books are gold to the people." He holds up the two Books. "The sale of these two Books will feed my parents for a month! I am their sole provider, lad. Without me, then..." He stops.

We stare at each other.

I am blown away by his confession, and I suddenly realize that this goes way beyond me. Good and bad have always been clear in my head: Uncle Denesius is good, Roddrick's bullying is bad; protecting the Books is good, the Roarim are bad. But what Pedregal tells me falls somewhere in between, in a grey area. What must I do?

"The rules say I must report you to the Grand Protector," I say.

Pedregal nods slowly.

"But..." I continue. Something has entered my mind, an agreement of sorts. Would Pedregal accept it?

Pedregal looks at me.

I have made up my mind, even though going against Uncle Denesius's orders makes me feel terrible. "Teach me to fight!" I say. "If you put those Books back, I will not say a word to the Grand Protector. You will no longer need to steal the Books. I will find a way to get you food for your parents. In exchange, I ask only that you teach me the fighting techniques that you teach the other Seekers."

Pedregal raises his eyebrows and, after a while, says, "Well, I'll be!" He stands, and as he does so, a smile creeps up from the corner of his mouth. "You are wise beyond your young years, lad. It is a fair trade, indeed. And one you deeply deserve. I still do not understand why the Grand Protector does not want you trained in battle like the others. You are old enough."

Now it is my turn to look at the ground. I lean my weight from one leg to the other. "He says he does not want to lose me. The Roarim almost killed me, you know?" I show him my maimed hand, even though I know he knows of it. "The Grand Protector says I should never again have to face battles at so close a range. He will protect me. He says I am destined for the Library, and he is right."

Pedregal's eyes are piercing. "And yet... you wish to be trained?"

I nod feverishly. "Of course! The next time the Roarim come, I will slice them in two, like this..." I simulate a whizzing sword.

Pedregal chuckles. "Of that, I have no doubt, little Termite."

I blush and grin. Even though he called me Termite this time, I do not mind it because he said it in a gentle, poking way. Uncle Denesius is the only other person who treats my nickname as a term of endearment.

"Well," he says. "You make me a generous offer, but I cannot accept it."

My hands drop to my side. "Why not?"

He rubs his bearded chin. "I cannot accept turning you into a thief yourself, lad. I would stop stealing the Books, but you would start stealing food. That does not seem like a wise trade."

I stomp my foot, my indignation quickly turning to desperation. "Please, Pedregal!" The fact that all the other orphans my age started their training a year ago has been excruciating for me. I understand that Uncle Denesius fears for my life after my close encounter with the Roarim and that he cannot bear to see me close to a sharp blade, but I wish he would understand that this exclusion is causing my companions to mock me.

"Is it because of Roddrick?" Pedregal says.

My head snaps up. It is as if he has read my mind. I

did not think anyone else had noticed Roddrick's bullying.

I nod.

Pedregal sighs and rubs his thumb over his forehead, thinking. "Very well," *he says.*

I break into a smile.

"I accept your trade, Eodain. I will train you in fighting, I will never again touch the Books, and you will provide food for my parents."

I beam.

"However," *he adds.* "I will not teach you so you can fight Roddrick."

My smile wavers.

"If Roddrick suspects you are learning fighting skills from me, he will betray us, and that would be the end of our agreement."

My elation vanishes. However much it pains me, I know he is right. Not that I ever intended to attack Roddrick, but I had hoped to at least be able to defend myself from him.

* * *

As I lie at the bottom of the rift, drifting off, I remember Roddrick's cape. "Roddrick!" I say.

He is leaning against the opposite wall. He opens one eye and peers at me.

"Where is your Seeker's cape?"

Draxis raises his head from the ground and leans on his elbow to get a better look at Roddrick.

"What happened to it?" I insist.

Roddrick leans his head against the rock and shrugs. "Don't know," he mutters. "Lost it in the fight."

I stare at him quizzically.

Draxis lies down again, and Roddrick closes one

eye.

I keep looking at him, though. He was not wearing it when we left the West Tower. Come to think of it, he did not even fight in the Tower... Anger wells up within me.

He left it behind!

It always takes me a moment to figure out Roddrick's statements because I never know when he lies or tells the truth. But in this case, there is no doubt in my mind: Roddrick heard the Roarim soldiers call out to each other about a Knowledge Seeker hiding in the Tower. Roddrick does not want to be that Seeker. He is deflecting the danger towards me.

Just like that, he has cast aside his sacred oath to the Atheneum, to the Books, to Uncle Denesius. He swore to protect his Talisman and take his own life if he lost it. He is no longer a Seeker and is fleeing like a dog with its tail between its legs. As usual, his actions make my stomach churn. My jaw sets so I will not say something nasty. I wish he were not part of this group. Having him around makes me feel unsafe, and with good reason.

The others fall asleep, but Roddrick's betrayal bounces around in my mind. The hard ground digs into my back. I think I will never rest, yet Pedregal's tap on my shoulder wakes me with a start. He is looking back the way we have come.

"Thoron arrives," he says.

I sit up in a hurry, unexpected tension releasing from my shoulders at the sight of the guardsman jogging towards us.

As I stand and wait for the guardsman to catch up with us, Roddrick approaches me and says, "What about your Seeker's cape, Termite? You do realize tens of thousands of soldiers are now looking for a red-caped boy, don't you?"

I glare at him. "I am not ashamed of who I am, *Hyena*," I seethe. "Unlike you."

Roddrick takes a menacing step in my direction, but Thoron comes running up to us. He catches his breath and looks at me, then at Roddrick. "What are you standing around for?" he snaps. "We have a long way ahead. Best get on with it."

Roddrick and I step away from each other. We head out again.

Thoron's authority reassures me. I was taken aback yesterday when the others waited for me to signal a break in our exhausting flight. I would much rather have Thoron take the lead.

"Did you get the Roarim off our tracks?" Pedregal wants to know.

Thoron nods. "For now, at least. I left enough clues to make them believe we are hiding near Eliadys. I saw groups of scouts combing the mountainside, searching for us. That said, the bulk of their army is preparing to head back to Roarim City. We will have to stay one step ahead of them. Hopefully, we will be across the plains by the time they realize we tricked them."

With that threat momentarily out of the way, we head out again, at a slower pace this time. Thoron shows no sign of weariness and leads the way further into the scorched plains. Fortunately, it is early evening by now, and the sun is more forgiving.

My head feels clearer, and I can finally ask the questions burning in my mind. "Draxis! I still cannot believe you made it out of the tunnels! What happened?"

The giant keeps walking before me, and for a moment, I believe he has not heard me. But then he turns. He gestures with his fingers to show he ran for a long time, then his hands blast apart and fall back inwards.

The tunnels collapsed!

He clasps his heavy hammer and makes a movement with it to show he hammered his way out of the rubble, then makes a gasping sound as he catches air.

He points at his eyes, then makes the shape of a hill with his hands. A thick tear rolls down his cheek.

He saw the burning Atheneum! My throat constricts, and I nod, unable to speak. It is nothing short of a miracle that my friend is still alive.

"What about you?" I ask, turning to Pedregal because I cannot bear to linger on Draxis's sad face.

The swordmaster does not answer right away. He looks at the ground as he plods forward. He lifts his head and looks at me. "I tried to save my parents..." he says. His voice breaks. "But I was too late."

I stop and stare at him in horror. "Pedregal!" I clasp his shoulder. "I am sorry."

He nods, then weakly gestures for me to walk on. But I do not budge and continue to stare at him intently. "The Roarim will pay for what they have done," I say vehemently.

Pedregal nods again, his face pale. "Let us get out of this desert alive first, Eodain."

I watch him walk on, realizing we all carry a heavy burden of loss.

Roddrick passes me by, knocking into my shoulder, and mutters under his breath, "How's that crossing-the-desert idea working out for you, bookbug?"

I ball my fists and glare after him.

CHAPTER 11 *The Newarkers*

I am fourteen when Roddrick almost kills me.

Roddrick became a Knowledge Seeker a year ago and, in that small span of time, he has already been on two expeditions in search of the Books.

Fourteen. That is the age when the orphans of the Atheneum receive the great honor of becoming Knowledge Seekers. They receive their own Talisman, greatsword, and cape; and their own quarters within the Atheneum. It is also the year when their nickname is replaced by their official name. Thus, Hyena becomes Roddrick Atheneumson. The Atheneum is his mother and his father. It is his caregiver and provider. He will never go hungry.

In exchange, he must tend to the elegant old building and head out into the land in search of the lost Books of the Enlightened People. It is a dangerous task, for tribal peoples roam the north while pirates and Roarim soldiers patrol the south.

That, too, is my path, my destiny. Despite all their

flaws, I feel a deep bond with the Enlightened People. I believe this awe, respect, and kinship that I have for them has come to fill the void left by my absent parents.

Whoever my parents were, sometimes I feel grateful to them for having left me at the foot of the Atheneum—as all poor parents do when they cannot afford to care for their children. I miss not knowing them, but at the same time, the Atheneum is my home, and my destiny is to become a Knowledge Seeker.

I have just turned fourteen and am preparing to be Anointed a few months from now.

However, my prospects at becoming a Knowledge Seeker are hampered by Uncle Denesius. As usual, he is being overly protective of me. He has hinted that perhaps I am not ready for such a dangerous burden. I stop him in his tracks before he can continue this line of thought.

"Give me a task, Uncle!" I beg him. "I will prove my worth. You will see. You will have nothing to fear, and I will be ready to join my companions on the day of the Anointing."

And so, after much insistence, he agrees to let me join a Knowledge Seeker on a quest to the land of the Newarkers. Except, this Seeker turns out to be Roddrick. My face goes from cold to hot.

For Spirit's sake! Why Roddrick?

I almost say that out loud, but I bite my tongue because as quickly as Uncle Denesius has given me this quest, he can take it away.

Fine, *I think.* I will show him what I am made of.

And so, the next day, I head to the stables, only to find that all the horses are gone. Roddrick must have made sure they were taken out on errands at daybreak.

The trip to the Newarkers is almost eight hundred

miles! The trip on horseback will already take us two months there and back. Following Roddrick on foot is out of the question.

I think this is the end of my ambitious trip, but then it hits me. I rush to the back of the stables and convince the Atheneum gardener to lend me Olive, his donkey. I find Roddrick on a black horse in the main courtyard of the Atheneum, looking proud and imposing with his burgundy Seeker cape. He is followed by a couple of soldiers who are also on horseback.

"You are late," Roddrick says, even though I know I am not. The soldiers guffaw, and the three of them head towards the Atheneum gates and down the hill into the city, with me in tow.

Compared to the people of Eliadys, I look dressed like a prince. I am reminded of the privileged life that we lead in the Atheneum, thanks to the collection of taxes from the northern cities that we protect. It does not seem fair that we should live in opulence when ordinary citizens are going hungry.

The human race is still grappling to survive after suffering through five centuries of apocalyptic changes to the Earth. And Uncle Denesius is so desperate to save the ancient Books before they disintegrate that he sometimes forgets about the struggles of regular citizens.

Even I am guilty of that, I realize, and I make a mental note to talk to Uncle Denesius about it.

The rest of our trip continues without incident. Olive, the donkey, is slower than the horses, so by the time I catch up with the others, they have settled down before a fire and have finished eating. There are only scraps left for me.

After a month like this, Roddrick slows down his horse. "We are approaching Wakingdon. The leader of the Newark tribe has promised to deliver us with a rare Book as a tax payment. That said, do not expect any welcome here. I will be doing the talking." He looks at me as he says this. "There are certain traditions one must uphold in order not to offend them."

I know Roddrick wants to keep the glory of recovering rare Books for himself, but I do not really care at this point. I have never traveled anywhere, and I now find myself in the remains of an ancient city of the Enlightened People.

The wind blows dust and tumbleweed over the ancient road we are treading on, and people step out of crumbled-down homes to observe us. I nod their way as we continue, not stopping until we reach a massive, white building. An equally giant statue of a bearded man in a chair sits inside it.

"A great leader of the Enlightened People," Roddrick says with awe in his voice. "Entrance to the sacred building is forbidden. The Newarkers believe spirits of the Enlightened Ones inhabit it."

At once, my curiosity spikes. What else could be hiding in this ancient building?

We pass by the sacred monument, which looks mostly intact, and approach a row of large tents set up on dirt in the middle of the ruins of another building, which must have been five times the size of the Atheneum.

Roddrick points out that this is where the Capitol once stood—that ancient building that the Atheneum is a copy of. For once, I believe he is telling the truth.

Roddrick gets off his horse and ties it to a horizontal log with a water basin below. We do the same. A group of important-looking people approaches us. They are all bald, and their skin is dark brown.

Roddrick bows. "Noble ones of Newark. I thank

you for receiving us in your northern city of Wakingdon. I am Roddrick Atheneumson, son of the Library, protector of the Books, wielder of the Talisman. I come to you upon the request of the Grand Protector to meet with your noble Chief, Elaine O'Brian."

The group of men stares at us, as if considering whether to welcome us or kill us. A tall one in the middle glances at me for an unnerving amount of time. Then he nods and gives a short bow. "Follow me," he says.

Roddrick glances back at us, then tells me, "Tend to the horses, Termite."

He turns to follow the Newarkers, but the tall one has stopped and is looking at him. "No," he says. "Chief O'Brian will see all of you. Your horses will be fed and groomed."

Roddrick casts me a look that could kill, and we all follow the men.

We are taken to one of the central tents, which sits in the middle and is bigger than the others. It can easily hold twenty people.

A woman with dark skin sits on a leather chair. The sunspots on her forehead and cheeks tell of her age, while her head is smooth and hairless. There is an odd look in her eyes as if she were partially blind, yet her posture is strong and commanding.

We are led before her, and the four of us bow deeply.

When I straighten, I catch my breath because Chief Elaine O'Brian is giving a little bow as well, and as she does so, an object hanging from around her neck slides out from under her tunic.

It is a Talisman.

Roddrick has seen it too, because he glances over

his shoulder at the two soldiers and gives them a brief, meaningful look.

Chief O'Brian tucks away the coveted object in a natural, untroubled move.

The tall man who greeted us outside whispers something in the seated woman's ear, and he glances my way. A frown crosses over the woman's forehead. It is fleeting, yet it makes me uncomfortable.

Roddrick fidgets and clears his throat. "Greetings, noble Chief O'Brian," he says. With that, he proceeds to present himself. This time he names the two soldiers and me— Termite. He signals with his head for us to sit by the entrance.

I obey, feeling the Chief's eyes follow me. I shudder involuntarily and glance away. There is a hand-woven tapestry to my left, made from different shades of lamb wool, hanging from the tent ceiling to the floor.

I focus back on the front because the negotiations begin.

Roddrick states the case of the Atheneum and the Grand Protector; how Uncle Denesius protects the lands from marauding pirates and the power-hungry Roarim; how he protects the Books and how costly it is to maintain the Atheneum and the defensive wall. He thanks the Chief for understanding that tax payment is required and that payment in Books is accepted.

Chief O'Brian remains seated without moving, nor showing any emotion. Seeing this powerful woman makes me wonder why orphaned girls are not allowed to become Knowledge Seekers, but it is one of those questions I instinctively know Uncle Denesius would not approve of me asking.

One day, I will ask him.

Chief O'Brian returns some polite words of welcome and allegiance to the Atheneum, then gestures for a guard to step forward with a box. The guard places the box in front of Roddrick and opens it.

I stretch my neck. I know this is the payment we are receiving, but the way Roddrick tenses, I know it cannot be good.

He dives his hand into the box and lifts a thick, dusty Book. My heart sinks. Even from here, I already recognize it: it is an English-French/French-English dictionary. We already have three similar tomes in the Library. I had hoped for something new. Had the Newarkers not promised something unusual?

I sit back again as Roddrick politely returns the dictionary and starts negotiating for something else. I guess I should have expected it. The Newarkers weren't going to hand over anything priceless at the snap of a finger.

My mind wanders, and I am attracted to the finely-woven tapestry again. There are black lines, grey and white patches, and a lump in the middle... So, why then, does it look so familiar?

And then I realize my eyes are focusing on the details when, in fact, I should take in the design as a whole. I lean back a little and tilt my head to the right. The whole design rotates with me, and suddenly the image clicks in my memory.

At my gasp, the tent goes deathly quiet. I snap my head around and find that Chief O'Brian's eyes are set on me. This makes Roddrick turn and bare his teeth at me for taking the Chief's attention away from him.

I gulp and clear my throat. I had not meant to interrupt the meeting, but Chief O'Brian seems to be waiting for me to acknowledge the artwork.

"A satellite!" I say nervously, pointing vaguely to my left. "This tapestry... ahem... it is beautiful..."

Roddrick rolls his eyes at me, then faces the Chief

again and says, "It is quite unheard of, for a woman to be carrying the weight of so much responsibility."

I tense up. *He would not dare ask for the Talisman as tax payment, would he?*

But Chief O'Brian has not moved an inch. Then, she rises, dismissing Roddrick altogether by glancing past him towards me. "You must be weary," she says. "A tent has been provided for you, as well as food and refreshments. Get some rest. We will speak again in the morning." And just like that, she turns and disappears through a slit in the tent.

When we arrive at our sleeping quarters, I discover that our tent is split in two, with a group of guards occupying the other part. *Are they protecting us? Or are they holding us prisoner? Maybe a bit of both.* In any case, it means the food is hard to swallow, and there is a tenseness in the air that does not allow me to rest as much as I would like.

Yet, by some miracle, I fall asleep and am awakened at dawn by the sound of a boot scraping the ground near my head. A Newark guard nudges my shoulder and indicates I should follow him, but does not summon my sleeping companions. My heart constricts, yet I have no choice but to follow the guard.

Chief O'Brian is waiting outside the tent with another three guards. Without a word, she turns and strides away with the guards and me in tow. The further we walk away from the tent, the more anxious I become. It is a while before I realize we are heading towards the ancient building with the seated statue.

Curiosity sets in.

We walk along beside the massive statue and reach a side door to the monument. Chief O'Brian takes out a huge key and unlocks the door. It is here that she looks at me and nudges her head to say I should enter.

I gawk at her. She wants ME to enter the forbidden building? The one that is supposed to contain spirits of the Enlightened People?

A guard shoves me in the back, but I resist, confused. "But..." I stutter, "...it is forbidden!"

The smallest of smiles passes over the aged woman's face. "If I allow it, then it is not forbidden."

I stare at her. I do not have much choice, and, in any case, if this is going to be the last thing I see in my life, I feel like it is going to be worth it. Goosebumps break out over my skin as I enter into the gloom.

Chief O'Brian follows me, and, to my surprise, she shuts the door, leaving the guards outside. It is just the two of us, now.

"Come," she says.

We walk down a corridor, our boots echoing on the marble floor. The air feels musty and old. We pass through another door, and I gasp.

Half-a-dozen pigeons take flight in a hurry. We have entered the center of the building. Except, there is nothing left. Some shrubs peek out from between large slabs of marble on the ground. My arms drop at my side in disappointment.

"Who are you?"

Chief O'Brian's unexpected question makes me whirl towards her.

"Er... They call me Termite. I will become a Knowledge Seeker soon. Then they will call me Eodain Atheneumson."

"Hmm," she says, as if my answer does not satisfy her. "You look familiar. You have the face of someone I knew when I was your age. Who are your parents?"

She is obviously confusing me with someone else. "I do not have parents. I am an orphan, as are all the Seekers who live at the Atheneum."

She blinks once, then sighs. "I will not hide that I do not like the Atheneum, nor the one who runs it." Her eyes are hard, and I start to sweat. "But a Chief must know when to stand back in order to protect her people. Pirates raid our livestock and steal our women. We are not strong enough to defend ourselves. I have no choice but to rely on the protection of the Atheneum. I will pay the tax, as is customary. And I will do more than that. Your Grand Protector will be satisfied." Without warning, she turns and heads to the right, where a door leads to a small, dark room.

"You do not believe in spirits," she says, not as a question but as a statement.

I clear my throat. "The Grand Protector says..."

"My people would have been terrified to enter this sanctuary," she interrupts. "I see that you are not afraid of the Enlightened People."

"Oh, no!" I burst out. "I admire them. They were resourceful and brilliant and foreseeing..."

"So foreseeing that they destroyed themselves..." she says sarcastically.

"Er..."

Lighting a torch, she approaches a bookshelf, where she fixes the light into a metal ring sticking out from the wall. "And what of the Sky Spirits?" she asks. "Do you believe in them?" As she says this, she approaches a bookshelf filled with Books.

I do not know why but I decide to be honest with her. "I know that the Sky Spirits are satellites: artificial machines sent into space so people could exchange messages and information. The satellites connected the Enlightened People all across Earth." I fall silent and wait for her reaction.

A smile creeps up her face again. "You are so young," she says, carefully extracting a Book from one of the shelves. "And yet, you know of the satellites. Few still do."

She places the thin yellowish volume on a wooden table, and I read the words:

NATIONAL GEOGRAPHIC MAGAZINE
May 2087

Satellites: A Vision From Above

The subtitles read:

Evolving Sky Spirits.
Free Knowledge From Space.
The Rods of God.
The Fall of NASA.

My heart races.

She passes her hand lightly over the Book as if it were a delicate flower. Her voice drops. "As I said before, I do not like your Grand Protector. He claims to protect the Knowledge so the Roarim or the pirates will not misuse it, but he, too, is guilty of keeping it for himself. He has not yet fulfilled his promise to turn the Knowledge Seekers into teachers so they may educate the people."

I swallow.

"However," she continues. "I do realize that protecting the Knowledge within the Atheneum is difficult and costly at this time. We are all anxious for better times. Yet, this ancient monument we stand in is dying. I am surprised the pirates have not yet looted it."
She hands me the Book. "Some things are worth saving. Your Grand Protector will consider this a great gift, but it is not a gift. It is an attempt to save a piece of

Knowledge from the Enlightened Era. It will be safer in the Atheneum than it is here."

I stare wide-eyed from the Book to the Chief. "Thank you," I breathe. "I will protect it with my life. You have my word."

Her smile vanishes, and her eyes darken. "Beware of the other Seeker. I do not trust him. He does not understand the Old Ways."

I stare at her and wordlessly give a slight nod. She means Roddrick!

We are going to head out when my eyes fall on a glass display case. Small silver objects lie in a row, looking harmless and insignificant.

My eyes widen. "Are those... technetium storage devices?" My heart quickens. They look similar to the Talismans I have seen the Knowledge Seekers carry, and also the one Chief O'Brian is wearing around her neck right now. I know that the Newarkers do not have access to the Books or virtual files from the Atheneum, so that leaves me with the burning question: what type of other information might these technetium devices contain?

Chief O'Brian glides before me, cutting off my view of the ancient coveted objects. "Those are not for your Atheneum," she says, laying her milky eyes on me. "Only one worthy enough could wield them."

She does not move, and I understand that I have worn out my welcome.

We head out, and all at once, I wish I could spend more time here. I feel a blooming kinship with this wise Chief. I think I could ask her all the bubbling questions I have been holding inside for so long, and she would have answers. Yet, I say no more. It would be disrespectful. She has already given me much more than we could ever have expected.

We head out of the building. My mind is whirling. The Atheneum has indeed focused its efforts on saving the Knowledge while people are anxiously waiting for us to teach it to them. Organizing the Knowledge Seekers to become teachers instead of seekers is a massive undertaking, however, and with the constant interruption of wars, it has been hard for Uncle Denesius to focus on this task.

One day... *I promise myself.* One day, when I am a Knowledge Seeker, I will return...

The Newarkers bring us our horses and my donkey. Their fur is shiny, and they look rested and well-fed. We are provided with food and water for our return trip. All this is happening swiftly, and little is said. Our welcome has expired, and we must leave.

All this time, Roddrick's face is pale, and he does not speak a word. He seems bewildered at having been cast aside. I can almost see the questions gnawing at him. How? And... Why Termite? Why did a lower-ranking squire, who is not even a full-fledged Knowledge Seeker, receive such a priceless gift?

I wish I hadn't had to tell him about the magazine, but Roddrick would never have gone home empty-handed, and the National Geographic is the only thing the Newarkers have given us.

As we take our leave and head out into the dry wilderness again, I turn back for one last glance towards Chief O'Brian. Her milky eyes are set on me, and her words ring in my mind, "Beware of the other Seeker. I do not trust him."

Even so, our return trip goes by uneventfully. Roddrick and the two soldiers do not leave me behind this time. They know as well as I do that our tax payment must be protected and brought home safely. We travel at a slow but steady pace, always staying together despite not a word being spoken between us. I barely sleep at night. I lie on top of the magazine and pretend to sleep, but the smallest sound startles me awake. Roddrick would not dare steal the Book from me, would he?

Only once do I take a quick peek at the magazine. I flip through it, and my eyes fall on the title:

The Rods of God.

An image depicts a satellite with long poles attached to it. One end of the poles is slightly thicker, while the other ends have four small, wing-like things protruding from them. These objects have nothing to do with the Gods of the Ancients. Rather, their power was deemed so great that the Ancients compared them to the power of their Gods. For these plain-looking poles were attached to satellites and sent up into space, and when they were released, they would fall back to Earth, gathering such an impressive speed that the crater they would leave upon impact could destroy entire cities.

My eyes scan the words in the article: kinetic bombardment, orbital strike, global war, no defense...

The Enlightened People did not only create things for comfort or beauty. The satellites were not only there to spread Knowledge across the Earth. They were also there to kill. The Enlightened Ones learned how to kill themselves.

I feel someone observing me and look up.

Roddrick is there, watching me.

I close the magazine and rapidly wrap it in a protective cloth, then stuff it in my travel satchel.

He snorts. "Do you truly believe I would steal it from you, bookbug?" The soldiers snicker. Roddrick grins. "How lowly you think of your fellow Seeker!"

I glare at him, tighten the strap of my satchel, and get on Olive's back without answering.

As the days pass, I start to relax. My mind wanders back to Chief O'Brian and her dislike of Uncle Denesius. She may not like the arrangement with the Atheneum, but I believe her resentment goes deeper. I believe it is because she is a woman. Women are not allowed to hold high positions in the Atheneum, yet, the fact that Chief OBrian is a woman proves to me, once again, that women would be just as capable Seekers as men. Uncle Denesius must have a valid reason for barring women from this honor.

I sigh. There are so many things I will have to discuss with him when we get home.

When we reach a particularly pleasant stretch of road with golden fields spreading out to my left and trees with shade to my right, I hope we will rest here for the night. As I look at a rare sight—a gurgling stream—I am struck from behind. I fall off the donkey. With my head spinning and ears ringing, I reach for my sword, but a soldier's boot kicks it away. Olive brays in panic and gallops off.

Another boot kicks me so hard in the stomach the air is ejected out of me. For a second, I cannot breathe, and at that moment, I feel the weight of the satchel falling away from my shoulder. Another kick, and I hear a sickening pop inside my chest.

I try to pull myself up but cannot. While the world spins in front of me, I notice Roddrick on his horse, throwing a glance my way. "I told you I would never steal from you, Termite," he says. "However, I cannot speak for them."

A kick in the head from one of the two soldiers almost makes me lose consciousness. Hands grab me *under the armpits and drag me over the road. Emptiness greets me as I am tossed down the ravine, rolling over-and-over until I land headfirst in the stream.*

CHAPTER 12 *The Soldier*

I do not know why Roddrick's attempt to kill me keeps playing over and over in my mind. I guess it keeps my thoughts away from more terrible things, like the memory of the burning Atheneum.

We walk for most of the night and into the early daylight hours. My mind and feet are set on automatic. It feels like forever until Thoron finally signals for us to stop. The heat of the day beats down on us, and we approach the end of the rift.

I glance at the opening, trying not to think of what lies beyond: scorched plains followed by mostly barren mountains.

We drop to the ground and share small portions of food and water. Now that Thoron is here, we can ration his food and water, but my stomach gnarls at the thought that we will be out of both within a day. The fact that we could be walking to our deaths whispers at the back of my mind.

We fall asleep with the sun beating down on us,

then head out again as the night settles in deep colors of orange and red. We walk on through the night under a star-filled sky. When the sun rises, our feet take us over the plains, and our situation becomes dire. The mountains are still a day's walk away and our provisions are all but gone. A gnawing feeling in my gut tells me that I am deceiving myself: Roarim City is still days away, and we will find nothing in those mountains to sustain us.

We reach the flank of the first mountain by late afternoon, dehydrated and exhausted, and crumple to the ground in the shadow of a ledge. The heat from the ground seeps through my clothing. Heatwaves rise on the horizon.

I lick my dry lips, tasting dust and sand, and despair engulfs me. Out there, far away, on the other side of the plains, I can guess the outline of the mountain range where the City of Eliadys lay. For all the hardships faced by the city, it was a haven compared to this.

No one dares to speak. I think we all know that we are trapped, and my chest tightens in guilt for having been the one to suggest escaping through the rift.

"We need to get higher up," I say. My words do not really mean anything, for there is nothing higher up. I just feel like I need to take responsibility by giving us a goal.

Pedregal agrees. "I have heard there are pools of water among these mountains, collected from hundreds of years of dew dripping from the rocks."

I lean up on my elbows and stare at him. "Let's go, then." I know none of us have the energy to walk on, yet lying here feels like a death sentence.

We split up and look for a way up the mountain. I am about to start climbing when something shiny catches my eye. It is an object at the base of the mountain. I bend down to pick it up. It turns out to be an empty water bottle made from strong, transparent plastic. I stiffen. Roarim soldiers are known to travel with these ancient recipients, just like we would use recycled ancient plastic vats in the West Tower to store our water.

I glance around. It doesn't take long to locate footprints coming in from the plains. Footprints that are not ours. And they are heading right into the mountain behind me. I gesture at Draxis, who is some ways away, and signal 'Roarim' with my hands. He catches the attention of the others, then heads my way.

I am already following a natural path up the mountain. Several footsteps are imprinted in the dust before me. Whoever is hiding out here cannot be far off. Draxis's heavy feet thump on the ground behind me.

After a while, I realize there are only two different boot marks and, moments later, I find a discarded backpack. After a quick glimpse inside, I find it only contains another empty bottle and a knife. I store away the items in my satchel—we must carry anything that might help us survive.

I continue to forge my way up the mountain, adrenaline momentarily eclipsing my weariness. I reach a shaded area near the top of the mountain where the rocks are bigger and rounder. The path turns to sand and opens up into a wider area.

I round a rock that is twice my size and take a peek. I see a small lake. A movement in the far corner of the basin makes me jump right back! My heart quickens.

Draxis pants up beside me, and I hush him.

We listen for sounds, and I am surprised to hear sobbing. I lean forward and glance around the rock again. I see them: two Roarim soldiers clad in armor and helmets. One is lying on the ground; the other is kneeling beside him.

My companions catch up, and I signal *two* with my fingers, then point behind the rock. They nod, and before I can do anything else, Roddrick charges forward, sword in hand.

We rush after him, yelling ferociously.

The kneeling soldier leaps to his feet, and without hesitation, rushes to the side of the mountain. He scrambles up with incredible agility.

We watch him leap up onto a jutting rock, which sticks out above the unresponsive soldier. Roddrick rushes forward and nudges the soldier on the ground with his foot. "This one is dead," he says.

"Do not touch him!" The shriek comes from the rock, and I gasp because it is the voice of a girl. She removes her helmet and throws it at Roddrick.

"Hey!" Roddrick yells, lifting his arms to deflect the projectile, which lands harmlessly at his feet.

Before I can react, Draxis steps forward, raises his massive hammer, and swings it just below the jutting rock. An explosion of rubble flies all around. The shock loosens the rock, and it—along with the girl—comes tumbling down. She catches her balance at the last second and leaps effortlessly to the side, then lets herself roll to the ground to break her fall.

At once, she is on her feet again, dagger in hand and teeth bared under a flurry of sand-colored hair. Her dirty cheeks are marked by the passage of tears, and her face is as pale as a ghost's. She swings her blade at us, making us step back cautiously so she can drop back to the ground and embrace the lifeless soldier. "Do not touch him!" she shouts again, her eyes daring us to do otherwise.

We look down at the curious pair. Roddrick snorts, steps forward, and lifts his sword.

"Wait!" I shout, pushing down his arm.

The girl looks at us with wide eyes. Even though she knows she risks death, she stays by the dead soldier's side.

Roddrick glares at me but waits.

I look at the girl. "Who is that?" I ask.

Fresh tears spill down her face. "My brother, Simon Dundurn," she sobs.

Roddrick shakes his hand off his arm. "Who cares?" he snarls, stepping forward again.

"Hey!" I shout at him, shoving him aside.

His face contorts with anger, and he snarls at me, "What is wrong with you? This is a Roarim. Are you blind?"

Not long ago, I would have cringed at his vehemence, but right now, I do not have any patience. Roddrick irritates me. "That is enough! She is mourning her brother. Are you heartless?"

Roddrick swings around to face the others. Words spit out of his mouth. "Well? What are you waiting for? Punch some sense into him, will you?"

The others remain unmoving, and I catch a brief moment of hesitation passing over their faces.

It is Pedregal who finally replies, "He is the Seeker, Roddrick." His voice trails off. Those few words carry all their meaning: I am the last Knowledge Seeker, and I must be obeyed.

Roddrick turns to Thoron, who has just arrived after having scanned our surroundings. Thoron does not say anything, and by his silence, it seems he agrees with Pedregal.

"I see!" Roddrick snaps. "Stand by this traitor, then. I will have no part in it." He puts away his sword and lumbers off toward the shallow lake.

I turn to the girl. She is looking at me, her cheeks pale, waiting for my verdict. I do not know why I wish to save the life of a Roarim. Perhaps it is because it seems unfair to slaughter someone who is outnumbered four to one. Or maybe it is because I have been in her position before, when Roddrick would corner me with his buddies. "Hand over your weapon," I order.

She hesitates.

"We will not harm you," I assure her.

Thoron twitches beside me. "Do not trust her, Eodain," he mumbles under his breath.

She throws her dagger at my feet and turns to hug the dead soldier, rocking back and forth as she does so.

I sigh and pick up her dagger. "We will have our fill in water, and then we will help you bury your brother." I turn around, ignoring Thoron, who shoots me a look of disdain, and head to the lake.

I do not care what the others think. There is too much pain, too much loss around me right now. I cannot think. My body aches for water. Maybe I am making the biggest mistake of my life, and later I will pay for saving a Roarim, but right now, I am at peace with my decision.

* * *

I struggle out of unconsciousness and find myself face up, half-submerged in the stream. There is not a muscle in me that does not hurt. I groan and try to sit up, but pain shoots through my rib cage. It makes me terribly aware of my situation.

It is not pretty.

Roddrick and his two soldiers have abandoned me, half dead and with no way to get home. The magazine is undoubtedly in Roddrick's possession. That thought triggers a tsunami of anger within me. I ignore my aching ribs, roll onto my stomach and drag myself out of the stream. It takes me forever to make it back up the road. The sun beats down on me, and cracked mud dries on my hands and in my hair.

By the time I reach the side of the road, nausea washes over me, and I need to rest. Horses approach steadily from behind, and I force myself to stay conscious.

"Help!" I mouth, but I am not sure I make any sound.

A wagon, pulled by a couple of horses, slows down as it nears. I reach out my hand, willing it to stop. "Help!" I utter as I focus long enough to glimpse fear in the face of a man and a woman sitting on the wagon. Then, the pounding of horses' hooves accelerates, and the wagon rolls by in a hurry.

My heart sinks. That part of my brain that seems to have a will of its own transports me into one of the Books that I read many years ago. In it, there was an image of a white steel carriage used by the Enlightened People with the word AMBULANCE written on its side. The Book stated that one of these ambulances would arrive a few minutes after being hailed and transport a wounded person to a healing place called a HOSPITAL. This hospital was filled with people knowledgeable in medicine, and all who asked for help would receive it.

Where have the ambulances gone? *I wonder as I drift into darkness.* Where have the hospitals gone?

I stumble forward along the road and reach pastures filled with cattle. Someone is tending to a cow. His eyes widen when he sees me approach. I can tell the young man is going to run away, but I have thought up a strategy to convince him to help me. "I come from the

Atheneum. I was ambushed and robbed. If you help me, the Grand Protector will reward you," I say.

The young man hesitates, then runs off.

Great. *I sag to the ground. But it turns out my tactic worked because the young man returns with an older man who must be his father.*

"What is your name?" he asks.

"Termite," I reply. *They would not have believed me if I had said Eodain Atheneumson. I am not wearing a Seeker cape. I am not yet a Seeker.*

They help me into the back of a hay cart, and the father takes me into the poorest quarters of Eliadys.

He stops in the middle of a dusty street lined with shacks, and people start gathering around the cart, glancing curiously at me.

"I do not know what to do with him," I hear the father say. *"Says he was attacked. Says his name is Termite and that he is from the Atheneum."*

"Termite?" someone shouts. There is a commotion as an elderly man makes his way through the crowd. He peers at me. "You are Termite?" he asks. Without waiting for an answer, he grabs my maimed hand and looks at it. "Oh!" he exclaims before bowing profusely. "Master Eodain!"

I stare at him.

He turns to the crowd. "This is Master Eodain! Quickly, now! Help him off the cart!"

People break into excited conversation and stretch their necks to get a better look at me.

"Make way! Make way!" the elderly man shouts as two men help me off the cart and carry me through the onlookers into a tiny shack a few houses down. They drop me on a rickety bed.

The father who drove me into the city stands in the doorway. "What is your name?" I ask. "So I may repay you?'

He shakes his head vigorously and hurries off without a word.

An elderly woman's face appears before me. She takes my hand and squeezes it. "Master Eodain! My dear boy!" Her wrinkled face is beaming. "We are Pedregal's parents," she says. "Rest, now. We will take good care of you."

Pedregal's parents! *They are the ones I have been sneaking food out of the Atheneum for in exchange for the swordmaster's lessons! I cannot believe my luck. Tension releases from my muscles, my highly alert brain eases, and I drift into a deep, welcome sleep.*

When I awaken, my clothes have been cleaned, and my wounds have been tended to. Pedregal's mother bustles about a tiny kitchen, chopping and mixing vegetables into a steaming pot hanging over a fire.

After a while, the elderly woman fills a bowl with broth and comes to my side. "Your vegetables," she says, smiling.

I smile back. She is offering me the food that I have sent to them by means of Pedregal. "Thank you," I say shyly. As an orphan, I have never received this much personal attention and care before, and I do not know how to respond to it. I sit up with difficulty and sip on the soup even though it is burning hot. It tastes glorious.

Pedregal's father enters with chopped wood and feeds the fire.

"Look, honey," the woman tells him. "Our patient is awake.

He shuffles to her side. "Wonderful, wonderful!" he says, his eyes creasing with laughter.

I look around to avoid blushing more and notice that the window beside my bed is covered by a dirty, half-transparent sheet of ancient plastic. Also, the walls are constructed with ancient bottles of plastic filled with dirt, stacked one on top of the other, and covered with dry mud. I had told Pedregal about this building method, and he applied it to his parent's shack.

The elderly man realizes what I am looking at. He nods. "You have started quite a revolution, dear boy. The whole neighborhood is trading for plastic bottles nowadays. Everybody wants a house like this. It was very clever of you to come up with such a building strategy!"

I smile sadly. If only he knew what other things the Books could teach him. It reminds me of the conversation I had with Chief O'Brian, about Knowledge Seekers turning into teachers. This whole trip to the Newarkers and back has opened my eyes to the needs of the real world.

The woman looks down at her wrinkled hands. "We apologize for our humble home," she says. "But you are welcome in it anytime."

The man rests his hand on his wife's shoulder and nods. "Yes, young Master. You are much better off at the Atheneum. Our Grand Protector is such a generous man for taking in and caring for our orphans. Let us hope the Roarim have learned their lesson so that we can return to peaceful times again. It would benefit us all."

I frown. "Peaceful times?" I ask.

The woman pats her husband's hand. "Oh, honey, this child does not remember. It was way before his time."

I stare at them.

"You are right," the man says, squeezing his wife's hand. "It seems like only yesterday, when the cities of Roarim and Eliadys got along. It is too bad that greed *poisoned the minds of our enemies. Lucky for us, the Grand Protector realized their corruption and built the defensive wall just in time before the Roarim's first attack." He falls silent, then waves his hand at me. "Ah, but why am I talking about somber times. Today is a day of celebration!"*

My eyes turn to the open door that leads into the street. It is unnaturally quiet out there. "Celebration?" I ask. "But it is so quiet out there."

Pedregal's mother nods. "Of course! Today is Anointing Day. Everyone has gone to the marketplace for the festivities."

"WHAT?" Some broth spills on my lap. I wince as the burning liquid seeps through the blanket. "How... how long have I been out?" I gawk at them.

Before they can answer, I hand the bowl to the elderly man and swing my legs to the side of the bed. The ground sways beneath me.

Pedregal's mother clasps her chest. "Oh, do be careful, dear. You could open your wounds again."

I look at them intensely and force the words out of my mouth, "How long have I been unconscious?"

The woman looks at her husband before saying, "Three days, dear. You were not well. Not well at all."

I stare at her blankly. Three days! *I stagger to my feet. I left the Atheneum weeks ago to visit the Newarkers and have completely lost track of time.*

"Please, child. You must rest," Pedregal's father says, urging me to lie down again.

"No, no! Anointing Day... I must go..." My stomach squeezes in panic. I stuff my feet into my boots, not even bothering to tie the laces. "...must go. No time." My fingers tremble as I try to button up my shirt. I give up after three buttons. "I am sorry. I must go."

Pedregal's parents stare at me.

I swallow, trying to remember my manners as I stumble out of the shack. "Thank you! You have saved me. I will never forget..." Bright sunlight startles me. I lift my arm to shade my eyes and grab onto the wall.

"Master Eodain!" Pedregal's father exclaims, reaching out to help me.

"No! I must go!" I mutter, turning away and heading down the street. The Atheneum shines, clean and beautiful, on the hilltop overlooking the city. Colorful banners blow in the wind. I glance back at Pedregal's father. He has wrapped his arm around his wife, and she is clasping his hand. Both stare after me with the deepest concern.

I almost burst into tears.

The way to the Atheneum seems endless, and my rib cage screams with pain. How could I have lost track of the days? The road takes me to the back of the hill, and I climb hundreds of stairs cut out of the rock, then follow the Atheneum's outer fortifications to the main entrance.

Cheers reach my ears. Drums, flutes, and mandolins play festive tunes. When I turn the corner, Knowledge Seekers are parading down the hill on their shining horses, banners flying, capes flowing. Flowers are thrown before them, and city dwellers shout their admiration and servitude.

The last soldiers file out of the Atheneum grounds after the Seekers, and the gates are being closed.

"Wait!" I moan, slipping through the gates before they thud shut behind me. The sound of the crowds diminishes. I wobble across the silent courtyard, which is littered with flowers, and burst into the building. I head down the cool hall towards the Library. My boots echo on the marble slabs.

I shove open the heavy Library doors.

"Wait!" I shout, my cry bouncing off the walls.

A handful of people, who are cleaning up inside, glance up at me.

I collapse to the floor, my back resting against the door. There is not an ounce of energy left in me.

Footsteps rush to my side. I grab the shirt of the first person who bends over me. "Anointing..." I beg feverishly. "Must be Anointed!"

"It is Termite!" someone yells. "Call the Grand Protector! Call him at once!"

I am picked up and placed on a marble bench in the great hall. I recognize Uncle Denesius's hurried footsteps long before he reaches my side. "I am h-here!" I hiccup. "I am ready f-for the Anointing!"

"Termite!" he gasps. "Oh, Termite! I feared the worst!" He looks me over. "Who did this to you? I will have their heads!"

"Rod-drick," I stutter. "It w-was Roddrick."

"What?" Uncle Denesius pulls back, frowning. He places his hand on my forehead. "You are delirious," he says.

"It was R-Roddrick!" I repeat.

Uncle Denesius's face hardens. "Come, now, boy. Don't be foolish. Roddrick would never lay a hand on you."

I open my mouth, but nothing comes out. Roddrick: sitting on his horse, standing some way back, watching the soldiers punch me. He did not lay a hand on me. "N-no, but..."

Uncle Denesius is no longer listening. He addresses the ones standing around us. "He is burning up. Tell the healer to hurry."

"U-uncle. The Anointing. I am r-ready..."

He turns his worried eyes my way again and shakes his head. "Oh, Termite. I knew I should not have let you *go. This is all my fault."*

"N-no! I am r-ready..."

Someone places a wooden cup in Uncle Denesius's hands, and he lifts me into a half-sitting position. The faces sway around me as a thick liquid goes down my throat. I take two gulps before I almost choke.

"Shh," Uncle Denesius hushes me. "You are safe now. When Roddrick returned without you and told me about the pirate attack, I was sure I had lost you forever. I sent out troops looking for you, but all they found was Olive, wandering alone. My heart is blessed. Today is a fortunate day, indeed!"

"B-but the An..."

Someone taps Uncle Denesius on the shoulder and whispers in his ear. "Forgive me, Grand Protector, but the people are waiting for you down at the marketplace."

"Yes, yes," he says impatiently. "Get my horse ready."

I grab onto his sleeve, but everything seems so distant. It is as if I am in a deep tunnel looking out, and my arms no longer obey me. "I want to be Anointed," I say, but the words must not come out because they ignore me, and Uncle Denesius is giving the healer instructions to get my fever down and get me back on my feet as soon as possible.

"I want to be a Knowledge Seeker," I beg in my mind as I drift into a deep sleep.

CHAPTER 13 *Lullaby*

I plunge my head into the lake. The liquid acts like a thunderbolt, waking my mind and bringing life back to my tired body. I drink to my heart's content—as do the others. It is only after we have had our fill and have rested that I focus on the girl again.

She is kneeling next to her brother. She is no longer crying. Her gaze is lost, and she seems indifferent to what is happening around her.

Thoron approaches me and says, "I have scanned the area. There are no other Roarim about. These two came on their own."

I nod without taking my eyes off the girl. I realize Thoron is much better prepared at all of this than I am. Why had I not thought of checking our surroundings as soon as we arrived? Thirst had gotten the better of me, and that is not a good thing. I need to be more alert. I walk over to the girl. "What is your name?" I ask.

"Elysa Dundurn," she says in a numb voice.

Pedregal comes up beside me. "A bit young to be a

Roarim soldier, don't you think?"

I have to agree. She cannot be older than I am.

She glances at us, then looks away again. "I am training to be a healer. I could not let my brothers do all the fighting and not be there to help the wounded. I dressed up as a boy and joined the army." She trails off, and her chin shivers. "I guess the war was a bit more than I could handle."

"What are you doing here, then?" Thoron snaps, and I wish he wouldn't be so harsh. "A deserter, I bet!"

Her nostrils flare. "I am no deserter! Nor was my brother! The fire at the Atheneum caught us by surprise. We got separated from the army and lost our bearings in the cloud of dust and smoke. By the time daylight arrived and the sky cleared, we..." she catches her breath, "...we were halfway across the plains. My brother was wounded. I headed for the nearest mountains, thinking I was going in the right direction..." She cuts off. Her head drops, and she shuts her eyes.

Thoron snorts. "Well, had your people not started that blaze, you would not be in this predicament." He glares at her, then turns and stomps off.

Her head shoots up, and she opens her mouth to retort. There are small frown lines on her forehead as if Thoron's statement caught her off guard. When she does not speak, I bend to the ground and begin digging.

Silently, Pedregal and Draxis join me, and we make a hole to bury Elysa's brother. She is clasping her hands together the entire time, and thick tears roll down her cheeks, but she remains stoic and unmoving. Thoron and Roddrick stand off to the side, clearly uninterested in helping out the Roarim, and I am lucidly aware that Pedregal and Draxis are only doing this for me—not for her.

When we are done, I go and sit by a welcoming

fire. The night is growing cold, and I am relieved to be able to wrap myself up in my Seeker cape.

"Tomorrow, we hunt," Thoron says as he lies down for the night.

My empty stomach rumbles, but exhaustion takes over. I lie down as well, briefly wondering if I should offer my cape to the girl. She is lying out in the dark, exposed to the elements, near the boulder that toppled down earlier. I quickly discard the thought. Why would I want to continue to help a Roarim? And, in any case, my companions would go into an uproar.

As I drift into sleep, I briefly wonder if Elysa will still be there in the morning.

* * *

The next day, Thoron catches two hares with his crossbow. Not too bad for a first hunt. The hares are crisping over a crackling fire, and the smell makes my mouth water.

I glance at the girl for the hundredth time. She did not flee nor try to slit our throats during the night. In fact, she comes over and presents a handful of dark-blue berries.

"Trying to poison us, then?" Roddrick snarls.

Her face falls. She glares at him, then shoves all the berries into her mouth. When she bites into them, thick blue liquid spurts between her lips and trickles down her chin. She keeps chomping, taunting him, then turns and walks away.

I lift a hand to my mouth to stop a snicker.

Roddrick jumps to his feet, glaring after her, but just then, Thoron arrives and dumps a dead falcon in Roddrick's arms. "Clean this bird, will you?" he says.

I stare at the scene, trying to suppress my rising

grin. Either Thoron's arrival was fortuitous, or he acted in the moment to force Roddrick to calm down. Roddrick sits again and gruffly plucks the bird's feathers.

My shoulders relax. I realize I have lived most of my life on edge, waiting for Roddrick to act out. And now this girl—this Elysa—just made him the laughing stock of a joke.

It bothers me that I am completely fascinated by this Roarim girl. Maybe it is because she is not at all the way I imagined the Roarim to be. I have never really seen the face of a Roarim because of their helmets. I expected ugly, ferocious people with pointed teeth or gnarled hands or distorted faces; something— anything—that would justify our hate and fear of them.

But this girl? Well, she is just a girl. There is nothing odd about her. She is just like any other girl in Eliadys. Until I think about her hazel eyes and pixie face, and just like that, I have to turn my focus on keeping the fire going as my cheeks heat up. This will not do. I have to think about our present situation. This girl is a Roarim. Her people destroyed my home, killed Uncle Denesius, and obliterated the Books.

Then, a humming reaches my ears, a haunting tune that is coming from the lake. When I look up, I find Elysa combing her wet hair with her fingers. Quiet words drift through the air.

"Twinkle, twinkle little star...."

I am struck by lightning.

"How I wonder what you are..."

My back tenses like an icepick.

"Up above the sky so high. Like a diamond in the sky..."

I rise to my feet, ignoring my companion's stares. My feet carry me over the ground in large strides. My heart almost beats out of my chest, and my mind roars with three words: *How dare she!*

Somewhere far away, I hear laughter. "You show her, Termite!"

Elysa lifts her head, her fingers still caught in her hair.

My hand lifts high, fingers extended, ready to strike.

The tune dies in her throat, her eyes widen in terror, and she lifts her arm before her face to deflect the blow.

Except, the blow does not come.

I stand there, muscles tense, ready to hit. But I do not. Hot and cold flashes wash over me. "How *dare* you!" I growl.

Her eyes dart everywhere. "Wh...?"

"How *dare* you sing that song! It is forbidden!"

She glances around as if seeking help. "B-but it is just a l-lullaby..."

I lift my arm higher, then stop. I hesitate. *What am I doing?*

The fear in her eyes is poignant. "It... It is just a l-lullaby, a song we sing to soothe our sadness or put our children to sleep..."

Goosebumps burst out on my skin. I have become Uncle Denesius. His rage has become my own. The only thing stopping me from slapping her is the look in her eyes. They show the same terror I felt when Uncle Denesius struck me on the West Tower when I was little.

My arm shakes, and I lower it slowly.

She stares at me. "It is just a lullaby," she whispers.

I stand before her, shaken to the core. I do not know what to do with myself. "Just..." I breathe. "Do not sing that song ever again."

She stares at me before rising to her feet and sprinting off behind the rocks.

I back away, stunned by my actions. I cannot face the questions from my companions, who grumble at my weak spirit, and make my way to a ledge overlooking the desert plains. There, I drop down against a rock. I grab my hair in my hands and squeeze my eyes shut, trying to calm down.

My heart is beating fast as if I had been transported back to that night on the West Tower, and I can still feel the outline of Uncle Denesius's fingers on my cheek from where he slapped me.

I am so confused. Why did he hate that song so much? I go over the words. They are innocent words that talk about the stars. Come to think of it; it is almost as if the song referred to the Sky Spirits.

Twinkle, twinkle, little star,
How I wonder what you are...

I shudder. The song itself does not explain Uncle Denesius's hatred for it. And although I may never discover the reason for his reaction, what bothers me more than anything else is Uncle Denesius's action itself. How could he have struck an innocent child like that? How was I supposed to know the song was forbidden? I remember spending my childhood looking for approval and love from Uncle Denesius only to end up in shock and fear more than once—the same shock and fear that reflected on Elysa's face moments ago.

CHAPTER 14 *A Plan*

I simmer in dark thoughts for a while. Pedregal brings me a rabbit leg. I tear at the meat with my teeth, grinding the food down between my jaws like some savage beast. Pedregal is wise enough to leave me alone. Showing signs of weakness and emotion in front of these men will only lead them to think of me as a child. I kick at the dirt with my boot.

The food entering my system does me a world of good and calms me down. I am still hungry, but I am not in the mood to chat with my companions. In any case, they are talking about our encounter with the Wraith Lord and his mighty dragon. A shiver runs up my spine. That is another theme I do not want to linger on, so I rise and approach the ledge to look out over the plains.

Somewhere beyond the horizon, to the south, lies Roarim City. And, within it, the NASA Ground Station—at least, according to Uncle Denesius's maps. I grasp the Talisman. As long as I am the only one holding Knowledge, I will draw danger to myself—from the Wraith Lord, first and foremost. With the Books gone and the other Talismans gone, the Lord of the Roarim will want to get his hands on the one I carry. Nothing makes sense! He conquered the Atheneum and its contents. So why did he destroy them? Did his rage against Uncle Denesius blind him that much?

I clasp the Talisman tighter.

Four days have passed since we left the West Tower. The satellite will pass over the Ground Station in sixteen days. If it takes us another six days to reach Roarim City, that will leave us more than enough time to come up with a plan of action.

"Well, I think we have found ourselves a nice spot," Pedregal says. "We have water and can survive on our hunting skills. We should be safe for a while."

"You are deceiving yourself," Thoron says. "Summer is around the corner. This lake will not last. Trust me. A month from now, there will not be a drop of it left. We cannot stay here."

"A month?" Pedregal replies. "Fine, then. A month gives us time to explore the area. There must be other lakes out there. And caves. We can establish a base in a safe and hidden location, gather herbs, dry meat, and fill water flasks. We can survive for years in hiding."

"What kind of a life is that?" Thoron retorts. "The Roarim have taken everything from us. My wish for revenge is great. We have the Talisman. We have great power in our possession. Many would pay handsomely to obtain Knowledge from it. The Talisman will gather much wealth, followers will come to us. We could build an army..."

"An army?" Pedregal snorts, rubbing his blonde beard. "That would take years! Gathering an army strong enough to withstand the Roarim would take a lifetime. Where would we find soldiers? The people of Eliadys are decimated. And you can bet on it that the Newarkers and the Southern tribes will not lift a finger to help us. We have no choice but to hide until a safer opportunity presents itself."

"I will not hide..." Thoron bursts out, then stops because Roddrick is waving a hand at him to calm down.

"Gentlemen, you are both blind to the obvious. We do not need to hide. We do not need to spend a lifetime raising an army. We have everything we need within a three to four-day walk from here," he says.

I glance at him from the ledge, already tensing at what he may propose.

Thoron glances at Roddrick. "Oh, yes? And what would that be?"

A smile appears on Roddrick's face. He straightens his back and places his hands on his knees. "It is quite simple. Our group is defenseless against an encounter with the Roarim. So why not use an existing army? One that is already strong and anxious for a fight?"

"Roddrick!" Pedregal exclaims. "You do not mean the pirates?"

Roddrick's smile widens. "Of course, I mean the pirates, Pedregal. Who else, but the pirates, could we turn to at this point? They understand the worth of the Talisman; they strive to get their hands on the Knowledge of the Enlightened Ones. They are skilled in fighting, their lair is said to be well protected, and they have storages full of food and water." He lifts his hand to stop a protest from Pedregal. "Yes, I am fully aware that they are erratic and disobedient, but their hunger to have access to the Talisman will allow us to keep them in tow. They will do anything for a promise of Knowledge. Their pirate overlord will understand the value of having two Knowledge Seekers, a swordmaster, and a guardsman in his inner circle. The Talisman will bring him great wealth—something we will also be able to profit from. We can negotiate a comfortable life, protected and hidden from the Roarim."

"I know of this pirate overlord," Pedregal says, spitting at the ground. "He cannot be trusted."

"At least we would face him together, knowing this fact," Roddrick argues. "The pirate overlord would not dare let anything happen to the Talisman. That will be our protection. It is our best option."

Draxis, silent until now, grunts and waves his hands in the air, communicating his discontent.

Roddrick argues with him, and Pedregal joins in. Thoron jumps in next. The four men quarrel back and forth, their conversation becoming ever more heated.

Next thing I know, Thoron stands and shouts, "Hold it! HOLD IT!" Silence falls over the company, and they stare at him. Thoron turns my way. His voice softens. "What of you, Eodain? You have said nothing. Shall we hide out in the mountains, gather an army from the Southern tribes, or join the infamous pirate overlord?"

Now they are all looking at me. It takes me a moment before I can reply, but only after I turn to stare out over the plains with a sigh. "I will do none of those things."

Roddrick mutters. "What is that supposed to mean? Joining the pirates is the only way. There is no other option."

"Shut up, Roddrick," Pedregal snaps, then says, "What do you mean, lad?"

I glance at them at last. "I will not hide, and I will not raise an army or join the pirates." I pause, then plunge on. "I am going to Roarim City. I am going to the NASA Ground Station. I will connect the Talisman to the communications satellites and spread Knowledge across the world again, to whoever is still able to receive it."

Their eyes almost pop out of their heads. Roddrick turns every shade of red.

I continue, unfazed. "The Knowledge of the Enlightened Ones belongs to everyone. It cannot remain exclusive to one person, or one tribe. As long as the Talisman remains the only source of Knowledge, it will wield power over others. He who gets his hands on the Talisman can rule in illegal impunity and with immoral wealth. He will be a danger to all living things. To spread the Knowledge to all humans is to spread hope for a brighter future. Men and women will have a chance to extract the Knowledge they need to live better lives. They will learn once again to restore broken environments, build stronger homes, and live in just and fair societies. Who knows, one day we may reach for the stars again."

I look at them each in turn. "This Knowledge was once freely available. Men and women could access the information they needed by using a program called the internet. That is what we must aim to do again. Never before has this been attempted, for the simple reason that the Ground Station sits at the heart of Roarim City. But today, we have no choice because only this Talisman remains. Either its Knowledge is spread equally and freely, or it must be destroyed before it falls into the wrong hands. Knowledge must belong to all, or to none," I say.

Roddrick jumps to his feet. He is on top of me before I have time to brace myself. "ARE YOU MAD?" he screams. He grabs me by the collar and almost chokes me.

At once, Pedregal and Thoron are at his side, pulling him away. He fights to come free, but they pin him in their grasp.

I am shaken. Resolute about my task, but shaken.

"He wants to deliver the Talisman to the enemy!" Roddrick bellows. "Are you going to let him have his way? He is a traitor! You cannot let him do this!"

All three are looking at me. I am not surprised that they think me mad. Had I still been Termite, perhaps I would have wavered. But that part of me was lost in the fire. I stare at Roddrick and am surprised to find that I am slightly taller than him. Today, for the first time, I realize that his growing spurts must have stopped a while back. I have caught up and even surpassed him. Feeling bolder, I stare him down as I state, "I am Eodain Atheneumson, son of the Library, protector of the Books, and wielder of the Talisman. I have made my decision, and you will respect it. I am taking the Talisman into the heart of Roarim City, and I will succeed in connecting it to the satellites." I pause. "You revoked your right to being a Knowledge Seeker the moment you lost your Talisman and removed your Seeker cape. The burden is no longer yours to carry, and I do not ask you to join me."

Roddrick's face pales. He knows I am hinting at the Sacred Pledge: forsake your Talisman, forsake your life. He has been on borrowed time since we met up four days ago. I am surprised he keeps pushing his luck.

Roddrick calms down, and the others let him go. "You are a fool," he snarls. With that, he heads back to sit by the fire.

Pedregal, Draxis, and Thoron glance at each other. It is Pedregal who speaks next. "Eodain," he hesitates. "There is a great risk that the Talisman will fall into Roarim hands long before we make it to this Ground

Station..."

"I will not allow it," I interrupt. "If the Talisman risks falling into Roarim hands, it must be destroyed." I pause. "And I must be destroyed along with it."

The men fall silent.

Pedregal nods slowly. "Well, that settles it. I will not let something like that happen on my watch! The Seeker has spoken. He has decided on our course of action. We are men of the Atheneum. We have sworn our allegiance to it. The building is gone, our Grand Protector is gone, but the last Seeker still stands. There is no doubt in my mind: Eodain *is* the Atheneum, and it is our duty to obey and follow him. I dare anyone to think otherwise."

To my astonishment, a smile creeps up on Thoron's face. It is a cold smile, but he says, "Yes, it is the correct course of action. We must go to Roarim City."

Draxis stands and nods gruffly.

That leaves Roddrick. Roddrick's eyes narrow as he stares our way, cracking his knuckles. Yet, he knows he has no choice. If he backs out, he will be deemed a coward. He stands, unsheathes his greatsword, and holds it upright before him. "If that is the will of the Seeker, then I will follow it, as will my sword."

We sit back around the fire, and I suddenly remember the girl. Elysa had run off after I almost slapped her, but now she is looking at me from her spot by the lake.

How much has she overheard?

* * *

Our circle is silent for the rest of the evening. The desert air is cold, but we dare not feed the fire too much as it could be seen for miles. I wrap myself up in my cape to keep warm.

My thoughts shift to the girl. I realize she has not eaten. I pick up a remaining piece of meat, glad to have an opportunity to speak to her.

"What a waste of perfectly good meat," Roddrick mutters behind me.

I ignore him and approach Elysa.

As soon as she sees me, she scampers back, her eyes wide.

I slow down, realizing she is now afraid of me. My stomach twists. "I am sorry," I say, "for my actions earlier. I do not know what came over me. That song... that song triggered a memory in me."

She stares at me, her hazel eyes standing out against the dusk.

"I am sorry," I repeat, then show her the meat. "I have brought you some food. You should eat..."

"Why are you apologizing?" she snaps.

I gape at her. "Huh?"

"Why are you apologizing?" she repeats. "And why are you being *nice* to me? Is this some sick form of torture you use against your prisoners? Be nice one moment, then turn into a monster the next? Do you think this is some kind of game?"

I am stunned. *Prisoner? Torture?* "You... you think you are my prisoner?" I ask.

She wraps her arms around her legs and hides her face in her arms.

Her comment upsets me. Here I am, trying to be *nice* and apologize, and she rubs it right back in my face. Does she not know we are all stuck out here in the desert? Does she not know I am the only one standing between her and my companions, who would rather see her dead? "Fine," I grumble, throwing the meat on the ground next to her. "Eat your food, *prisoner*. We leave at daybreak, and you are coming with us."

She lifts her head, and her mouth drops open.

"I was going to offer you a place to sleep by the fire, but you might as well stay right here." I turn and stomp away with a tightness in my chest. I had come to make things better, not worse. This idea of taking prisoners, seeking revenge, and making the enemy suffer is not for me, yet she just made me act like an insolent rival. I lie down next to the others, and roll up, preparing to sleep. Only, sleep will not come. I want to kick myself. I sounded like Roddrick just now. What is wrong with me?

I lie on my back among the boulders that surround us, watching a patch of the starry sky right above me. I wish I were not in this situation. I wish I did not have to make drastic decisions, take prisoners, or ache for things gone.

I am about to drift off when I hear soft footsteps approaching. I tense up. I know it is the girl. My hand closes over the sword hidden under my cape. I wait, fully alert.

Elysa steps quietly beside me and lies down as close as possible to the fire.

I relax my grasp on my sword and watch her settle with her back to me. I remain tense for a while, then see her shoulders shaking. She is crying silently.

My throat constricts, and I find that it is hard—really hard—to hate the enemy.

CHAPTER 15 *Altercation*

When I wake up the following morning, Elysa is no longer by the fire. What I do find, however, is a handful of black berries. I eat them and am pleasantly surprised when the sweet liquid coats my throat.

I vow to be nicer to everyone. We are all suffering in one way or another. I glance at Draxis, who has just pushed himself up into a sitting position. The giant is rubbing the back of his head and lets out a massive yawn.

I have not had much time to talk to my friend, and it is time to set things right.

"Draxis?" I say, approaching him.

"Mmm?" he looks at me through puffy eyelids.

"Draxis, you do not have to come with me, you know that, right?" I lower my voice so the others will not hear. "Your bondage to Uncle Denesius no longer exists. You can finally return to your land and look for your family, the way you have always wanted."

He waves a hand at me and grunts in annoyance as

if I said the stupidest thing in my life.

"I am not kidding, Draxis," I insist. I place my hand on his arm and wait until he is looking at me. "You are not bound to me."

A sad look crosses his face, and he looks away. It is as if he were ashamed of something. Then he pulls out the hairpin from within his shirt. There is not much left: the purple flower has faded, and the yellow bead fell off long ago. He thinks for a moment, and after a long pause, answers with hand gestures and grunts: *I will go with you, then I will look for my family*. He pockets the hairpin and rises, leaving me staring after him as he plods off. I feel like he is holding something back, something he does not want to burden me with, but pressing him will be of little use. I know where my boundaries lie with Draxis. Whatever inner conflict he is dealing with, he wants to deal with it alone.

I sigh and gather my things. I check the contents of my satchel, and my hand brushes the National Geographic Magazine. I do not know exactly why I picked this particular Book from the Library. Maybe because I promised Chief O'Brian, I would protect it with my life, or maybe because I never got to read it. As soon as Roddrick handed the precious magazine to Uncle Denesius, it ended up in the forbidden section of the Library, where I could not reach it.

"Time to go, Eodain," Thoron interrupts me. "We have to make good use of the early hours before the sun gets too hot."

I nod and leave the magazine in my satchel. One day, I will get to read it in full. I fill both my flask, and the plastic bottle that belonged to Elysa's brother with water. I pick more berries. We eat the remaining rabbit from last night, even though it is cold and far from enough to satisfy our hunger. I glance worriedly at the giant, who would need at least five entire rabbits to feel full.

We head off, and I take one last look back at our relatively safe hiding place among the rocks, with its fresh lake.

Elysa stands for a moment by her brother's grave, then follows us from a distance. At least she should be happy that we are heading towards her homeland.

We must travel south-east along the edge of the plains, following the foot of the mountains. The land shows signs of having gone through many deep and violent changes. We should be within Roarim borders within six days but could be hampered by ancient landslides, surface ruptures, or sharp escarpments. I think back on Uncle Denesius's old map of the area, and it looks nothing like it. The cataclysms caused by the merging of climate change and war altered the topography forever.

I am still amazed that an entire army was able to cross this harsh region in such stifling heat. Putting together an expedition of this magnitude would require strong leadership and an impressive supply of provisions. My heart sinks at the idea that Eliadys and the Atheneum could never have organized such a feat. We devoted our lives to the Books and the Enlightened Era.

I glance back at Elysa and wish I could ask her questions, but that would look odd in the eyes of the others. So I trudge on, focusing on placing one foot before the other as the bright sun rises higher.

"Eodain..." Roddrick comes up beside me. His eyes dart, and sweat pearls his forehead. I wonder if he is suffering from a heat stroke. Although he used a normal tone of voice for once, I raise an eyebrow because he called me Eodain, not Termite. *He wants something.*

He walks beside me for a while, looking down at his feet as if in deep thought.

I wait.

"Eodain," he starts again. "I understand that you wish to distribute the Knowledge of the Enlightened Ones in a fair and equal manner. But don't you think that taking the Talisman into the lion's den is nothing short of suicide? And the NASA Ground Center... Who is to stay it is still functional? It has been five to six hundred years. That is a long time for those machines to still be working, even considering the ingenuity of the Enlightened People. You know as well as I do that all iron structures of the past have long since rusted away."

I glance at him. "Not if they were made from titanium-erzats like the solar panels at the Atheneum," I say. "Uncle Denesius assured me the NASA Ground Station was still standing. One of his spies saw it with his own eyes. I believe the Roarim have maintained it across the generations, as it would be something of pride to them. It is similar to the Newarkers who protect their sacred monument."

Roddrick twitches, and I know I have irritated him by the mention of that unfortunate trip. "But what of the satellites, then?" he insists. "Even if we make it through the midst of the Roarim stronghold, enter the Ground Station, figure out how to make it work, and our signal captures a passing satellite, we must still hope there is someone at the other end capable of receiving the message!" He looks at me sternly. "That is a lot of *ifs*, don't you think?"

I bite my tongue because I want to retort with something nasty, but instead, I remain calm and say, "Yes, Roddrick, that is a lot of *ifs*." Because he is right, of course. I am holding on to a thin thread of hope that this plan will work, and the truth is there are many more things that could go wrong, than right.

But I cannot help it. I feel that as long as there are satellites in the sky, there is hope. I think of the great Logbook in the West Tower and how fewer passing satellites have been recorded in it. Time is not on our side.

"Are you doing this because of the Wraith Lord?" Roddrick asks suddenly.

His question startles me. "The Wraith Lord?"

Roddrick studies me, and his mouth is curled down. "Did that dragon not instill fear in you? You were there, six years ago, when Uncle Denesius attacked Lord Erawan and left him for dead. The Roarim Lord must have seen you. He has already carried out his revenge on Uncle Denesius. Are you afraid he will come after you next? Is your plan to hand him the Talisman so he will spare your life?"

I freeze on the spot, shocked. "Roddrick!"

The others stop and turn to look at us.

"Well, is it?" Roddrick insists. His face is becoming red.

I stare at him in disgust. "I should not even have to answer that," I say. "But if you must know, I am following a direct order from Uncle Denesius. He is the one who sent me on this mission, and I, for one, intend to fulfill it."

He gapes at me as if I had just turned into a braying donkey. "What nonsense! Uncle Denesius would never ask such a thing, least of all from you!"

"But it is tr—" I object.

"For Spirit's sake! Stop lying! You are playing with our lives. Did you not see the dragon? Did you not see the ten-thousand soldiers and the rage with which they destroyed our home?"

Thoron backs up. "Leave him to me," he tells me,

passing me by with quick strides. He reaches Roddrick, swings his arm, and punches him in the chin. Roddrick flies back, and falls flat on his backside.

Thoron stands over him. "We have voted, Roddrick," he says. "We have agreed to go to Roarim City. Did you notice that I, too, voted in favor of this plan? Pay attention, for once!" He whirls around and takes the lead again.

I stare after him, dumbfounded. Thoron has defended me once again, and yet his choice of words leaves me feeling uneasy.

Roddrick follows Thoron with his eyes as he rubs his chin.

Elysa has almost caught up to us. When she spots Roddrick on the ground, she sprints past him and hurries to my side. She stays at a safe distance, though closer to me than to anyone else.

We resume our walk, this time with Roddrick lagging behind. The afternoon is approaching, and we will soon have to stop to hunt for game before the night falls.

Elysa glances back. "I do not like him." She shudders.

"...and you should not," I say a little too sarcastically. I see the fear in her eyes and add, "Do not worry. He will not try anything as long as I am around."

She looks me up and down. "Because you are a Knowledge Seeker?"

Something stirs within me. I feel a sense of pride mingled with timidity at being called a Knowledge Seeker by a stranger—especially a Roarim one. "Yes," I say.

"I think you are doing the right thing," she says.

I stare at her. "You do?"

She nods. "I am training to be a healer," she

reminds me. "I would love to have access to this internet you mentioned, to go over the knowledge of the Ancient Ones to find the correct treatment to heal people. Perhaps," her voice dulls, "I could have saved my brother."

I walk on in silence, trying to find the right words. "I think you did a brave thing, following your brother into battle like that."

She shrugs. "Little help that did. If only I had reached that lake sooner..." She trails off.

"It is not your fault. You could not have predicted that you would encounter a lake up on a mountain."

"Oh, but I did!"

"Huh?"

"I *did* head straight for that lake, but I was too late."

"I do not understand. You knew you would find water there?"

She nods. "Of course! I followed the sparrows and the trail of moss hidden between the rocks."

I stop and stare at her. "You know how to find water in these mountains?"

She shrugs again. "Of course! Only a fool would head out here without some basic survival skills."

My mouth drops open, then closes again. I am too dumbstruck to feel offended at having been called a fool. I think of the edible berries. "But, who taught you these skills?" I ask as we start walking again.

My questions seem to bore her. "It is just something we learned at school."

I gasp. "You have *schools* in your city?"

The shock in my voice makes her frown at me. "Well, yes... Don't you?"

I stare at her. I do not answer.

She shakes her head in disapproval. "Makes sense," she says, walking away. "Barbarians!"

Heat rises to my cheeks. The part of my mind that is always alert and stores every piece of information in vivid detail, skims over the memory of a Book called a *Dictionary*. Although several sections were missing, the letter *b* was complete. I could have named all the words in that tome, along with their definition.

Barbarian = a person from an alien land, culture, or group believed to be inferior, uncivilized, or violent.

"Hey!" I shout after her. I am about to retort when my eyes catch something so astonishing that my voice dies in my throat. I follow the outline of the mountains, up and up, into the sky. The mountain tops off like a pointed hat, so sharp it would seem a giant chiseled it to resemble the head of a spear.

Elysa looks at me questioningly. "What is it?" she asks, turning to glance at the mountains.

I am still stunned by what I see but am not sure I should speak out loud. "Uh... nothing," I mumble. "I thought I saw something."

She glares at me and continues walking.

I fight to calm my beating heart. I recognize that pointed mountain all too well. I have visited this place in my dreams for years. It is the place where, as a child, I spotted a satellite falling to its untimely death.

CHAPTER 16 *The Rods of God*

I hesitate to tell the others about the satellite. My plan to go to the NASA Ground Center was already hard to swallow, so a detour to see a possible Sky Spirit that may or may not have crashed nearby will be too much of a stretch.

Fortunately, Thoron provides me with the perfect excuse. We find a relatively flat area higher up in the mountain to protect us from the cold air that sweeps across the plains during the night. It is a good place to set up camp. Thoron sends us in opposite directions to hunt for food and water. I have about three hours ahead of me before night falls.

I am off without delay. I think back on the night up in the West Tower when I saw a flash of white light illuminate the south side of the mountain. I give myself two hours to find it or abandon the search and return. I make my way through the rocky mountain, climbing a natural path worn by animals, but the sound of loose pebbles makes me whirl around.

Elysa comes up from behind a rock and looks at me.

"Are you following me?" I snap.

She nods.

I am not sure what to do about that. "Why?"

She looks down the way we came. "I am not staying with *them*." She nudges her head, indicating my companions.

"So you would rather stay with me when I almost struck you the other day?"

She shrugs. "You apologized."

I shake my head and sigh, exasperated. "You should focus on finding water instead, since you say you are so good at it." I head off again with her in tow. It is annoying, this idea that she is the enemy and I should treat her like a prisoner. I try to sound tough and in command, but I know it does not come off right. I would make a terrible chief. *One of the reasons I miss Uncle Denesius so much...* I swallow my grief as we reach a good viewpoint halfway up the mountain.

She follows. "What is it you saw, earlier?" she asks, unfazed by my comment about finding water. "What are you looking for?"

We gaze at a jumble of rocky hills interspersed by dunes that stretch southward, away from the mountain. In the far distance, the hills and dunes turn into a far greater desert than the dry plains we crossed a few days ago. I cannot see the end of this desert, which stretches out as far as the eye can see. This would not be a good place to end up in. The sun is dipping on the horizon to my right, casting long shadows.

But it is not this new desert that fills me with wonder. "This," I breathe. "This is what I was looking for."

She steps forward carefully towards the edge of the

elevated ledge and catches her breath.

Below us, at the foot of the mountain, is the satellite. Judging from up here, it seems in better shape than I expected, though one of its large solar panels tore off and is sticking out of the sand like a drowning person waving for help. Some other bits and pieces are lying around, but what strikes me is that the core module seems practically intact. It lies askew in the middle of a sand-crater. I know that most celestial objects burn up as they fall through the atmosphere, yet this one suffered much less damage than I would have expected. My heart races when I realize it never really lost control. Instead, it must have deployed an emergency landing mechanism.

"What *is* that thing?" Elysa breathes, startling me out of my thoughts.

"It is a Sky Spirit," I say in awe.

"A what?"

"Well, not a spirit, exactly, but a machine that the Enlightened Ones sent into space. It must have lost its orbit and landed back on Earth. We call it a satellite."

"Ah! A satellite. Why didn't you say so in the first place?"

I look at her. "You know about satellites?"

"Of course. We learned about them in school."

My stomach constricts. Why is it that the Roarim learned about these things in school when the people of Eliadys did not? Sure, Seekers had to learn how to read and write as part of their training to search for the Books, but not the common folk. This girl does not seem to come from a privileged family, yet she was taught many things. It is another sign of the amount of resources available to the Roarim.

"Eodain?" she says, cutting off my thoughts.

"What?"

She is looking at me intensely. "Can I ask you something?"

"What?"

She hesitates, then reaches out and takes my left hand in hers.

A tingling sensation travels up my arm. Her skin is soft and warm. I resist the urge to pull back. If I do so, she will notice my bashfulness. But if she keeps holding my hand like this, my legs will turn to jelly. What is she up to?

She turns my hand palm upward and looks at it. "What happened to your finger?" she asks, placing her hand flat over mine. The coolness of her touch soothes the sharp tug left behind by my ghost finger.

My shoulders slump a little. "Do you really want to know?" I ask.

She frowns slightly but replies, "Well, I asked, didn't I?"

"All right, then. A Roarim soldier cut off my finger when I was ten."

She blushes. "Oh!" She lets go of my hand.

I kind of wish I hadn't had to tell her that.

We stand there awkwardly.

A breeze blows a strand of hair before her lips. She strokes it away. "I am sorry," she mumbles.

I shrug to try and brush off the seriousness of the moment. "It is not your fault. It is not as if you had cut it off yourself."

She shakes her head vehemently. "I would never... I..." She raises her hands helplessly. "I hate war!" she bursts out.

"Humph! If only the other Roarim thought the same."

"Hey!" she protests.

I should not have said that, but I plow on because I

still cannot deal with what the Roarim have done. "It is true!" I say. "Your people have attacked us over and over for decades! Clearly, they do not share your hatred for war. When have we ever threatened you?"

She balls her fists. "Well, it is not our fault if your Grand Protector kept the Knowledge to himself! How else were we supposed to get to it?"

My jaw drops. "Why would he share the Knowledge with *you*? Your people's greed has destroyed everything!" I lift my maimed hand in front of her face. "This? This is nothing! Did you know that they slaughtered Pedregal's parents? I am surprised he even talks to you! And Odwin Atheneumson, he was only fourteen. He had just been made a Seeker. And now he is dead!"

She raises her hand to her ears. "Stop it!" she shouts. Tears are forming in her eyes. "I told you! I want it to stop! I hate war!"

"Well, the Roarim made sure of that, didn't they?" I say quietly.

She shuts her eyes tight.

Great, now I made her cry.

Really, that was an unnecessary outburst on my part. It is not as if she had killed Pedregal's parents or Odwin Atheneumson herself. But she needs to stop being so naïve: her people did this, not mine.

I turn and gaze at the unusual landscape as the sun sets over it in a ball of fire.

Talking about this will get us nowhere. "Come on," I say to try and break the ice. "Night is falling. We do not have much time."

We head down the mountain towards the satellite, which becomes bigger as we approach it. It is at least eight or nine times my size. The fact that it had a landing mechanism indicates it belonged to one of the last generations of satellites created by the Enlightened People. And its size means it was of some importance. Most of the small cube-like satellites used by common folk to connect to the internet disintegrated in the atmosphere long ago because their low orbit pulled them back in eventually. Major communications corporations or scientific organizations would have used big satellites like this.

"Eodain?" Elysa says as we climb down the mountain.

"Hmm?"

She pauses, and I think she will want to talk about our people's enmity again.

"What?" I ask.

She sniffles and looks at me. "I am sorry for what my people have done to your people. Truly, I am. But, still, I have been meaning to tell you something. I have been thinking about your plan to connect your Talisman to the NASA Ground Station. I understand that you want to share the Knowledge contained in the Talisman with whoever is still able to receive it. I think that is a courageous move, and part of me thinks our Roarim leader would approve of it. I think you should consider presenting your plan to..."

"What?" I blurt out. "Present my plan to the Wraith Lord? Are you crazy?"

She looks at me a little strangely and bites her lip.

I cannot believe she just said that. "I would never approach your Wraith Lord! He is a despot and a murderer. I cannot believe you would suggest something like that." I walk off, wanting to distance myself from her. A sense of deep wariness grips me. Was she trying to charm me just now, up on the ledge? Why do I keep forgetting that Elysa is the enemy?

I hear her footsteps behind me.

"It is just that..." she says cautiously. "I have this feeling that our leader would understand..."

"STOP!" I snap, whirling to face her. "Just, stop! This leader you speak of killed the man who took me in and raised me like he would his son. He cared for me when I had no one else. So I will not hear another word about this tyrant of yours. Do you understand?" My heart beats wildly. Just when I thought we could be allies. Just when I thought maybe she wasn't so bad, for a Roarim.

She clasps her hands and lifts them before her mouth, blinking at me.

I walk on towards the edge of the crater. I need to get back to the others, and quickly. This girl is toying with my senses. Thoron was right: she cannot be trusted.

As she comes up beside me, the edge crumbles beneath my feet.

"Watch out!" she yells, grabbing me by the arm and pulling me back. Sand slides down into the hole. I wish I could slide down with it to get closer to the satellite, but I would have no way of crawling out. Elysa just saved me.

Still, I am in no way reassured by her presence. I glare at her and head one way around the crater. She heads the other way, glancing back at me with a pale face.

I will ignore her from now on. We will go to Roarim City and then she can be on her way. Until then, I quickly search for a way down to the satellite. Finding none, my attention falls on the solar panel, a little way off. As I walk towards it, another object catches my eye. It is a long pole. One end is slightly thicker, while the other has four small, wing-like things protruding from it. My breath quickens, and cold sweat pearls my forehead because I feel like I have seen something like this before. Something that is evil.

That part of my mind that is always alert searches for a likeness. It is something I saw in one of the Books, but which one? I go over hundreds of tomes that I read in the Library, but nothing seems to fit. A shudder goes down my spine as if my body already remembers what it was before my brain has time to catch up. And then it hits me. It was not in one of the Books at the Library that I have seen this object before. It is in the National Geographic that I have in my satchel. Only, I left my satchel at camp, thinking I would not be gone long.

A title flashes before my eyes: *The Rods of God.*

I catch my breath. Yes, that is it. This is a Rod of God. I drop to my knees. If this satellite had crashed instead of landed years ago, it would have released its deadly cargo.

I stare at the object, feeling numb. Of the many Sky Spirits I observed throughout my life, not all are purely innocent. Some spirits are evil. I reach out and touch the cold metal, wiping away the sand. Faded letters appear. My eyes widen. My heart beats faster. I rub harder.

MASA

I stare at the letters. Not *NASA.* But *MASA.*
How strange...
Elysa shrieks.
I whirl around, searching. Dusk has settled; stars are visible. It is hard to see among the shadows of the mountain.

"Elysa?" I call, jumping to my feet. The cry came from the satellite. She must have slipped into the crater. I rush to the edge and look down. At first, I do not see anything in the gloom, but as I walk around the edge, I can just make her out down below. She is picking herself up. She turns and glances up at me, and her posture stiffens. Her eyes widen, and her mouth opens.

A large shadow approaches me from the left.

Elysa screams, "Eoda...!"

Too late.

The last thing I see is Roddrick's fist slamming into my face.

CHAPTER 17 *Lies*

I am eight when I enter the city of Eliadys for the first time. Orphaned children are allowed in the procession, following behind the new Knowledge Seekers. First, the new Seekers are Anointed in the Library. They are given their Talisman, their greatsword, and their cape. After that, all the Knowledge Seekers file down the hill towards the city, on beautifully groomed horses, with Uncle Denesius leading the way. Us orphans follow at the back, packed into hay carts drawn by horses.

This particular day is memorable. Musicians accompany the procession, playing joyful tunes. The Atheneum banners fly high, and women and children pave the road with petals. Roddrick is one of the Atheneum orphans in the hay carts with me, but even that does not dampen my spirit.

There is much clamor and laughter in the central square: theatrical plays, hilarious clowns, and women sweep by dropping buns glazed with honey in our carts. This goes on until nightfall, when the festivities end with a beautiful display of fireworks. By then, we children are exhausted and are falling asleep in the carts.

A raucous laugh awakens me, and I realize we are being driven back to the Atheneum. I glance around and notice a stark contrast from earlier this afternoon. Now, dirty children are standing along the walls of the houses, unsmiling, and with big eyes. Drunken men are staggering along side streets, mumbling to themselves, and thin mothers, with babies clinging to their bosoms, lift their hand to us, begging for food and coins.

A heaviness settles in my chest, and I draw my limbs close.

As I follow them with my eyes, I also become aware of a couple of cloaked men walking alongside our cart. Dark eyes glance my way, and I cringe. I look around, but most of my companions are sleeping.

It must be my imagination, yet I swear I hear someone whisper, "It is him."

A hand closes on my arm. I feel a tug and, without warning, I am flying off the cart. I land in the dirt as the cart rolls away.

"Help!" I yelp, but sturdy hands are dragging me away towards a side street.

Their hands are all over me as I struggle and yell for help.

All at once, a horse charges into the side street. It neighs angrily, making the thieves scramble. There is a confusing jumble of men and horses and swords. People scream in pain; others run off.

I am again grabbed by the arm and lifted from the mess. I yell and fight, but it is Uncle Denesius who is now holding me. He swings me up onto the horse of a Seeker and shouts, "Get him out of here!"

The bandits run for their lives, a group of Seekers

hot on their trail, while Uncle Denesius and the others gallop up the hill towards the Atheneum.

Tears stream down my face. I hold on so tightly to the horse's mane that my knuckles hurt. We are heading up the hill when some of the Senior Seekers approach Uncle Denesius, and I hear them argue. They are saying that it is folly to bring children into the city. And so, from then on, it is decided that we orphaned children will no longer be able to take part in the celebrations.

My heart constricts, and more tears spill out of my eyes. I am torn between terror because of what happened and anguish that we will no longer be able to go to the celebrations.

We finally enter the gates of the Atheneum and get off the horses. I rush to Uncle Denesius's side and lock my arms around his leg.

"Termite," he says. "What is this?"

I look up at him. He is like the Atheneum itself, made of strong marble and deep foundations. Nothing can knock him down. Through sobs, I say, "Th-thank you, U-uncle."

"For what, Termite?"

"F-for ad-dopting me." I gaze at him, hesitating, but the words slip naturally out of my mouth. "I l-love you."

He looks at me, a brief moment of surprise passing over his face. Then, he lays a firm hand on my back. "Ah, son. As long as you stay close to me, you are safe." He smiles. "I will protect you, always."

My heart bulges. He called me son. I feel safe and never want to leave his side. I have a home and someone who cares for me. I am not out there, sleeping in the dirt on city streets, homeless and abandoned. I will always stay by his side.

Uncle Denesius ruffles my hair. "Now, hurry along and clean up for dinner. You will sit next to me tonight."

I grin at him through wet eyes, and rush off to the sleeping quarters. Uncle Denesius saved my life, he called me son *and he wants me to sit next to him at dinner. That is enough to wipe the city thieves out of my mind.*

Only, when I get to the dormitory, Roddrick is waiting for me. His face is flushed, and his hands are balled into fists. He must have heard about the children no longer being able to attend the festivities.

I freeze and turn around in panic. "Unc..." I begin, the cry dying in my throat. Roddrick has brought his accomplices, and they are blocking the way out.

I do not sit next to Uncle Denesius that night. In fact, Roddrick makes sure I miss dinner altogether.

* * *

Here I am, dangling over Roddrick's shoulder with my hands bound behind my back and a painful black eye forming as I come to. I struggle and kick, and Roddrick drops me on the ground like an animal ready for slaughter.

"What do you think you are doing?" I yell, trembling with rage.

"Finally," he pants, stretching the muscles in his back. "You walk from now on."

I look around, trying to spot Elysa. Is she still stuck in the crater?

We are in the middle of the hills and dunes I spotted earlier, and the mountain with the satellite is shrinking in the distance. Roddrick has managed to carry me much too far from my companions. My stomach roils.

"Elysa! Where is she? Is she all right?"

Roddrick shrugs. "Who cares?" He lowers his backpack off his other shoulder, pulls out a water flask, and takes a gulp from it.

I notice that my scabbard with my sword is no longer attached around my waist, so I kick at him instead, but he side-steps my weak attempt to hurt him.

He switches the flask from his right hand to his left so that he can draw his greatsword. He places the tip on my throat. "From now on, you walk, or I leave you out here to die from thirst."

Walk? Walk to where? In the pit of my stomach, I already know the answer. "I am *not* going to the pirates," I snap at him.

He puts away the sword and takes another gulp of water. "I gave you a chance," he says. "I tried to reason with you in a conciliatory manner. I tried to shed light on your idiotic plan, but you would not listen. You left me no choice."

I swallow, my throat dry and scratchy. "Roddrick," I say as calmly as I can muster. "Your plan has as many faults as mine. We do not know these pirates. We do not know what they are like or how we can convince them to help us. There is no guarantee that they will not take the Talisman and kill us."

Roddrick returns the flask to his backpack and heaves it onto both his shoulders once more. "They cannot operate the Talisman without you," he says. "You are my guarantee."

I stomp the ground with my foot. "Stop it, Roddrick! These are not children's games anymore. It is time for you to make choices without involving your emotions. I cannot help it if you hate me. You have had many chances in life to prove yourself. Now prove to me that you can set aside our differences so we can focus on the greater picture. This is not about who is carrying the Talisman and who is not; who is a Seeker and who is not. This is about obeying Uncle Denesius's last wish. We owe it to him! But you are right; maybe I should not have made such an important decision without telling you first. All we have to do is talk about it some more, until we can come to an agreement together."

Roddrick is bored. He rolls his eyes and bends down next to me. "I have had enough of your lies," he mutters. The next thing I know, he is ripping off a large strip from my cape with a small knife.

"Hey!" I protest.

He stuffs the strip of material over my mouth and ties it at the back of my head. Then, he stands and wipes his hands. "There," he says, sighing in satisfaction. "I have been meaning to do this for a long time." He wipes the sweat off his brow with the back of his hand as if thinking of something.

"Look, Termite," he begins. "You think you know Uncle Denesius, but you know nothing. Why do you think he did not want you trained to defend yourself? Why do you think he never made you a Knowledge Seeker when you turned fourteen? Why do you think he chose me to accompany you to the Newarkers? 'Make sure Termite does not return in time to be Anointed,' he told me. 'Make sure it is you who brings back the tax payment, and not him.'"

He sneers. "I swear. That is what he told me. I figured he worried you would leave the Atheneum one day. Maybe he wanted you to be so fearful of the outside world; you would never leave his side. I have always wondered why. Did he want to make you his heir?" He shrugs. "Whatever the reason, he had a strange way of showing he cared."

I go deathly still. Roddrick's words mean nothing to me. He has always been a liar, but this new level of depravity is troubling. How did he come up with such nonsense? Uncle Denesius, ordering Roddrick to make sure I did not make it to my Anointing Day when I was fourteen... *ludicrous!* It makes me nervous—not of Uncle Denesius, but of Roddrick. What is he up to? Has the heat fried his brain?

I shake my head to show him I do not believe a word he is saying.

"Let's go!" he orders.

I cannot get up on my own, so he has to pull me up.

"Now, let us have a nice, *quiet* walk, shall we?" He shouts the word *quiet*, then kicks me in the thigh to make me move.

I glare at him with my strong feelings of hatred probably marking my face. But he has the greatsword. I have nothing. There is nothing I can do except obey and start walking across the rugged landscape with this madman.

CHAPTER 18 *Alligator*

My stomach twists with anger and desperation. I know nothing of the area we are crossing, and I suspect it is treacherous. Roddrick has the only water around, and that means I must depend on him.

We walk on into the night, the stars illuminating our way. Our path takes us along the edge of the hills bordering patches of dunes to avoid sinking into the sand while not having to climb too steeply.

Sometimes, I pretend to stagger so that I may leave a trail in the dusty ground. Thoron and Draxis can be swift, and I half-hope they will be able to follow my footprints. Only, I suspect my companions have barely noticed my absence, and Elysa is stuck in the pit with no way out.

My heart beats faster, and I want to hit something. I was reckless. I should have told the others about the satellite; we would have gone together. Or at least they would know to look for me.

To make matters worse, a storm brews in the

distance. Lightning strikes the horizon. The center of the storm is far enough away, but the wind still blows sand in my face. The stars veil over.

I already walked all of today and now well into the night with only a sip of water before I headed out to search for the satellite. That is another reason I know I cannot take on Roddrick. I can feel my energy draining with every step.

It only takes one gust of wind to knock me off my feet. I could get up, but I lie there anyway—anything to slow down our march. I look back and watch my footprints fade away with the wind.

A distant sound reaches my ears, like rumbling that is not made by thunder. Its intensity rises and falls with the wind, causing goosebumps to rise on my arms. The memory of the toothy dragon flashes in my mind.

Roddrick has heard it, too, because he tenses. He picks me up, and we rush towards a rocky hill. I sink to the ground, listening. It might just be the wind rasping against the ground, mingling with distant thunder, that we are hearing. Except I do not think so.

The Wraith Lord is out there, searching for me.

After a while, Roddrick removes the gag and gives me a sip of water. He takes another gulp as well.

It worries me. How many flasks of water does he have? Does he not realize we could end up walking for days? Does he even know where he is headed? "You should save it," I pant.

That statement earns me the gag again, so I sink back and rest my head against the rock. The wind blows through cracks, making wailing sounds.

I know I should be thinking of an escape, but I can barely keep my eyes open. I slip into bursts of nightmares where Uncle Denesius and Roddrick are plotting against me. Then the nightmare switches, and a terrified Uncle Denesius is fleeing from sharp dragon fangs. He screams at me for help.

I startle awake and settle back, deeply troubled. What has gotten into Roddrick, telling me such absurd things about Uncle Denesius? Why does Roddrick think I am lying about Uncle Denesius's instructions? I simmer in dark thoughts for a while, realizing that Roddrick's erratic attitude has reached a dangerous new level.

* * *

I seem only to have closed my eyes for a moment when Roddrick nudges me awake. Early morning light seeps over the rocky hill.

Roddrick feeds me some berries and dried meat along with another sip from a new flask of water. He must have emptied the other one. It is not much. Just enough to keep me alive. No matter how much I hate it, Roddrick is now my lifeline.

We cautiously leave our hiding spot and search the skies, but there is no sign of the Wraith Lord or his dragon in the cloudless sky. The day is promising to be long and scorching. Instead of heading south-east, like we were supposed to, Roddrick steers me south-west. It makes me mad that I have gotten this far, only to be heading away from my original destination. I should have told Roddrick about our limited window of time to connect to a satellite. It strikes me that I may not make it to Roarim City in time to capture its passing.

By midday, we reach the edge of the desert that I had seen with Elysa up on the mountain. I think back on the map Uncle Denesius showed me years ago, when he pointed out the NASA Ground Station to me, and it comes to my attention that this desert may not always have been one. Uncle Denesius's voice resonates in my mind. "The pirates are thought to live at the edge of a former sea. The Gulf of Mexico, it was called."

No wonder the swirling sand is leaving trails of sticky salt on my cheeks. I can even taste it in my mouth. I briefly wonder if the shores of that sea merely retreated. Maybe it still exists out there, across the desert.

Still, if we are walking along the former edge of this Gulf of Mexico, who is to say we will run into the pirates? If I recall, this sea was gigantic. The pirates could be anywhere. They are cunning, and experts at vanishing without a trace. It could take us weeks, months even, before we locate them. And at the rate Roddrick is gulping down water, we do not even have days.

We walk south for two days along the edge of the desert, and by mid-afternoon of the second day, we notice something on the horizon. It is a dark line that shimmers in the heat. I am apprehensive, yet curious as to what it might be. Unfortunately, to get there, we must walk over a large, unprotected stretch of desert in the burning sun.

I suspect Roddrick is becoming anxious because we head on without delay.

As we advance, I note that the dark line is a dead forest shrouded in mist. It is a strange contrast with the dry land. It does not look welcoming, but anything is better than this desert hell.

Black spots swim before my eyes, and I begin to slow down without intending to. Roddrick keeps having to shove me in the back. Weariness from long days of walking is too much to bear, and I collapse on the ground, barely conscious. Now Roddrick has no choice but to snag me under the armpits and drag me the rest of the way.

Finally, late afternoon arrives, and we enter the shade of the leafless mangroves. They are about twice our size, and the branches are twisted, looking like gnarled fingers. The grey mist that clings to them only adds to the ghostly effect, and I am not sure this is a better place than the desert.

We lay splayed on the ground for several minutes, panting.

I shoot Roddrick a desperate look, but he gets to his feet and points his sword at me. "Move," he says through cracked lips. There is an air of panic about him as if he finally realizes his mistake, but it is too late to turn back. I have not seen him drink from his second flask in a long while, or pull out a new one.

I head into the trees, certain that it is a bad idea, but our time is counted if Roddrick has finished his water. Also, it crosses my mind that if there is mist here, perhaps there is also water.

And I am right—partially. As we head on, the ground becomes softer and, before long, soggy. My boots splash a little deeper with every step. We rush forward, eager to reach an area with clean enough water to drink.

Roddrick gets down on all fours and is about to plunge his face into the water.

And that is when I see it: slimy green threads that float on top of the black liquid. "Mmm!" I groan through my gag and push Roddrick aside despite my hatred for him.

He growls at me, then realizes what I am looking at.

The black liquid is some sort of chemical substance that releases a foul odor. Not only that, but as I look deeper into the dead mangrove forest, I see greenish fumes bubbling out in the shadows.

I shake my head. Whatever this is, it looks deadly. Perhaps it is poisonous, or perhaps it is flammable. Either way, we will have to keep walking until we make it out of here.

Something splashes some way off, and I swear I see movement out of the corner of my eye. My heart races. I have heard of toothy animals called alligators, but they are extinct, aren't they?

I hesitate.

"Move!" Roddrick barks again, his voice thick. "Just move!"

We wade on; the sloshing noises we make only increase my thirst. About an hour later, I stop. I cannot go on like this.

Roddrick huffs behind me. He seems as exhausted as I am. "Do not do this to me," he warns, lifting his sword weakly.

I want to resist, except I would be wasting what precious energy I have left.

Suddenly, yells bounce through the silence, chilling me. Loud noises of splashing and shouting root me to the spot. Roddrick nudges me forward cautiously. After a while, we see the outline of a cart pulled by a couple of horses.

I squint. How could a cart have reached the middle of this swamp? But then it starts making sense. A raised patch of ground indicates there is a path.

Four men are standing around the cart, looking at the swamp. There is a great commotion in the water as a huge animal splashes before them. The men howl with laughter and excitement.

Roddrick pushes me against a tree trunk and lifts his greatsword against my throat. "Not a word," he whispers as if I could talk back through the gag. He grabs me by the collar, and we continue onward as cautiously as possible.

When we get as close as we can, I understand the situation. These men have caught a vicious-looking alligator with a snare trap attached to a long pole. The beast is so strong it takes two of them to control it, which they seem to find hilarious. There is a cage at the back of the cart, and another man pulls out a goat from it.

"Last one!" he shouts, then hurls the poor animal at the alligator, which snaps its massive jaws and pulls the goat under.

The men hoot and laugh.

Roddrick and I observe the horrible scene, and I am all for backing away. The men wear green-brown shirts, camo pants, caps, and a couple of them have bows and arrows strung over their shoulders. We recognize them at the same time because Roddrick gasps, "Pirates!"

Before I can protest, he pushes me forward towards them. Our splashing footsteps alert the men, and they shout in warning. Two of them load arrows on their bows faster than I can blink.

"Gentlemen! Do not shoot!" Roddrick yells.

I struggle. *This is not a good idea. Not a good idea at all.* Except, to my dismay, we are reaching the edge of the raised path.

"Who goes there?" one of them barks. The pirates with the pole release the alligator, and it disappears under ripples of liquid.

Roddrick and I leap hurriedly on to the path. Roddrick hides behind me to avoid any stray arrows heading our way. "Gentlemen," he repeats. "Do not shoot. There are only two of us, and we mean you no harm." After a moment of hesitation, he lifts his greatsword from my throat and throws it on the ground before us to show he is unarmed.

He plows on. "That thing you did there—catching that beast the way you did—requires intelligence and expert hunting skills. Only the renowned pirates would have courage enough to attempt such a feat."

The bows raise higher.

The men look at us, then the same pirate barks, "What's with him? Why is he bound like that?"

I can hear excitement building in Roddrick's voice. This is what he had been hoping for all along. "He is the reason I was looking for you," Roddrick says. "I wish to offer a gift to your overlord. I know he is wise and will appreciate what I have brought him. I request an audience, for my gift will make him a wealthy man."

Silence falls over the men.

"Identify yourselves!" the pirate snarls.

I hear Roddrick swallow. Finally, he says, "They call me Hyena. I survived the attack on the City of Eliadys." I tremble in rage. So, he has truly given up on his Seeker vows. "And this," he continues, "is Eodain Atheneumson, the last surviving Knowledge Seeker of the Atheneum."

Roddrick reaches for the chain around my neck and pulls out the Talisman to show it to them.

The pirates glance at each other. The bows lower slightly.

Roddrick knows he has won them over. "You know what this is, don't you? It is the last functioning Talisman you will ever find, and this Seeker can operate it."

The pirates stare at us.

"He does have the Seeker cape," one of them says in a hushed voice.

"That does not mean anything," another one says.

"He could have stolen it."

"I don't think so. Look at their fine clothes. Those are Atheneum fabrics, without a doubt."

The first pirate speaks to Roddrick. "If what you say is true, then that is a mighty gift, indeed."

Roddrick pushes me forward, and I land on my knees. "He is yours," he says. "All I ask for is a small quantity of gold and a comfortable life among you fine men. I will be useful to you."

"Will you, now?" the pirate says.

I shudder because there is the faintest tone of mockery in his voice.

A terrifying silence follows before the pirate resumes, "Are you not betraying one of your own? What is to say you will not do the same to us?" He pauses, considering Roddrick. Then, he chuckles, and the others follow his lead. "I am toying with you," he says, speaking lightly. "Coming into the forbidden swamp, and surviving it, is unheard of. You should be rewarded for your bravery. And you are right. I do indeed believe you will be of use."

I look at him, and he smirks.

The bows rise again, and there is a sound of the strings tensing.

Roddrick stutters, "But... N-no, w-wai...!"

It takes the time of a breath. The bowstrings loosen, and the arrows whizz past my ear. I hear thuds as they plant themselves into Roddrick's body.

"MMM!" I moan, whirling.

Roddrick's eyes are wide as saucers. He glances down at the arrows sticking out of his chest. His mouth drops open, then he staggers and falls flat on his back.

"MMM!" My scream comes out muffled as I wriggle towards him.

A trail of blood leaves the corner of his mouth. He

stares at me. "You..." he mutters. "...you were always his favorite."

Behind me, the pirates are laughing, and I hear their heavy boots coming towards me.

Roddrick's eyes become glazed. "Why you?" he asks.

Then he is gone.

"MMM!" I shout as the pirates pick me up.

One of them nudges Roddrick with his foot until he rolls into the swamp. I can see a trail of movement in the water as the alligator approaches.

I shut my eyes, hard.

CHAPTER 19 *Close Enemies*

The pigeon coop is one of the dirtiest places in the Atheneum—aside from the pigsty, that is. I have regularly been tasked with cleaning both.

I do not mind the pigeons as much. They are located in one of the towers of the building, which is shaded and relatively cool because a breeze comes in through the narrow windows. The messenger pigeons coo quietly and flap their wings but are mostly content watching me sweep and scrub the floor.

Once in a while, a pigeon lands on the windowsill with a message attached to its little leg. I must drop what I am doing, go down the winding stairs of the tower, and deliver it to whichever Senior Seeker is in charge that day. Sometimes, though, I finish cleaning first, so I do not have to clamber all the way up again after delivering the message.

A few weeks after Uncle Denesius reveals the existence of the NASA Ground Station to me, I am sitting in the coop with my back resting against the wall.

I have finished my task and am in no rush to report to the Senior Seeker. If I report to him too quickly, he will certainly send me to the pigsty. So, instead, I relax in the coop, enjoying a moment to myself without anyone bossing me around or tormenting me. My only companions are the feathered creatures resting on their perches.

The messages that arrive with the pigeons come from Knowledge Seekers who are away traveling the land. They report back to Uncle Denesius on their findings. It still astounds me that we have had to return to the basic use of birds to transfer messages. Before, during the Enlightened Era, people called each other through some small handheld devices—again using those fascinating communication satellites. It is said that people could even see each other directly on small screens.

As I close my eyes and try to imagine what it must be like to call a Knowledge Seeker who is located in a distant land and being able to see what he is seeing, feathers ruffle above my head, and a pigeon makes its appearance on the windowsill. I stand and talk softly to the bird, making sure it has grains and fresh water. Once it is settled, I check its leg for a message, and startle back.

There is indeed a tiny scroll rolled around the pigeon's leg. I look closer. A skull and crossbones are imprinted on the outside of the paper.

My heart races.

A skull and crossbones! That is the symbol used by the pirates!

I start sweating. This is serious! I have to inform someone, but who? The Senior Seeker?

I back away with the sealed message in my hand, breathing fast. No. I have to tell Uncle Denesius directly.

But interrupting Uncle Denesius is not something one does lightly. It is severely frowned upon and could get me whipped. I glance at the small paper in my hand. Failing to deliver this message, however, could lead to something worse.

I tighten my grip on the message and make a swift decision. I race down the stairs and cover the ground quickly, checking to make sure the Senior Seeker isn't around to stop me. I must get to Uncle Denesius before anyone sees me.

Panting, I climb the stairs to Uncle Denesius's office. The door is closed, meaning he is busy. I hesitate and think about the consequences. If the message is not urgent, he will shout at me for interrupting him. But if the message is urgent, then not showing it to him immediately could get me banished.

There is my answer.

I knock softly on the door before opening it slowly to give whoever is inside time to compose themselves. Then, I enter.

Uncle Denesius is sitting at the head of a large table. Important-looking men—some of them Knowledge Seekers; others, city-leaders—sit around the table. They have fallen silent and stare at me.

I step forward, realizing too late that I must look a mess after having just cleaned the pigeon coop. My boots clobber too loudly on the marble floor, and it seems to take me forever to reach the head of the table.

"Yes, Termite?"

Some of the men chuckle at my name.

I consider Uncle Denesius's voice. It is stern with a sharp edge to it. Yet, if he is angry, he does not reveal it to his attendees. If he is angry, he will deal with me later.

I clear my throat, reach out my hand, and give

Uncle Denesius a small peek at what I am holding in my fist. "Forgive my intrusion, Uncle," I say, trying to contain my twelve-year-old not-yet-turned-man's voice. "I was told to bring this to you at once."

I am not sure why I say that. No one told me to bring anything. But it would come off as offensive to tell Uncle Denesius in front of everyone that I wish to speak to him. A meaningless orphaned child does not tell the Grand Protector to do anything. I think he will forgive this lie as soon as I explain it to him.

Uncle Denesius shows no emotion whatsoever. He swipes my hand away and sighs, then addresses the attendees. "Gentlemen, our meeting comes to a close. Other matters call for my attention." He stands, and his chair screeches on the floor. "We will meet again in a month. Good day to you."

His words are final.

The attendees glance at each other, then hurry out of the office. Uncle Denesius lights a pipe while exchanging some calm words with a couple of Seekers. Then they head out as well, and he and I follow at a slow pace.

Uncle Denesius closes the door to his office, locks it, and we begin strolling down a corridor flanked by columns and statues of Enlightened People who were famous in their time.

"Give it to me," he orders, holding out his hand as he puffs smoke through his pipe.

I obey at once and watch him unscroll the message. I cannot tell what it says.

"Hmm," he says, reading slowly. When he finishes, he crunches up the paper and throws it into the dying embers of a fireplace in the vast hall we have entered.

I cannot take the suspense. "I am sorry if I interrupted your meeting, Uncle. No one has seen this *message. I took it upon myself to bring it to you at once. I hope I did the right thing."*

"I see," Uncle Denesius says, taking the pipe out of his mouth. "A child with a mind of his own. I will have to watch my back." He chuckles.

The tenseness in my shoulders dissolves, and I grin. He is not angry, after all. I did the right thing. The message still worries me, though. "Uncle," I whisper, even though we are alone as we stroll into another corridor. "Was that a message from the pirates?"

Uncle Denesius puffs at his pipe while walking with one hand behind his back, deep in thought. "Yes, Termite. That was a message from the pirate overlord, John McNeil."

I gasp and stare at him. "The pirate overlord? What did he want? Is he going to attack us?" The terror brought on by the Roarim war two years ago is still fresh on my mind.

Uncle Denesius pauses. "No, Termite. I am doing everything I can to avoid that."

"What?" My head jerks back. "But how?"

He sighs. "There are many things a leader must do to protect his dominion, Termite. You will learn that as you grow older. John McNeil and I regularly exchange correspondence."

My jaw drops. I am appalled. Uncle Denesius? Corresponding with a murderous thief?

"You will understand one day, Termite. The Enlightened People had a wise saying for this sort of situation: keep your friends close and your enemies closer."

I stare at him, then at the floor, absorbing his words. I analyze them, and when I begin to understand, I cannot help but shudder. Uncle Denesius is maintaining a delicate relationship with the pirate overlord to keep us safe and avoid more warmongering. We could never defeat a joint attack by both the Roarim and the pirates. I cannot begin to comprehend the delicate situation Uncle Denesius is in. He is a master in diplomacy and war tactics. He must be dealing with so many secret matters. At once, I can almost feel the staggering weight on his shoulders. Once again, his cunning intelligence astounds me.

"Keep your friends close and your enemies closer," I repeat, understanding the deep and wise burden of those words.

Uncle Denesius places a comforting arm around my shoulders. "That is right, Termite," he murmurs, "Keep your enemies closer." Then he draws me nearer. "That is right."

* * *

Horrible images play over and over in my mind: Roddrick rolling into the swamp, the alligator approaching, sounds of jaws snapping...

His sudden and violent death hits me deeply. Roddrick has been on the periphery of my mind my entire life, simply because his tormenting has taught me to always watch my back. He was the one threat I could always count on. Being released from this mental weight makes me feel giddy.

Yet, for all his mean actions, I cannot help but feel sorry for him. Roddrick and I grew up with the same loss, a void that we never really managed to fill—the absence of our parents. We came from nothing. Our background is a blank slate.

I have never wanted to admit this to myself because doing so would be too painful, but growing up without parents is hard. I learned to hide this acute emptiness by replacing my absent parents with the Atheneum. The Atheneum was my purpose. It gave me something to look forward to in life.

I suspect that Roddrick never found anything tangible to fill his void—except, perhaps, tormenting me. Maybe, at some level, he realized that I had gotten over the loss of my parents and had given myself something else to look forward to: becoming a Knowledge Seeker. Perhaps I associated the Enlightened People with my parents—both having been lost in a murky past. Over the years, the search for ancient Books has painted over the ugly wound left by my parents' rejection.

Even Uncle Denesius must have noticed that silent ambition in me. It would make sense, then, that Roddrick's last words expressed wonder as to why I was always Uncle Denesius's favorite and not him.

The cart jolts, and I knock against the cage bars. I have replaced the goat in the cage. Who, I wonder, will I be fed to? The thought makes me nauseous. I am about to slide from a sitting position to a lying one when the full might of the pirate stronghold comes into view.

The cart lurches through the last, gnarled trees from the swamp and enters the strangest place I have ever seen.

To the left and right of the path, two ships surge out of the sand and tower above me. From atop the half-inverted bow of the ships, pirate watchmen look down at us. A fortified wall made of wooden beams stretches from one vessel to the other.

Loud sounds of chains and grating wood indicate something large moving, and soon we pass through the shadow of massive, arched gates, set in the middle of the fortified wall. The wall is topped by black flags with insignias of a white skull and crossbones.

What lies beyond is even stranger.

Row after row of ancient ships lie side by side. Some lie straight, others are tilted and resting against the next one. Some are whole, while others are scarred or broken in two. All of them are stuck in the sand.

A ship graveyard!

The size of these ships is breathtaking. I count nine levels on the biggest one. My brain goes haywire with images from ancient pamphlets: *7-day luxury cruise for two*, *Win an all-inclusive family trip to the Caribbean*, *Follow your heart and travel the seas...* How could these things have floated? They look so heavy! To think the Enlightened Ones mastered water and space! I remind myself that distance was not a problem back then, but a comfortable adventure.

The cart reaches a group of tugboats and trawlers resting against each other. The cart goes up a ramp and onto a large flat area on top of these boats. The pirates must have removed the bridges of the boats and connected the decks to form a wide square to accommodate events for what looks like a healthy pirate population. The cart travels above the boats, from one to the next, using a makeshift road that leads to the tallest cruise ship. The fact that these ancient seafaring machines are still relatively intact and have not rusted away over the centuries makes me believe they are made from titanium-erzats, a strong yet malleable metal used extensively before the Final Wars.

I lie down and listen to the chatter, shouts, and footsteps that echo around the metal walls of these ancient seafaring machines. Sometimes there is a loud guffaw of laughter, or arguing, or the sound of pottery clanking. I see heads pop out of portholes in the cruise ship's hull just before we enter a big hole in its side.

My ghostly digit throbs painfully. I am starving,

dehydrated, and emotionally drained. With each horse's step, the cart draws me further away from my goal and deeper into the pirate stronghold.

The cart stops in the middle of the metal giant, and I vaguely register men carrying me down a narrow, white corridor, their boots clanging on the metal floor of the ship. They thrust me onto hard ground, and the gag and binds are removed. There is the sound of a door shutting and a key turning in the lock.

Faded letters soldered into a metal plate of my prison stare at me:

Property of *Joy of the Tropics*, 2035.

Joyful, indeed...

* * *

Keys jingling. A door opens. Footsteps and gruff voices. Hands lift me by the armpits to drag me once more down the narrow corridor. However, this time we go up endless metal stairs, and I stumble several times even though I am half-carried, half-pulled. The stairs seem to go on forever. I catch glimpses of massive halls bordered by rows of windows on each level. Each hall is filled with people bustling about, although the higher we go, the emptier and more elegant the halls become.

I glance at the heavy brown boots and trousers with random green and beige patterns of the pirates carrying me. A sharp memory of an image in a Book gives me chills. It is an image of row upon row of men marching in some kind of parade—a *military parade*, the Enlightened People called it. Each carried deadly weapons that were used back then, and they seemed proud of the whole event. It must be true then, the rumor that the pirates descend from these soldiers of the past—soldiers who were complicit in the destruction of the Enlightened Era.

My chest tightens. *Uncle Denesius!* I call for him in silence, knowing that my plea for help is useless. Uncle Denesius is dead. He would have known how to deal with these men. He would have known their ways. He would have known what coaxes or flusters them. What did he promise the pirate overlord? How did he manage to keep the pirates at bay? I should have been more attentive. I should have asked more questions. But I grew up living in the past, in the Books, in the Enlightened Era. I have never had much interest in the present.

A door opens, and I am dropped unceremoniously on the floor. For a second, spots swim before my eyes, but survival instincts push me to get to my knees to avert any new danger that may come my way.

My eyes dart around the room. A row of windows adorns the left wall, letting in the sharp light of mid-day. A canopy bed with fine bed linen and drapes takes up most of the space. I squint. I know several pirates surround me, but the light hurts my eyes, and I have to look away.

Beside me, to my left, is a small, low table laden with fruit, meat, cheese, bread, and a jug.

My mouth waters. I resist the agonizing urge to reach for the jug, almost physically feeling the cool liquid contained within it sliding down my throat.

One of the men standing in front of the windows steps forward, but the sun is too bright, and I cannot make out his features. "Go on, then," he says.

I briefly consider that the food and water could be poisoned, but if the overlord is after the Talisman, he will not opt to do something as heinous. He must know only I can access it. So I do not wait to be told twice, as I turn on my knees, and throw myself on the jug, almost dropping it in my haste. The muscles of my hands and arms are so weak I can barely hold on. Water splashes onto my face, into my mouth, and down the front of my clothes. I try to contain my desperation and focus on holding the jug, so I do not waste a single drop. When the pitcher is empty, I stare at the food. Unable to decide where to start, I chomp down on everything at once. I must look like a pig and am acutely aware of the silence in the room, but I cannot help myself.

It takes superhuman effort to slow down and restrain myself from reaching out for another chicken leg. I swallow hard, wipe the water and grease from my mouth with the back of my arm, and glance sideways at the man by the window.

He has not moved an inch, except he finally takes another step forward, so he is standing in the shade of the wall between two windows. Now I can finally make out his features. He looks only slightly taller than me, but he is stocky, and there is a commanding air about him. His straight, brown hair is thinning, and he probably does not know which way to flatten it: backward or to the side. I do not like the smirk on his face.

I should not have stuffed myself. My stomach is not used to so much food.

"Well, well," he says. "We have ourselves a Knowledge Seeker." He bows a little, but it looks more like a mocking gesture than a respectful one.

I tense at once.

He straightens and places a hand over his heart. "You must forgive such rough treatment. My men are fools and could not recognize a mule from an ass." He lifts his eyes to the men standing behind me. "The men who brought in the Knowledge Seeker and killed his companion," he orders, "take them to the square. Fifty whips each."

My jaw drops, and I am about to object, but the men are already gone. Goosebumps rise on my arms, and now my stomach hurts. I am still on my knees but force myself to stand. I cannot show any more weakness in front of this man.

A bit late for that...

"I am John McNeil, commander of what you would call the pirates. Welcome to my humble abode." He spreads out his arms and gestures at the room. "Is this luxury cabin not a better-suited accommodation for a noble Seeker like yourself?" He looks at me. "For, you *are* a Knowledge Seeker, are you not?"

I hesitate for a fraction of a second. I do not think lying to this man will benefit me. I suspect he would be insulted if I tried to play games with him, so I say, "I am Eodain Atheneumson, son of the Library, protector of the Books, wielder of the T..." I catch my breath.

"Yes?"

I glare at him. I cannot get myself to say it: *wielder of the Talisman.*

A smile appears at the corner of his mouth. He is looking at me intensely, then nods at someone behind me. A steel arm comes over my chest. A hand grasps my wrist.

John McNeil approaches and pulls out the delicate chain from around my neck. The Talisman dangles at the end. He stares at it, a gleam passing before his eyes. "Hmm," he says, then drops it as if he has already lost interest. Hands and arms release their grip on me, and I can breathe again.

The pirate overlord takes the air of a pleasant man who has no worries. "Please, Sir Eodain," he says. "Make yourself at home. Rest, take nourishment. You will be much more comfortable here than in the engine rooms, don't you think?" He lets the question hang as if to make sure I understand that I could end up back in a cold cell at the snap of a finger.

A couple of women enter the room, and John McNeil glances at them. "Prepare a bath for the Seeker," he says. "He reeks." He heads out and, without turning, adds, "We talk in the morning."

CHAPTER 20 *Back from the Dead*

After filling a bath with buckets of steaming water, the women leave, and a guard locks the door. I am left in a room with a soft bed, food and water, and clean pirate clothes. Everything one could need.

Except for my freedom.

I decide to make the most of it. I scrub myself clean, put on the clothes, and munch on a thick slice of bread and cheese, even though I still feel full. I need to get my strength back if I am to get out of here. In any case, once I refuse to give John McNeil access to the Talisman tomorrow, I can say goodbye to this comfort.

I approach the windows and notice they do not have window panes. They do not even have prison bars. There is no need: the ground is hundreds of feet down. I stop munching. Slipping out of the window would mean instant death.

I must be on the top floor of the *Joy of the Tropics.* About nine floors below me lie the group of middle and small-sized boats that form the bulk of the town, with the main square half-hidden between masts and ship chimneys. I wonder if the pirates who brought me in are now getting their punishment there.

I lean forward more carefully. To my right, more abandoned ships lie cluttered across the desert.

A sudden ruffling sound makes me jump. I pull back and watch a dozen pigeons fly before my windows.

Messenger pigeons!

That makes me wonder who the pirate overlord is communicating with. I shudder and lean forward again, turning my head to the left to try and figure out where the pigeons came from.

My jaw drops. I am near the front of the ship, and I have a partial view of superimposed terraces. Each terrace is covered in solar panels. A gust of wind almost destabilizes me, and I pull back hurriedly.

The pirates have solar panels!

I lean against the wall, heart thumping. There is something about those solar panels. I glance out the window once more and take another good look at them. A troublesome thought makes its way into my mind. These solar panels look very much like the ones from the Atheneum.

My mind races. Solar panels from the Atheneum? Is that the price Uncle Denesius had to pay so the pirates would leave us alone? I think back on the storm three years ago, when half of the solar panels disappeared. The Seekers concluded they had been torn off by the wind, never to be seen again.

But Uncle Denesius knew where they were.

I lie down on the bed, stunned by the thought. What else did Uncle Denesius have to part with to keep the pirates at bay? How did he pull this off without being noticed? He must have given the pirates access to the City of Eliadys so they could carry off the heavy objects. My blood turns cold at the thought. What a dangerous feat! How could Uncle Denesius have been sure they would not invade the Atheneum in the process? How could he have been sure they would not kill him? My hand clenches around the bedsheet.

Uncle Denesius! What were you thinking? You played with fire!

But then I realize that tomorrow, it is I who must play with fire. Tomorrow, I will confront the pirate overlord, and it will not be pretty.

With that thought eclipsing all other thoughts, I try to sleep when night falls but am unable to do so. I twist and turn, wondering if I will be brave enough to resist whatever it is the pirate overlord will throw at me when I refuse to cooperate.

I think of the Sacred Pledge—the one where a Seeker must destroy his Talisman and take his own life, so the Knowledge does not fall into the wrong hands. The problem is this: there is no other Talisman. This is the last one. Do I have the courage to smash the last remaining link to the Enlightened Era?

Not while there is still hope.

I roll around on the bed again, my mind searching for a shred of that hope but finding none. Doubt creeps into my mind and gnaws at my stomach. The Wraith Lord, the pirate overlord... They all want exclusivity to the Knowledge to satisfy their greed. Is there still room in the world for Knowledge? Do we deserve it? I catch my breath, waiting for the answer. A lump forms in my throat.

Probably not.

I listen to the silence, afraid of the conclusion I have just reached. I pull out the Talisman and look at it in the darkness. This is the gateway to a better life. It contains information on how to travel great distances, treat crippling illnesses, and heal this dying world. Yet, it also reveals how to create weapons of mass destruction and how to win wars. If we do not deserve the Knowledge, then that really leaves me no choice.

All I need to do is stomp on the Talisman. I could break it in an instant. I glance at the window. Gravity would take care of me.

My breath quickens. When it comes to the Knowledge of the Enlightened People, my life is meaningless in the grand scheme of things. All that counts is what I will do with the Knowledge. It should not be up to me to decide its fate. There should be a hall full of the wisest people, led by the Grand Protector, discussing what I should do with it. Instead, the choice falls on my shoulders. How can I make such a decision, one that could affect generations to come?

Uncle Denesius said that, until we found a way to spread the Knowledge to all mankind, only the bravest should carry these Talismans. *But what do we do now that we have run out of the bravest?*

I roll on the bed again. Either I break the Talisman and jump to my death, thereby dooming the human race to centuries of darkness, or I resist the tortures of the pirate overlord and find a way to get out of here.

I swallow. Without realizing it, the night has passed, and the first light of dawn seeps through the window.

I promised Uncle Denesius I would take the Talisman to the NASA Ground Station. He entrusted me with this quest. But how to make it happen? As I ponder this thought, Elysa pops into my mind. Did she find her way out of the crater? She was training to become a healer—could I entrust her with some of the Knowledge contained in the Talisman to help her achieve her goal?

Yes. In spite of everything, I believe I could, yes.

And Pedregal's parents. Could I have given them the necessary information to grow their own crops, teaching them how to avoid drought, save water and protect their harvest from vermin?

Yes, I could have.

What about Chief Elaine O'Brian, leader of the Newarkers? She would know what to do with the Knowledge, wouldn't she?

That glimmer of hope I was looking for grows within me. These are the people I must stand up to the overlord for, no matter what he throws at me. I sit at the edge of the bed, hands clasped nervously before me.

When the guards come, I have not destroyed the Talisman. I have not jumped out the window—because of the people who would use the Knowledge for good.

* * *

When the guards come, I am ready. *Ready* would be an overstatement; *resigned*, more likely. I am resigned to my fate. I will not give John McNeil access to the Talisman, no matter the cost. A sharp jab travels through my hand where my finger was cut, and I figure I may lose more limbs before the end of the day.

The guards lead me down a flight of stairs, then through a confusing set of narrow corridors that go deeper within the ship. Finally, we enter a vast hall that seems fit for a king. Windows align the left and right of the hall, meaning it stretches from port to starboard side. There are rows of columns throughout the room, but other than that, the place is empty. At the end of the hall is an ancient sign that reads CASINO, and, below it, on an elevated platform, is an oversized chair covered in rabbit skin. The pirate overlord is sitting on it.

I am brought before him like a serf before his master, and I feel my legs becoming weak.

John McNeil looks down at me with a touch of scorn. "Hmm, holding true to your vow, I see."

I know he is referring to the Seeker cape. It would never cross my mind to discard it the way Roddrick did at the West Tower to deflect danger. The cape represents who I am, and by wearing it, I am making a statement. Not long ago, Pedregal said, "Eodain *is* the Atheneum." His statement holds truth. It is not me the pirate overlord will be dealing with today, but with the Atheneum.

There is no point in delaying the inevitable, so I do not answer at this point.

John McNeil seems to think likewise. "So," he says, standing and clapping his hands together. "This is how it works."

I clench my jaw.

John McNeil walks back and forth on the platform. "This is the hall where I receive noblemen and chiefs. We talk about business. We help each other out."

I raise an eyebrow. *Noblemen and chiefs? Thieves and cutthroats, more likely.*

"I have sent messages far and wide, praising your fortunate arrival."

Praising? Or gloating?

"And this afternoon, my first visitor arrives. Each of my guests will bring with them a request—a question—which they will provide to me. I, in turn, will transmit these questions to you. You will access the Talisman and provide the answer. The bigger the question, the bigger the payment. I have made it clear: I allow one question per guest only. You see, I am not naïve. We would not want these fine people to lay their hands on too much information at once. No. We will feed them bits and pieces so that they will have to return, time and time again. This will provide us with a comfortable income for the future."

I ball my fists.

John McNeil nods to himself as if that little speech had been for his own benefit. "But let us not dally. There is something I wish to show you. It is something only a Seeker would appreciate. Come." he whirls around and heads towards a side door.

A sharp nudge to my back indicates I must follow. I have not yet had a chance to say that I am not going along with his plan. The real test will come this afternoon when I do not deliver the answer to his *fine guest*.

I think about that for a second. What would this *fine guest* do to John McNeil if he does not get what he came for? I hold on to that idea. Maybe there is something there that could work to my advantage.

We cross a corridor and enter through a door on the opposite side with CLUB LOUNGE written above it. What I discover in this room leaves me astounded. About half the size of the CASINO, this room is much gloomier. There are only small, round windows on the opposite wall, just large enough for archers to shoot arrows from should an enemy attack. The room is cluttered with piles of indistinguishable objects— indistinguishable to the untrained eye, that is. I know exactly what I am looking at: broken computer screens, smashed keyboards, all kinds of cables, and disk drives. There is a treasure trove of ancient technology here. I feel a pang of sadness. Uncle Denesius and I would have spent hours sifting through all of this. I suspect we could easily have put together three functional computers from the parts lying around.

John McNeil's eyes glint in the shadows, and I

know he must feel pleased with himself for having gathered such fabulous treasures. He paces the room with his hands behind his back—a smirk on his face—and watches me from the sidelines.

I try to ignore him by walking around the room, looking at the different piles. Every pile is categorized: cables, hard drives and motherboards. I am blown away by the possibilities.

When I reach the front of the hall again, I check out a large table with a decent computer on it that, I suspect, is fully functional. My fingers tingle as I pass my hand over the keyboard. I can see the cables sticking out of the back of the computer and going into the wall.

"That is right," John McNeil murmurs. "Switch it on."

My finger reaches for the 'ON' button, and my heart races as I feel an urge to press it, but then I pull my hand back and swallow hard.

A silence falls over the room.

"Is that how it is going to be?" John McNeil's voice is low.

I brace myself. "You know very well I will not give you access to the Talisman. You are wasting your time. You may as well send me back to your prison."

"I could do that, yes," The pirate overlord says thoughtfully. He paces again. "On the other hand, I believe you will come to your senses." He snaps his fingers.

Firm hands grab me and drop me on a hard, wooden chair before the computer. I resist, but I am pinned down. I feel metal closing in around my ankle. I hear a snap and find myself shackled by a chain attached to the ground.

John McNeil gestures towards a couple of pirates who have just entered the room. "Show him," he orders.

Show me what? The throbbing in my left hand intensifies.

The men grab a large screen and place it on the table beside the computer. I believe this is a television screen. The pirates place a black device next to the television and aim it at me. I lean forward for a closer look. It has a small circle at the end with a glass or mirror within it—I am not sure which. I can see my distorted outline in it and recoil involuntarily. I have never seen this object before and am suddenly afraid it is some kind of weapon.

John McNeil nods at the pirates, and they press half-a-dozen buttons. Several things happen at once. The black device rolls awake, and a tiny, red light from it taunts me. The television screen switches on to horrible, loud static.

Someone lowers the noise, and an image appears— an image of *me*! I jump out of my skin. Never before has an invention from the Enlightened People terrorized me so. I can see my messy brown hair, my grey eyes, and the few freckles on my cheeks. I look older. I have never seen myself in such great detail before, and I feel as though the device is sucking the soul out of me.

John McNeil chuckles. "Impressive, isn't it? I wondered if you had seen one of these before. It is called a camera. Do not worry; it is harmless. You could say it is a complex version of a mirror, except that the images can be stored and replayed at will. It is quite brilliant, don't you think?"

"Turn it off!" I beg, unable to look at myself another instant.

John McNeil presses a button on the camera, and the image disappears.

I fall back in the chair, panting. It is one thing to

read about the inventions of the Enlightened People in the Books, but drastically different to experience them firsthand.

"The point of this exercise was not so you could admire yourself on the screen," the pirate overlord continues. "The point was to show you this..."

One of the pirates does something to the camera, and a new image appears on the television. I tense again, and hands press me down in the chair. At first, the image is unclear, then the camera lifts, and I am looking at a charred hill. A few broken walls line the top of it. "The Atheneum!" I cry, disbelief thick in my voice.

"Yes," John McNeil confirms. "Or what is left of it."

I stare at the remnants of my home. The hill is black, and wisps of smoke rise from it into a dust-filled sky. The image moves to the top of the hill, littered with marble slabs and carbonized wood.

"Why are you showing me this?" I manage to say, wanting to shut my eyes but feeling too numb to do so.

John McNeil lifts his hand. "Wait for it..." The camera explores the remnants of the once great building, and the pirate overlord explains, "I sent a small reconnaissance team into Eliadys some days ago. I wanted to see if anything—anything at all—remained to be salvaged from the ruins."

Of course...

"It turns out something did remain." He turns to look at me. "Or should I say, *someone?*"

My blood turns cold. *Someone?*

The camera reaches a round shaft in the ground that goes on and on, deep into the hill. The camera wavers then lowers into the darkness. For several minutes, there is nothing. I forget to breathe.

"My men attached a rope to the camera and lowered it into this hole. Now, observe."

I do.

Before long, the darkness on the screen changes. Instead of seeing a wall of black earth, the camera seems to illuminate a large cavern.

The vault!

The device turns slowly as it dangles from the rope. There is some light within the vault. I see overturned tables, computers on the ground, and a makeshift bed with a man lying on it. He is immobile. Just as the camera begins to swing away, the man turns, and I see his face.

I stifle a moan.

"Show him again," John McNeil barks.

The images go backward, then freeze on the face of the man.

"Uncle Denesius!" I cry.

CHAPTER 21 *A Shocking Discovery*

John McNeil waits until I am somewhat calmed.

Uncle Denesius! I cannot believe it! He is alive! He took refuge in the vault below the Atheneum and survived the inferno. Is he hurt? How long has he been down there?

"Did you get him out?" I exclaim. My steel resolve from the morning vanishes. Uncle Denesius is alive. He needs help. He needs *me*!

John McNeil's silence makes me shudder. I can feel the trap closing in around me. His voice is icy. "As I said before, this is how it works. As long as you provide me with the answers from the Talisman, you have my word that I will send provisions down to your Grand Protector. He will live. But defy me, and I will have the hole plugged so thoroughly he will suffocate, like a rat caught in a trap. The vault will become his tomb." He pauses. "I suggest you think carefully about what you will do next, Seeker."

I slump into the chair. My head sways. *Uncle*

Denesius! I am still reeling from the fact that he is alive. Every thought I had during the night—destroying the Talisman, jumping out of the window, resisting the tortures of the pirate overlord—everything dissolves in my mind. Only Uncle Denesius matters, now. "No! You cannot do this! You cannot leave him down there forever!"

John McNeil shrugs. "I can leave him down there for as long as I want—for as long as I need *you.* I know you are the only one who can operate the Talisman. I know it answers to your imprint only. The life of the Grand Protector lies in your hands, Sir Eodain. Handle it wisely."

A pirate presses a button, and Uncle Denesius vanishes from the television screen.

I barely notice when John McNeil and his men head out. He pauses by the door. "The Talisman stays here at all times. I would not want you to think that you can sneak away with it," he says. "Your task begins this afternoon. Do not disappoint me." Then he is gone.

One guard is left outside the door and one within the room. The door is locked from the outside.

A whirlwind of thoughts race through my head, chasing one another in a nightmarish jumble. A few minutes ago, everything was crystal clear in my mind. Now none of that matters, only Uncle Denesius.

I must get him out. But how? The hopelessness of the situation is agonizing, and I cannot think straight.

I sit there for a long time until I begin to find a thread of thought again. I must save Uncle Denesius— that is unquestionable. I will have to comply—at least until I can find a way out of this mess.

And so, I remove the chain from my neck and hold the Talisman in front of me. This belongs to Uncle Denesius. It has always been his. He only placed it in my care until I could give it back to him. And I will give it back, somehow. I will return the last Talisman to the Grand Protector. It is the honorable thing to do.

Against all my instincts, I must use the Talisman to protect the man who has saved me countless times. He took me in as a baby when my parents rejected me. He opened my mind to the wonders of the Books. He revealed the power of the Sky Spirits to me. Roddrick's absurd lies do not tarnish the image I have of Uncle Denesius. Quite the opposite. He is my rock and my foundation. Together, we will conquer those who are selfish and ignorant by spreading awareness and enlightenment.

"Hang in there, Uncle," I breathe, then insert the Talisman into the computer. I press my finger on the edge of the Talisman, and a faint light scans my fingerprint. The fingerprint is accepted, so I type some orders on the keyboard and gently maneuver the mouse with my hand. It is a clumsy thing, and I have trouble directing the arrow on the screen, but I am relieved to see that the overall functions of the computer are similar to the ones back home. Of course, that leads me to wonder if the computer came from the Atheneum as well. I bite my lip.

Uncle Denesius, what have you done?

As customary, a small file appears in the top left-hand corner of the screen. It is called 'TALISMAN_001'. This is the file where I will find a complete copy of the Knowledge of the Enlightened People. Every page of every Book in the Library has been scanned into the Talisman with great effort and after multiple tries, using faulty machines and a significant quantity of energy from the solar panels. Then, every scanned Book has been copied into every Talisman of every Knowledge Seeker and protected by a secret password unique to each one.

I click on the file and stare at the little grey box that appears on the screen. I freeze. Uncle Denesius did not give me a password. I stare at the screen.

He forgot to give me the password!

I suck in air and hold it there, causing the guard to observe me from the door. I try to hide my panicked state and type in: ATHENEUM. Rejected. I hesitate, then type in SKY SPIRIT. Rejected, again. I shake my head in frustration. What if the Talisman blocks after three tries? I believe all the Talismans were set up that way. Uncle Denesius's Talisman would be no different.

Bile builds up in my stomach. Time is not on my side. Soon, John McNeil's first guest will arrive.

The guards change, and food and water are brought to me, but I am unable to swallow either. I tap with my fingers nervously on the table. *Come on, Uncle! Talk to me!* I feverishly scan my memory for clues. And then it hits me. It is so simple I shake my head in annoyance. I type:

'TERMITE'

The screen blinks and changes slowly, line by line, going from black to blue. I let out a breath of relief. I have entered the protected file. Now I stare at the screen. Save for one document; it is blank.

Utterly, despairingly, BLANK!

My stomach drops to my feet. I should be seeing thousands and thousands of documents, each containing a copy of a Book. Spiders crawl up and down my back. What is this? Where are the Books? Where is the entire Library of the Atheneum? Where is the Knowledge from the Enlightened Era? There is nothing! It is all gone. There must be a glitch. An error. I try again. I remove the Talisman from the computer. I insert it again. I type in the password. Still nothing. Everything is gone. There is nothing left.

How can this be? Was Uncle Denesius in such a rush that he deleted everything by accident? Did he forget a step in the process? Is the Talisman defective?

It is useless now: traveling to Roarim City, searching for the NASA Ground Station, connecting to the satellites. There is nothing left to send. There is not a single piece of Knowledge to distribute among the human race.

There must be a mistake. Uncle Denesius would not be so stupid. He would not throw away his entire life's work. There is a reason for this—something I have missed.

I stare at the blank screen again. In the top left-hand corner, there is one tiny, dismal document. It is called: 'GROUND STATION.'

My left hand throbs painfully, and my breath quickens.

Ground Station...

I click on the document and am asked for a password again. Fortunately, 'TERMITE' works. The document is heavy and takes a long time to load, but when it does, I am met with a jumble of unintelligible letters and symbols. I scroll down, my patience waning when the upload glitches, but the whole text is pure gibberish.

My mind races. The password is 'TERMITE.' The document is called 'GROUND STATION.' It is as if Uncle Denesius had left me a hidden message: *TERMITE, take the Talisman to the GROUND STATION.*

But what for? What is this indecipherable text? Is the document corrupt? Or is it some kind of program?

Will it activate the Ground Station? And then what? There is nothing to send!

If Uncle Denesius is so smart, why did he make such an unforgivable mistake?

I feel weak in the knees. It is all gone! All the Knowledge! The pain in my chest is as sharp as when the Roarim cut off my finger. It is as if the one lifeline that existed between my world and the world of the Enlightened People had just been severed, leaving them to drift off into oblivion, and I have no way to pull them back.

I shut my eyes and hear footsteps in the corridor. There is the sound of a key in the lock, and the door opens. "The overlord says to give this to the Seeker," a voice announces. "He wants an answer within the hour." I hear someone placing a sheet of paper on the table, then leaving. The door closes again.

I keep my eyes shut. I am ready to give up. I wish to be swallowed into the same oblivion that is taking the Enlightened Ones away from me. Only, as I go down that dark path, I see Uncle Denesius's face. I need to save him. I need answers.

I open my eyes, close the useless document and open a blank one. I read the question on the sheet of paper from John McNeil's guest.

I do not have the Books, and I do not know how I will get out of here, but I have one last trick up my sleeve: my memory.

* * *

Uncle Denesius is the first one to notice my astonishing ability to remember. I am five when he comes to the Atheneum daycare to visit the orphans.

His visits are always memorable. Every child wants

to see, touch, and speak to the Grand Protector. He is tall and intimidating yet treats us with a calm smile on his face. We are awed and excited and long to impress him.

The women carers, led by the Old Nanny, have washed and scrubbed us. They have dressed us in our best clothes after having rapidly sewn the many holes together.

Today is a special day. The man we affectionately call Uncle is going to give we orphans a nickname. Until now, we have been called by a number: I am Nine. Ironically, it is my ninth digit that is severed five years later.

It is a fun and exhilarating day. Uncle Denesius arrives with a thick Book called Animals of the World. It is a special Book from the Enlightened Era that lists the animals known from that time. We gawk at it, and Old Nanny scolds us because we are having trouble sitting still.

We are in a semicircle, facing Uncle Denesius as he turns the pages of the Book, selects a passage, and passes it on to the first five-year-old child. She places her finger on the letters and starts reading slowly, stammering as she does so. Reading from this big Book is difficult, and reading for the Grand Protector is nerve-wracking.

My heartbeat quickens as I will her to read more smoothly.

"B-butter-f-fl-y," she stutters before continuing with the next sentence.

Unfortunately, Uncle Denesius becomes impatient and takes the Book from her. "We do not have all day, little Butterfly," he says softly. "Your companions are waiting to hear their names, too."

Butterfly glances shyly at him, then hunches in on

herself.

The Book makes its way around the circle. Cheetah, Hyena, Hummingbird, Panda... Each child gets their nickname, and I start biting my nails in anticipation. What will I be called? Lion? Dolphin? Rattlesnake? Oh, I hope not Rattlesnake...

"You, boy biting his nails. Come," Uncle Denesius says, pointing at me.

My heart leaps. "Yes, Uncle," I say, jumping up and standing beside him.

Uncle Denesius turns the pages of the Book for what seems to last a lifetime. Several markers stick out of it, meaning he has picked the nicknames beforehand. He stops and hands the Book to me, the faint smell of tobacco lifting from his cape. "Here," he says, pointing out a section.

The Book is heavy and smells of old dust, and I am exhilarated. I glance at the word and read in a clear voice, "Termite, noun, a small, pale soft-bodied insect..."

Laughter explodes in the room. Hyena howls and falls over with his arms over his stomach. "A bug!" he roars. "He is a bug!"

Even the carers, chuckle.

"Silence!" Uncle Denesius shouts, though I think he is amused by the general buzz of the day. "Show some respect for your companion!" His words are lost in the chaos. The children have bottled up their excitement for too long, and they chatter and giggle and begin to run around the room.

Thick, hot tears build up behind my eyes, but I force myself to read the rest of the passage: 'Termites will eat almost every part of a book including paper, cloth, and cardboard...'

Suddenly, I understand Uncle Denesius's choice. He knows how much I love the Books! But it is too late to explain to the others. They are now grabbing at the refreshments that just arrived.

Uncle Denesius takes the Book back absentmindedly, and I slink away, even though I wish to ask Uncle Denesius to change my nickname. A lump forms in my throat as I realize it has already stuck with my companions.

"Termite! Termite!" Butterfly chants as she skips by me.

I clench my fists and resist an urge to yell at them. Don't they understand? Uncle Denesius gave me that name because I love the Books, not because I am a bug! I want to shout my reasonings at the top of my lungs, but I know that no one will listen.

After the snacks, we are asked to sit in a semi-circle while Uncle Denesius reads us an ancient legend about a large, wooden sculpture called the Trojan Horse. After many years of war between two clans, one of them left a large wooden horse at the gates of the enemy city as a gift of peace. The enemy pulled in the sculpture and celebrated their victory. But when night came, soldiers hiding within the belly of the horse snuck out and opened the gates. He finishes the story, saying, "And that is how, through treachery, they vanquished their enemy."

We hang on to every word, fascinated by this ancient tale.

Then, each child gives Uncle Denesius a parting gift. One child gives him a drawing, another recites a poem, while yet another sings a song.

I have prepared a little speech, wanting to tell him how grateful I am that he took me in as a baby, but instead, another plan forms in my mind. The idea hits me so hard that I do not stand up immediately when I am called on.

"Termite!" The Old Nanny shouts. "Have you forgotten your name already?"

Snickers ripple through the room.

I glare at her, then stand slowly.

The Book Animals of the World is crystal clear in my mind: every letter, every smear, every indent in the page. Although I do not understand all the words, I recite by memory, "Termite, noun, a small, pale soft-bodied insect. Termites will eat almost every part of a book, including paper, cloth, and cardboard. Studies indicate that they are related to cockroaches, as they are the sister group to wood-eating cockroaches of the genus Cryptocercus."

The giggling dies down as I continue speaking. An uncomfortable silence replaces the joyous spirit of the day. Children are staring at me, then at Uncle Denesius.

The Grand Protector has his eyes set on me. He is as still as a statue, but a change flickers over his face. Is it wonder? Amazement? Something else?

When I finish, Uncle Denesius picks up the Book and turns the pages. He goes over the section with his finger, then looks up and says, "Very good, Termite. Very good."

That is the first time I become aware of my ability, but it takes another four years before it is explained to me.

It happens a few months after the West Tower incident when Uncle Denesius slaps me for singing a harmless lullaby. We have not spoken much since. To be honest, I have avoided Uncle Denesius altogether, though I think he feels somewhat remorseful because he regularly invites me to sit at his table at dinner-time—to Hyena's furor. I obey but eat quietly, focusing on my plate.

Then, one day, I am called to the Library after

dinner. Uncle Denesius wants to see me.

My body tenses, wondering if I did something wrong. I go over the past days in my mind, afraid to find I made some mistake, but find none.

Uncle Denesius is sitting at a table in the Library, pouring over stacks of Books. When he sees me, his face brightens, and he waves me over. "I found it!" he says excitedly. "Come quickly."

The knot in my stomach evaporates, and I hurry to his side, feeling stupid for fearing him. This is the man I know and love. He is curious about things. He is ingenious and witty. He is a pool of knowledge himself, and I wish I could delve more into his thoughts.

"Look," he says, turning a Book my way and pointing at the title.

"Mysteries of a Photographic Memory," I read. I glance up at him, frowning.

He urges me on.

I continue, "Photographic memory, also known as eidetic memory, is the ability to recall an image from memory with high precision for a brief period after seeing it only once." I break off and stare at him again.

He grins. "Well?"

"You... you think I have a photographic memory?"

He nods. "Yes. It is the only thing that makes sense. I have searched for years for an explanation. This is the only one that fits."

"But," I object, "It says I should only be able to remember for a brief period. That is not true. I can remember Books I read years ago."

"I know," he says, his face becoming serious. "I think you suffer from an extreme form of this condition. As you already know, the Enlightened People poisoned the land and the air. It may have affected you in some way, as it did with the giants, for instance."

I shudder at the words 'suffer' and 'condition.' "Is there a cure?" I ask, scanning the article.

"Why would you want a cure?" he says. "This is the greatest blessing the Atheneum could have ever hoped for."

My eyes widen. "It is?"

He beams. "Of course! Just imagine! You could memorize this whole Library if you wanted to. You are your very own Talisman! It is possible you may never even need to carry one!"

CHAPTER 22 *The Comedian*

The days that follow at the pirate stronghold are gruesome. It seems that, as word is spreading that a Knowledge Seeker is 'working' with the pirate overlord, more and more dodgy characters, as well as messenger pigeons, arrive with questions.

The requests for Knowledge trickle in, increasing as the days go by, and I have difficulty keeping up. John McNeil keeps me in the computer room until all the questions of the day have been answered, meaning I am working longer and longer hours.

At first, I worry that the questions will be something like *how to make sophisticated weapons*, but it turns out that most of them relate to basic needs such as farming advice, toothache problems, and marital counseling.

Since I do not have access to the Books, I must write everything by hand from memory. To be honest, I cut off large chunks of information and keep the answer to half a page.

Fortunately, one thing protects me. It turns out that no one else but me can read. "Learning to read is too time-consuming," John McNeil says. It is the task of his guests to decipher my writing. He tells his guests I am too busy and that they must find their own readers. Apparently, the guests are so in awe at seeing words on a page that they leave more than satisfied.

This is a boon. Getting the words on the page is exhausting enough. I pretend to consult the computer regularly, though I only typed up some gibberish that looks like a Book. I shiver every time John McNeil leans over my shoulder to look at the document, but all he says is, "Wonderful! Wonderful!" He does not see past my deceit.

After several days of answering mundane questions, I sit up when a customer asks about making bullets. These are precisely the types of questions that have me doubt whether we still deserve the Knowledge. Why would anyone want to make bullets? There is only one use for bullets, isn't there?

I only provide part of the answer. Or I substitute one element for another—something that cannot be found easily because the Enlightened People depleted the mineral, or the chemical.

It is a dangerous game. Once the pirate overlord's guests return home, decipher my writing, and discover the treachery, there will be consequences. If I stay too long, John McNeil may be the least of my concerns.

At night, I collapse in my bed, my head and fingers throbbing, and it seems I barely close my eyes before it is time to start over. Extracting the Knowledge from my memory is taxing, and I know I will not be able to keep this up for long. But John McNeil keeps pressing me to deliver more.

How am I to plan my escape at this rate? At first,

my head is still clear enough so that I can go over my options. Escaping the computer room would be too difficult. There is the ankle chain, the guards, and the locked door to consider. That leaves my bedroom. It is also guarded, but only from the outside. The only option I can come up with would be to escape through the bedroom window.

I glance down at the mind-boggling drop. If I could climb down in the middle of the night, that would give me a good head start before anyone notices my absence. That leads me to consider the drapes of the canopy bed and the linen covering the mattress. If I could cut strips of material and tie them together, perhaps I could make a rope. I read this in a Book once.

It feels like an unreasonable idea, but until I can come up with something better I decide to keep my mind busy by tearing strips of material—a few each night. I hide the strips under the mattress in the morning, praying no one will notice the narrowing drapes.

As the days pass, my plan seems less and less realistic. I do not think the material can support my weight, and I suspect the makeshift rope will not be long enough. It does not help that my brain is so foggy that I do not even have the energy to eat. And yet, the longer I stay, the more Uncle Denesius's life is at risk. I must find a way out!

I begin to lose track of time. I wake up in a sweat. The sun is high in the sky. The day is well advanced, and no one has come to wake me. I hear loud footsteps in the corridor, and my heart pounds in my chest.

What is happening?

I fell asleep while tearing a strip of material from the bedsheet, and it is clearly visible on the bed. I bundle up the sheet in a hurry, so it looks like a messy ball just as the key turns in the lock and John McNeil enters.

His face is beaming. "Good morning, Sir Eodain! What a fine day! Today we celebrate. We do not work. We eat and be merry. It is my way of showing gratitude for your admirable service. Come now, get dressed, and join me for an afternoon of entertainment."

Women appear in the doorway carrying clothes. They are *my* clothes, washed and scrubbed and repaired. Even my Seeker cape looks brand new. They want to clean my linen and make my bed. I pull the rolled-up bedsheet close and tell them not to bother; I will do it myself.

Once the small gathering leaves, I stare at the clothes, my ears ringing. No work today? An afternoon of entertainment? As a way of thanks? I do not have a shred of desire to party. And yet, I have no choice.

I hide the strip of material and make up the bed quickly, then step back with sweaty palms to make sure everything looks normal. Then, I dress and wait.

It isn't long before a couple of guards come for me. I expect the festivities to occur in the CASINO hall. Instead, they lead me out of the ship and across the makeshift streets built on top of the smaller boats. Are the guards taking me to the main square? Am I to be whipped? Did a guest uncover my treachery, and now the pirate overlord wants to amuse himself with a public punishment?

I stumble a couple of times and must be set back on my feet by the guards. I have been sitting for so long that my legs have weakened. The afternoon sunlight hurts my eyes, and the stench of alcohol and urine from side streets makes my stomach queasy.

Music and laughter reach my ears, rising and falling in volume as we approach the main square, and the nasty smell turns to one of sizzling meat and fresh bread.

We turn a corner, and the full power of the festivities assaults my senses. Banners made from different colored plastic bags are strung above the square. A multitude of men and women dressed up as comical characters swing and dance to violins and flutes. There are puppeteers, clowns, and jugglers. There are men on stilts and actors with hideous masks, red wigs, and puffy dresses. Pirates and town dwellers cheer at the comedians or sit in groups at wooden tables, downing jugs of beer.

To the left, there is a large tent—open on one side—with a row of tables. Some important-looking pirates sit there, dressed in their customary tactical shirts. The pirate overlord sits in the middle, his head covered by a dark-olive cap. Small medals and stars adorn his right chest pocket. There is an empty seat next to him, and I am brought to sit beside him.

He bellows over the noise, "Welcome, Sir Eodain. This is for you, for *us*. To our fruitful and lasting collaboration!" He lifts his jug, which spills beer onto the table.

A similar jug appears before me, and John McNeil pierces me with his eyes until I lift it to my lips and take a sip. Men cheer and holler around us, making my blood boil, but already the attention is shifting back to the performance.

Large, clay plates laden with mutton, potatoes, carrots, and cut apples are brought before me. The rich smell makes my head sway. This whole charade makes me nauseous, especially because I am forced to suffer through it.

I eat only enough to keep me going, then drop pieces on the ground when no one notices. Stray dogs are only too happy to pick up the scraps.

Evening falls, lanterns are lit, and alcohol starts to take its toll on the revelers. Some men have to be dragged away after they collapse, to the loud guffaws of their companions who remain standing.

I wonder if I dare take my leave. But just then, an actor dressed up as an old lady makes his way to the front of the carnival group. He is wearing a mask with a long nose and warts, and his ugly skirt is puffy from multiple layers of clothing. He hunches over as if suffering from back pain and makes funny, dancing moves that have everyone in stitches. I stare at the repulsive show while pirates shout obscene comments at the brave actor.

Just when I think it is finally over, the fake old woman steps forward and points a clawy finger my way. He (or she?) swings their hips suggestively at me to the raucous enthusiasm of the spectators.

"Well, what are you waiting for?" John McNeil bellows, his face red with glee. His forehead glistens with sweat. "Are you going to break this lovely maiden's heart?"

I ball my fist and am about to smash it in his face when pirates grab me by the armpits and shove me to the middle of the square. I stumble and catch myself. Music, howling laughter, and comedians whirl around me, and I have to close my eyes for an instant.

A hand clasps mine. I open my eyes and stare at the ugly mask of the old woman who pulls me into a clumsy dance. Her hand is surprisingly small and strong.

The crowd cheers, "Dance, Seeker! Dance!"

I feel sick to my stomach. I am about to pull away when the old woman tightens her grip on my hand. "No!" she says. "Just go along with it." She pulls me close, and I see the hazel eyes behind the mask.

Elysa!

I stare at her in bewilderment.

She places my left hand around her waist and laces her fingers around my right hand. "Swing!" she orders, and we dance around the bulk of the comedians.

The pirates hoot enthusiastically and spur us on, but my mind erases them. "Elysa!" I whisper in her ear. "Is it really you?"

"Yes," she says. "Follow my lead. Keep dancing until they forget to pay attention to us."

My heart bulges with hope. "Elysa! I am so glad to see you, but I thought you would have headed home!"

She leans back a little and stares at me. "And leave you here with *them*? Are you crazy?"

I pause and consider her. She seems to think it is totally normal for her to have come after me, her enemy, unless she feels guilty for the actions of her people and wants to make it up to me. "How did you find me? What about the others?"

She closes back in to talk in my ear. "Thoron, Pedregal, and Draxis found me and pulled me out of the hole. Thoron is a master in tracking. We followed your footsteps into the hills and desert but then lost you. It did not matter, though. Thoron knew Roddrick would have taken you to the pirates." She glances around. "Where is Roddrick, anyway?"

I catch my breath, thinking of Roddrick's body rolling into the swamp. I shake my head.

She understands and squeezes my hand without answering.

"Where are the others now?" I glance around, half-hoping to spot them.

"They are on the outskirts of the pirate boundary. We decided it was too dangerous for them to hide among the comedians. For one, Draxis is too obvious, and Thoron and Pedregal say their faces may be known to the pirates. So I took a gamble and volunteered to come instead."

I frown at her. *She volunteered? She is doing this for me?*

By now, we are panting from going around in circles, and the exhaustion from the past days is taking its toll on me. The pirates have lost interest in us, so we dance to the back of the troop, and Elysa pulls me aside behind a covered wagon.

I catch my breath and find that I am averting her eyes. "I am sorry for the way I acted when we were by the satellite. I am sorry for doubting you."

She pulls off her mask. "You should not be so quick to judge me, Eodain Atheneumson," she says. "There are many things you do not know about the Roarim."

I glance at her, worried that she is showing her face. "Put the mask back on!" I warn. "You should not be here. It is too dangerous!"

"And, what? Leave without you?" she retorts.

"No, but..."

"Then shut up and listen." She leans over the back of the wagon and reaches for a blonde wig and a woman's dress. "Put this on," she says. "We will mingle with the troop and follow them when they head out. They are camping just outside the fortified wall. We can slip away when no one notices." She shoves the disguise in my arms and pulls the ridiculous wig over my head.

The plan is solid. I am getting out of here. But something nags at the back of my mind.

"Come on!" she urges, noticing I have not moved. "We do not have all day."

Just then, a cry chills my bones. "SEEKER!" John McNeil's voice carries over the commotion on the square.

"Quickly!" Elysa cries, grabbing the dress from my hands and struggling to find the opening so I can put it on.

"Wait," I breathe, my head spinning.

She reaches out to put the dress over my head.

"Wait, Elysa!" I say, pulling back.

"What?" Her eyes fill with panic.

"I... I cannot go."

She freezes with her arms raised. *"What?"*

The dancing slows, and the music dies down behind me. I shut my eyes to try and order my thoughts. I am about to lose my nerve. "The Talisman," I burst out. "I do not have it with me!"

Her eyes widen in terror. "You... you do not have it?"

Behind me, John McNeil's roar carries over the square, making my skin crawl. "SEEKER!"

I shake my head. "I had to leave it in the computer room. I... I cannot go. Not without it." It hits me like a bucket of ice. The Talisman is empty. Do I really need to go back for it? A feeling of deep commitment to Uncle Denesius and the Atheneum surges within me, and I know I have no choice. I have to go back for the Talisman. I must return it to Uncle Denesius and find out what happened to the Knowledge. And, in any case, I cannot afford to have the overlord sniffing around the Talisman and discovering my treachery. "Wait for me!" I say. "I can get the Talisman and come back."

"Leave it!" Elysa says. "It is not worth it. Please, Eodain! Save yourself!"

I stare at her. She would rather save me than the Talisman? It is the first time anyone has chosen me over the coveted object that is the cause of so much envy. It makes me doubt my choice.

"SEEKER!"

Sweat plasters my back. It seems my mind is made up, but my heart is torn. I let go of her hand and step back.

She stares at me. I can tell she wants to stop me, but she knows I have made up my mind. She hurries forward, stretches on tiptoes, and pecks me on the cheek.

Then she pulls back, lowers her mask over her face, and takes me by the hands. "The troop leaves tomorrow. You have until sunset," she says, then leads me into a dance again. We swirl into the crowds, never letting go of each other's eyes, pretending we know nothing of the commotion we initiated.

A firm hand closes over my shoulder and yanks me away from her. A second pirate arrives, and I struggle to follow their fast strides as they drag me before the pirate overlord.

John McNeil has not moved from his chair. He is slumped against its backrest with half-closed eyelids. Spit drools at the corner of his mouth. He is struggling to stay conscious, but a sharp glint remains in the depth of his intoxicated eyes. He wags a fat, droopy finger at me. "Seeker," he pants, trying to straighten himself in the chair but failing to do so. "Dear Seeker. I thought I had lost you. I... I do not like it when you disappear like that. Do not get carried away by the charms of that old woman. I can provide you with anything you need. All you need do, is ask." He burps and seems to doze off, but then he pats my hand. "Do not test me, lad. I have my eyes on you, always."

I shudder.

John McNeil waves me off, and I am taken away from the square, away from the festivities, and away from Elysa.

CHAPTER 23 *A Last Performance*

Another sleepless night awaits me. Music from the festivities drifts into my bedroom on the top floor of the *Joy of the Tropics*. Elysa is down there, waiting for me.

I pace the room, back and forth, checking out the window every two minutes to look at the lights flickering on beyond the fortified wall. That is where the performers have set up camp. John McNeil does not even offer the troop the luxury and safety of staying within the stronghold.

I rub my maimed hand. Did I make a mistake? Should I have fled with Elysa when I had the chance? The very thought is panic-inducing, and it takes every fiber of my being to calm down and rationalize my actions.

If I had put on the disguise and if, by chance, we had made it out of the stronghold, the pirates would have caught up with us. I am certain of it. We would not have had enough of a head start. And, in any case, I could not face Uncle Denesius without the Talisman. He entrusted it to me. Not to Roddrick, not to Thoron, not to anyone else. But *me*.

Even if it costs me my life, even if the Talisman is corrupt, there is no way I can leave it behind. It is my responsibility, and it must remain the sole focus of my existence.

It helps to know that Elysa is near. I realize that, when we set our people's enmity aside, there is something there that I have never felt for anyone before. I yearn to be at her side, making our escape, but I will have to wait. I have to wait until tomorrow morning to be taken back to the computer room where I had to leave the Talisman. I will find a way to remove it, unnoticed, from the computer and bring it back to my room by evening. From there, I will clamber down the ship with my makeshift rope. I will join the performers, and no one will notice I am gone until the morning of the next day.

And so, I wait for the long hours of the night to pass, keeping myself busy by checking every knot in my rope.

I am not entirely sure, but I believe that I left the West Tower thirteen days ago. That means the satellite will pass over the NASA Ground Station in seven days. *Seven days!* I shudder. If I make it out of here tomorrow afternoon, that leaves me six days to travel back to Eliadys, save Uncle Denesius, then cross the desert plains again in time to reach Roarim City. If Uncle Denesius manages to fix the Talisman, that is. My stomach churns. I am fooling myself. We will never make it on foot.

I keep pacing. If I could get a horse and provisions from the performers, then maybe, just maybe, there is a chance we could make it. *So little time...* Yet, that is the way it must be. *Uncle Denesius first; the satellite, second.*

By morning, I am functioning solely on adrenaline. My eyes burn from lack of sleep, and my brain is foggy.

John McNeil does not look much better. He bursts into the computer room and leans against the doorframe. His eyes are bloodshot, and he missed a button on his shirt. He flattens tufts of hair, then rubs his temples.

I realize this would not be a good time to be at the receiving end of his foul mood.

"Back to work, Seeker," he growls. "I want you at your best. Today's guest is an esteemed friend of mine—one I would much rather keep as a friend, if you get my meaning. His question is simple. He wishes to know how to make nukes—whatever that means."

My jaw drops.

"His reward for this information is substantial. Never before have I been offered such generous compensation. You will, of course, provide him with everything he needs."

"Nukes?" I gape at him. "Are you out of your mind? Those are weapons that destroyed entire cities five centuries ag—"

"Shut up, Seeker!" John McNeil's face pales in anger. "Do not test my patience—least of all today."

I glare at him. If John McNeil had read the history Books, he would not accept these types of requests. Nukes! How is it people are still aware of them? How could anyone consider making one? There is not enough know-how, not enough material—is there? Goosebumps rise on my arms at the thought that someone out there still knows the meaning of nuclear weapons and wants to know how to make them.

"Be prepared," John McNeil continues. "It will be a long day and a long night. I must have this information by tomorrow morning."

"Wha...?"

"You heard me." He turns to leave.

I jump to my feet, almost toppling over the chair. "Wait! What of my uncle? You have said nothing of him. I will do nothing until you provide proof that he is still alive and that you are taking care of him."

John McNeil snorts and waves a dismissive hand at me. "Your uncle is alive and well. You can take my word for it."

"But..."

"...and make sure your notes are clear. Our guest can read."

I tense up.

The door shuts, and a guard places himself in front of it.

I fall back into the chair, stumped. *Nukes! The guest can read! Stuck here until tomorrow!* It will be too late, then. Elysa will be long gone.

* * *

The day goes by in a daze. I attempt to pull some information from my memory. I start with the history: what nuclear weapons did, how they destroyed nations and populations, how their poison still affects the ground we live on today, and the air we breathe. There is no chance I am going to reveal how to construct a nuclear bomb from scratch. And, in any case, I am not sure I am capable of pulling up such complex information from memory.

But that leads me to the troublesome question again: do we deserve the Knowledge? My hope was to spread the Knowledge of the Enlightened People back into the world—the good *and* the bad. No filters, no holding back. I would deliver everything.

And yet, as the only one with the Knowledge, I realize I have the power to decide what I want to share with the world and what I deem too dangerous. By unleashing everything, survivors could end up facing the same problems as the Enlightened People from the past. It is a dilemma I had not considered too deeply before, perhaps because I had never been asked to provide deadly Knowledge before.

I push the uncomfortable thought to the back of my mind. This is not a time to be solving such dramatic questions. This is a time to be planning my escape.

I am stuck in the computer room. I will be stuck here until tomorrow. What I need is to get back to my bedroom by this afternoon. What could I do to convince my guards to take me there? I could pretend to be sick. But that could cause too much attention. John McNeil would send healers to treat me. I need to be on my own.

I look around, searching for an answer. Computers and computer parts do not make effective weapons.

But electricity coming from the solar panels does.

The thought strikes me. I could cause a fire. I glance under the table. There is an extension cord with multiple outlets. All the outlets are filled with ancient electrical cords coming from the computer, the computer screen, the television screen, and the camera. If I switch on all the devices at once and place something highly flammable on top of the outlet, it could cause a spark.

I linger on the option. It is risky. What if I cause too big of a fire? What if the guard flees and leaves me chained to the floor? I start sweating. Could I pull it off?

It would have to be a big enough fire so it could not be put out easily. It will need fuel.

"Get me more paper," I order the guard before I can second-guess myself.

He straightens and obeys, opening the door and passing on the request to the guard outside. While he does this, I hurriedly drop a couple of the remaining parchment papers on top of the outlet. The second guard returns with a stack of paper. The first guard places these on the table and hurries back to his position.

My heart thumps. I pretend to be busy, filling the papers with technical drawings of a washing machine as pulled from my memory. Anything that looks sophisticated in the eyes of the guard should do. Once that is done, I cover the side of the computer with papers and pull the Talisman out. I slip it into my pocket. I wait, but the outlet does not catch fire.

"Get me more water," I bark at the guard.

He looks at me, annoyed, but obeys.

While he is fetching water, I switch on the camera and the television. Fortunately, there is a button at the bottom of the screen to darken the static, and the guard is none the wiser.

He plops down a jug of water and a cup on the table, throwing me a dark look that says, "That's enough."

That's enough, all right...

I serve myself a cup of water and promptly knock it over. The liquid spills on the table, and I hear it drip on the paper and cables below. I clumsily dry the surface of the table, all the while holding my breath.

An excessive power-load on a single socket, covered by highly flammable paper and a humid environment. That should do the trick.

The effect is instant. I barely have time to sit down again when I hear crackling and popping sounds, followed by a *whoosh*. In an instant, flames travel up the cables and over the table.

"Aah!" I yell, jumping up and fanning the flames as if trying to put them out. But this only feeds the fire.

It is working!

"Hey!" The guard shouts, rushing forward. He stomps at the cables with his boot, but the ancient material is like dry tinder waiting to be consumed.

"Put it out! Put it out!" I yell. I am thrilled that my plan worked, except that I had not foreseen it would be this successful. "It is spreading!" I shout, making sure my exaggerated panic transfers to the guard.

There are more crackling sounds; electrical sparks shoot up behind the computer, and hungry flames lick at the cables.

I lift my arms in front of my face. "Get me out of here!"

The guard glances back and forth, his eyes wide with terror. When he realizes there is nothing he can do, he rushes to the door and pounds on it. "Hey! Open up! Hey!"

I hear the jingle of keys and make the most of these extra seconds to drop sheets of paper, which quickly catch fire.

That should do it.

I glance down and notice a corner of my Seeker cape has caught fire. I throw the cape to the ground and stomp on it, but as I do so, a good gulp of black smoke enters my lungs. I break into a coughing fit.

The room is filling up fast with smoke. It is a closed space with very little ventilation. The whole room will ignite in a few minutes.

"Get me out of here," I yell again as the second

guard opens the door. His eyes widen when he sees the fire. The first guard shoves him aside and runs down the corridor.

The second guard enters, looks around, then hurries after the first one.

"Hey! Come back!" I shout. *For Spirit's sake! What if they leave me here?*

For a couple of terrifying minutes, I am on my own. I drop to the ground, coughing, and pull at the ankle chain. I kick at the metal ring attached to the floor, but it will not budge. The smell of ash in my nose reminds me of another inferno. The computer screen above me explodes. I raise my arms in front of my face, just as I am pelted with glass shards. The shards puncture my arms and land in my hair.

Loud voices make their way down the corridor, and half-a-dozen pirates burst into the room.

"Get the Seeker!" one of them shouts.

Finally!

Another pirate bends down beside me and feverishly tries to find the key to the ankle chain. His hands are shaking.

"Hurry up, already!" I shout, breaking into a coughing fit.

The chain releases. I stumble after the pirate and collapse in the corridor outside.

"Put out that fire!" I hear the bossy pirate shout. "And lock the Seeker in his quarters, quickly!"

I let the pirates lead me back up to my room while shouts and thumping boots fill the corridors. As soon as the door is locked, I grab a chair and secure it under the door handle. At least that should keep the pirates out for a while if they try to get in.

I rush to the bed, lift the mattress and pull out my makeshift rope. I attach it to one of the legs of the bed and throw the rest out of the window. The rope uncoils into the void. I glance out the window, and my heart skips a beat. It does not reach the tugboat stationed below. Far from it. The prospect of the drop makes me woozy, and I pull back. I lean against the wall, shutting my eyes. This is suicide! Yet, I have no choice. It is now or never. I glance across the room and notice the wig Elysa placed on my head the other night. I slip the chain with the Talisman around my neck, then stuff the wig down my shirt.

I pause and consider the candle on the nightstand beside the bed. The fire-tactic worked in the computer room. Why not do the same here?

I hesitate because I really, *really* will need to get out of here fast if I do this. I pluck up some courage, snatch the lit candle with its holder, and place it under the bed.

Alea iacta est. The ancient Roman phrase pops up in my mind from the part of my brain that is always alert. *The die has been cast.*

I intertwine the rope around one arm and step towards the edge of the window. I crawl out backwards, but to my dismay, my foot slips, and my full weight goes down.

I yelp.

The rope tenses around my arm, and I find myself dangling out the window, a hundred feet from the ground. Then the rope jolts as the bed slides forward, making me slide down several inches. I stifle another yell and cling to the rope for dear life. I spin to face the wall and will myself to control the overwhelming sense of panic.

I glance down carefully. The tugboat sways beneath me, and my stomach turns over.

The rope holds, the bed stops sliding, and I have

not fallen to my death, so I start climbing down with care. One wrong move, and I am dead, a fear that gets me to check every knot between the strips of material before I grab on to the next one. Some sections do not seem sturdy, but it is too late to head back. I glance through portholes as I make my way past the multiple floors of the *Joy of the Tropics*, praying no one will notice me from inside. I make it down to the hull when the rope ends. The muscles in my arms are screaming. No time for a break, though, as I need to assess where I will land. The tugboat below me has a nasty-looking masthead protruding from it.

A nudge in the rope, and I slip down a little more. My gaze snaps up to the bedroom. Flames are billowing out of the windows. The bed must have caught fire. Either I jump, or the fire will cut the cord for me.

The decision is made. I swing a little to the left, and I jump.

I narrowly avoid getting impaled on the masthead and whack a black flag attached to it instead. I land flat on the deck. My breath is knocked out of me. I look up, panting, and watch the rope floating down the cruise ship while flames continue to consume everything above.

Not a minute too soon!

I stand and check my limbs. Nothing is broken. I ignore the throbbing pain in my back and make my escape by jumping from one boat to the next.

Once I am in range of the square, I pull the wig over my head and fold my Seeker cape inside out around my waist, so it looks like a dark-pink dress. As a makeshift comedian, it will have to do. I glance at the open area and notice one last performer wagon preparing to leave.

I rush forward, no doubt looking like some sort of

madwoman with strands of blond hair flopping on my head.

Some pirates hanging around the square spot me and laugh. One of them hollers, "Move those legs, woman, or you'll be stuck with us!"

I ignore them and dash to the covered wagon, where a handful of performers are actively preparing to leave. One of them detaches herself from the group and rushes to me.

"What took you so long?" Elysa scolds in a hushed voice. She is holding a young child in her arms. "I had to tamper with their wheel, or else we would have been long gone." She throws me a startled look, no doubt noticing my soot-filled face. Without waiting for an answer, she shoves the child into my arms.

I am too shaken to focus on improving my comedian skills. Either this works, or it does not.

The die is rolling.

A woman within the wagon holds out her arms, and I give her the child. She has rearranged the luggage, and invites us to climb in next to her. Two other children and an old man are also in the covered wagon, resting against the back of the driver's seat, so we sit opposite them near the opening.

As the wagon begins to roll away, pirates throw unsavory comments at us, inviting us to come back soon.

We make it down the ramp that descends from the tugboat and advance towards the fortified wall bordered by the two towering ship's bows sticking out of the sand. We travel unencumbered through the gates. Guards chuckle from the top of the guard towers, enjoying our last performance as we make our way along the wide path leading away from the stronghold.

The procession of wagons takes a left turn in a

direction that leads away from the dismal swamp that took Roddrick. A plume of black smoke makes its way into the sky behind us.

Elysa points at it. "Is that your doing?" she asks.

I nod.

She lets out a low whistle, then states, "The pirate overlord is not going to like that."

I stare grimly at the sight. "No," I agree. "He is not going to like that at all."

CHAPTER 24 *Risky Ground*

I glance back the way we came, tense as a bowstring. Eventually, John McNeil will notice I am gone, which leaves me in a rigid silence until there is a good distance between us and the ship graveyard.

Elysa is leaning against the side of the covered wagon. The young child has crawled into her lap and has fallen asleep. She smiles at me, all the while stroking the child's hair. She looks softer, not like the girl who entered the lion's den to save me.

Her eyebrows draw together, and she mouths at me, "Are you all right?"

I do not know if I am all right, but I nod and look away again. My escape is bittersweet. The Talisman bobs under my shirt as the wagon moves along the graveled road. It is an empty Talisman. Once we find Thoron, Pedregal, and Draxis, we will have to head back to the Atheneum to save Uncle Denesius. I sigh and close my eyes, nodding off as the afternoon fades into a hazy sunset.

The voice of the old man awakens me, and I find Elysa and the children listening attentively. There is still enough light to see the wide road ahead, but night will fall upon us shortly. The ancient shores of the Gulf of Mexico stretch out to my right, while hills and mountains pop up to my left. The road is leading into them.

I approach Elysa and whisper, "I am surprised these performers are willing to travel by night."

She shakes her head. "They will not be traveling by night. They do not have far to go." She nudges her head to our left. "Do you see that mountain outpost reaching into the desert over there?"

I nod.

"They will stop and set up camp before we reach it. There is an ancient dump from the Enlightened Era that they will scavenge. It is full of treasures and trinkets which they will sell as they travel from town to town." She points behind me. "Look," she adds. "We are already on its outskirts."

An ancient dump from the Enlightened Era?

I glance hurriedly out of the wagon and stare. A wide area to our left seems different, as if the earth had been sifted several times over the years. All types of shapes stick out of the surface. I see remnants of rubber tires, broken glass bottles, rubber sandals, and heaps of plastic. My mind races. Would I find Books here? My first instinct is to stop and dig around. I snuff out my excitement. This is no time to be playing the archeologist. "We cannot stay here, Elysa," I say. "We have not traveled far enough from the pirate stronghold."

"I know," she says. "But Thoron and the others are waiting for us on the outskirts of the pirate territory, by that mountain. We will regroup and continue together from there."

Tension releases from my body. "Thank you!" I say earnestly, feeling overwhelmed that my friends are looking after my wellbeing.

She smiles and turns to the old man. The children are hanging on to his every word, yet I do not understand what he is saying.

"It is a form of old Spanish," she explains. "These travelers come from way down south, from beyond this desert."

Excitement builds up in me again. "And you can understand what he is saying?"

She shrugs. "Most of it. I only studied it for three years."

"...at school?" I say with a touch of wonder.

She nods again.

"So, what is he saying?" I urge her to go on.

"He is telling the legend of a place filled with trees and animals. The land was rich with rivers and rain. You could not take a step without spotting some form of life. Fruits cascaded from the trees. All you had to do was reach out and pluck them. But the Gods became angry because the people took too much. The Gods punished the people by sending dark angels from the sky. These dark angels left deep gashes in the land. He says it took only a month to destroy forests that had taken millions of years to grow. Such was the wrath of the Gods. His people have been roaming aimlessly ever since, hoping to find remnants of their ancestors' mystical paradise." She trails off.

I stare at her while the old man's voice drones on in the background.

She looks at me and shrugs. "It is just a legend," she murmurs and crawls back to lean against the side of the wagon.

A legend... If only she knew... I have read of such a place in the Books. I have seen the pictures. My mind goes back to the great tome, *Animals of the World*. I wish I could show her the wonders I have seen in it.

The wagon lurches to a stop, and I almost lose my balance. Somewhere far away, the sky rumbles. The old man stops talking. The smallest child begins to cry in its mother's arms. The driver of the wagon lights a lantern.

I listen in the falling darkness, alert. "Have we arrived?" I ask.

Elysa frowns. "I do not know. Wait here." She hops off the wagon.

A lightning bolt hits the ground in the distance, briefly illuminating the desert and scaring the children.

Long minutes later, Elysa reappears. "They want to head back!" she exclaims.

"What?" I jump off the wagon in haste.

"They say there is a storm coming. A pretty bad one from the looks of it. They do not want to get caught in the middle of it."

Thunder rattles the ground, making spiders crawl up my back. I glance around in a hurry. We are still some ways off from the jutting mountain where Thoron and the others are waiting. Reaching it would mean traveling through the treacherous storm. Storms rarely bring rain these days. Instead, it is the wind and dust and, most of all, the lightning that I fear.

Loud voices erupt from the front of the procession.

We glance forward, but the performers are looking our way—in the direction we have come from.

My head snaps around, and my blood turns cold.

A lightning bolt illuminates the night, and I see horses piling out of the cliffs behind us, filling the path we have just used. A leading horseman raises a black banner that, no doubt, displays a white skull and crossbones.

The performers' voices are thick with confusion and urgency. Clearly, they do not understand why the pirates who hosted them are now brandishing swords and letting out vicious war cries. What did they do wrong?

"Piratas!" A woman screams, the fear in her voice unchaining general terror.

"Eodain!" Elysa yells, grasping my arm.

It is as if I have been struck by the lightning that shatters the night. I had hoped we would have made it much further than this.

Children wail in the back of the wagon. "Quickly!" I shout, urging the mother to hand down her children. I lower them to the ground, one after the other.

"Eodain! What are you doing? We have to get out of here!" Elysa yells.

I bore my eyes into hers. "The overlord is not going to forgive them for hiding me, Elysa. You have to lead the women and children into the hills."

"But the Talisman!" she insists, picking up a child and resting it on her hip. "Eodain, think of the Talisman!"

I resist a powerful urge to agree with her. My sole purpose is to save the Talisman, isn't it? But I know that, although true, the thought is backed by fear. If I run away to save the Talisman, I will be riddled with guilt later, if I leave the male performers to face the pirates on their own. I call up the last shred of courage I have. "These men will be slaughtered if I do not surrender," I say.

Her eyes widen, and she shakes her head.

"Go!" I order, before she can object. "Hide the women and children. Find Thoron and the others. They are our only hope."

She places her free hand on my cheek. Tears spill out of her eyes. The way she looks at me, I want to kiss her, but the child wriggles, terrified.

Another lightning bolt strikes the ground. The storm is still some ways off, but it approaches relentlessly.

Elysa gathers herself and nods. She urges the women to follow her, then turns and shouts above the wind, "Eodain! Your sword! I brought it with me. You will find it in the wagon!"

I nod and watch her disappear into the night. Then I rush into the swarm of male performers who are bumping into each other, aimlessly trying to organize themselves but not knowing how to. I hop back into the wagon. And not a minute too soon.

Thudding hooves and horses neighing furiously arrive with such force that the wagon rattles, and I am flung to the side.

What follows is a terrible chaos of howling battle cries, and stifling dust rising from the ground, and for an instant, I think the pirates are going to slaughter all that remain.

I stay down, grab an empty potato sack and throw it over myself. Not a second later, a pirate jumps from his horse into the wagon. I stop breathing and watch through the burlap as the light from the lantern glows on his sword. Fortunately, a companion calls him, and he leaps out again.

I throw the potato sack aside and search frantically for my sword among the belongings of the performers.

After circling the wagons several times, I hear the horses slow down.

Where is it?

My heart races, and I think I am going to have a

full-fledged panic attack. That is when my clumsy, trembling hand touches the familiar leather scabbard of my curved sword, which I find hidden behind a trunk pressed against the driver's seat. I tug it free and attach it around my waist.

I crouch down and peek through a tear in the canvas that covers the wagon. Groups of pirates are leaping on to the wagons ahead of me and kicking the performers' belongings out. Next, they will be searching thoroughly through this one again.

John McNeil is pacing on his horse from one end to the other, pausing in the middle, facing his victims. His voice carries over the wind, "Show yourself!" he bellows. "You know who you are!"

CHAPTER 25 *Death by Blade*

The pirate overlord does another round of inspection, occasionally stopping before whimpering performers. As soon as I see him reach the front of the procession, I grab my Seeker cape and slide out of the wagon without putting it on. Fortunately, I am closer to the back of the column of travelers and can mingle unnoticed among the performers lining up in front of their wooden vehicles. The night rumbles with thunder, and lanterns attached to the wagons swing on their hooks, their light casting swaying shadows on the ground.

"You!" John McNeil screeches at the other end. "Step forward!"

A caped man takes hurried steps forward with his head hunched down. John McNeil lifts the man's hood with the tip of his greatsword, checks his face, then swings the blade in a swift, decisive gesture. The man topples to the ground, dead.

Shouts of alarm echo down the line.

"Who will be next, then, Seeker?" John McNeil

rages.

Bile rises to my throat. I shut my eyes and close my hand tightly around the pommel of my sword. It is all that stands between this madman and me. "Run like the wind, Elysa," I mutter. Then, I wrap my cape around my shoulders.

An elderly performer speaks up from the crowd. "Mighty overlord! Have mercy! We do not know this Seeker you speak of."

John McNeil trots his horse over to the man and lifts his greatsword. The poor man locks his hands before him, imploring.

I step into the clearing. The wind billows around me, lifting my cape.

I am the Atheneum; I am the Atheneum...

John McNeil freezes with his weapon raised. He kicks the old man away with his boot and nudges his horse towards me. Lightning bolts illuminate the horizon, striking the earth one after the other. If the storm passes right above us, we risk being incinerated. Dust lifts around me, but I stand firmly, the scabbard holding my sword hidden beneath the folds of my cape. John McNeil must come close enough if I am to have any chance of outwitting the force of his heavy greatsword against my lighter curved weapon. At least he is not wearing armor like the Roarim. Out of the corner of my eye, I spot a pirate on a horse lifting his bow my way and tensing the string.

"Hold it!" John McNeil shouts at him.

The pirate lowers the bow.

John McNeil stops his horse before me. His eyes gleam in hatred. Soot runs down the right side of his face. He leaps off his horse.

Since this morning, I had sensed that this was not a good day to exacerbate his temper.

"You think you can defy me?" he roars. "*No one* defies the pirate overlord!"

He is close enough. I grasp my sword and give it a mighty swing, pouring all my anguish and revolt into it.

John McNeil catches the blow midstride. Our weapons clash in midair. The pirate overlord staggers back, caught briefly by surprise, then he lunges. He is stronger than I expected, meaning that I will have to rely on my speed to outwit him. I side-step, narrowly avoiding his stab, and kick him hard in the side as he leaps by. He falls but uses the motion of his body to roll around and lift himself up again. Now I am the one lunging at him before he can swing his heavy weapon at me. Our blades clash as he swings his sword up, and it takes all my concentration and willpower not to get disarmed by his powerful strikes.

He seems to understand that I am a more skillful opponent than he expected because he steps back and wipes sweat from under his nose, taking a moment to assess me. Clearly, he did not expect a bookbug to be this savvy in sword-fighting. We dance around for a brief moment, sizing each other up.

Now he is ready again and leaps forward, swinging his sword from the side, upward. I lower my blade perpendicularly to his to stop the blow, but the power of his strike ejects my sword out of my hand.

I throw myself on the ground and roll away. His sword zips past me, the blade grazing my upper arm. I let out a cry, but I am where I need to be, lying right next to my sword, which I pick up to deflect another attack.

John McNeil swings his sword down, straight at my head, and I stop it in the nick of time. That leaves his chest open and vulnerable. While still on my back, I kick him hard in the side, under the ribs. He draws a sharp breath and trips, the sword slipping from his hand.

I am up in a flash, ignoring the burning sensation in my arm.

John McNeil gathers his balance and bends to reach for his greatsword.

I kick him in the calf.

He keels over with a grunt.

I lean down, roll him onto his back in one swift movement and shove my knee into his chest. "Surrender!" I yell, thrusting the tip of my sword against his neck.

He flaps his arms around, looking for his sword.

"Tell your men to back off!" I order, pressing harder on his chest.

He gives in. "Yes! Yes! I surrender!"

I check his eyes to make sure he is not fooling me, then stand with my blade still pointed at his neck.

I hear the twang of the bow, the hiss of an arrow. A sharp jab explodes into my right side as the arrow rips into my flesh. The stormy night swims before my eyes, and suddenly I am on the ground with the air knocked out of me. I let go of my sword and press my right hand against the wound, feeling the arrow jutting out of my gut. Warm blood gushes over my fingers. I am so shocked that, for a moment, I believe this is not really happening.

John McNeil is on his feet again. He stomps on my left hand with his boot, and I grimace, certain that he broke all the bones in my fingers. He kneels beside me, pulls me halfway up by the shirt, and removes the Talisman from around my neck. He holds it up before me. "This belongs to *me*," he growls. He clenches his fist around it and pulls me up even further until we are almost nose-to-nose. "*You* belong to me!"

A sudden silence falls around us, making John McNeil glance up.

I pick up the sound of low humming, and at first, I think it is blood rushing to my ears. But then I twist my neck and notice people pointing upwards. Hushed voices turn to loud exclamations. I look up and see it, too: fearsome red eyes piercing through the clouds. Without warning, a terrifying beast drops from the sky.

"*UN DRAGÓN!*" The chilling cry electrifies the crowd. Whoever screamed unleashes a wave of frenzy.

The beast bears down on us, zipping by our heads in a deafening roar with his giant fangs bared, taunting us. Horses rear in fear, thrusting their riders to the ground; men run in all directions, screaming. The beast turns and comes back, slows its flight, and drops to the ground before us.

John McNeil and I have not moved an inch.

The beast's wings flap so fast I can barely see them as they cut through the air. I squint as the wind pelts my eyes and thrashes through my hair. I must be delirious. I see light within its massive belly, splashing out onto the dusty ground. I focus my gaze and notice that its fangs are not protruding from a fearsome mouth but painted under its snout. Its light and dark green body is long enough to be confused with a dragon.

My terrified mind searches through the Books for the name of this thing—a man-made thing from the past.

A helicopter! Under other circumstances, I would be ecstatic. *A flying machine! A real, flying machine!*

But this machine brings deadly cargo. This is a Roarim craft filled with Roarim soldiers. Openings appear on its sides, and they pile out of the metal beast, one after the other, followed by a massive being clad in thick, shiny armor. His spiked helmet is set on top of his broad shoulders. He holds a gigantic sword in an ironclad glove, ready to kill.

"The Wraith Lord! The Wraith Lord!" John McNeil gurgles.

My brain explodes in terror. This monster looks just like the man from my memories—Lord Erawan! The stories are true. It is not a superstition: Lord Erawan and the Wraith Lord are one and the same.

But he is dead! He should be dead!

The Roarim soldiers attack the pirates, pushing them back and making way for their monstrous Lord, who steps purposefully towards us.

"No! No!" John McNeil begs, half-poised to run but too greedy to let go of me. "The Seeker is mine! I found him first!" He sobs and staggers back, but already the Wraith Lord is on top of him. The monster lifts his mighty sword and swings it.

There is not a sound as John McNeil's head detaches from his shoulders and rolls to the ground.

I look from the headless body back to the Wraith Lord and shrink as I realize what is coming next.

The Wraith Lord lifts his sword again, ready to strike at me.

I raise my maimed hand before my face, gaping at the razor-sharp blade that will be the death of me.

It remains suspended in the air, taunting me.

WOOSH!

Something heavy somersaults through the air and smashes headlong into the Wraith Lord. The force of the blow sends the enemy soaring and crashing to the ground.

I gape. Draxis's giant hammer protrudes from the Lord's chest. Roarim soldiers rush to his side.

I had been holding my breath, but as I let it go, the pain caused by the arrow embedded in my right side almost knocks me out. I let out a cry, breathing in short, painful gasps. I roll to my good side and stretch my arm towards John McNeil's body. Prying open his fingers with my throbbing hand, I grab the Talisman.

I glance back at the Roarim and their helicopter-dragon. The Wraith Lord staggers to his feet, helped by several soldiers. His armor is dented.

I gasp in despair. Any normal person would have been crushed to death by the blow of Draxis's hammer. Not so, the Wraith Lord. Either his armor is impenetrable, or there is no way to kill him.

Because he is already dead!

Terror surges through me again, and I drag myself further away, little by little, my clothes soaked in blood. I reach a boulder, and take cover behind it, but then a large shadow appears above me and I think I am done for.

The shadow bends down and picks me up with his huge, strong hands.

"Draxis!" I choke.

My giant friend sees the arrow protruding from my body, and a sense of dread paints itself all over his face.

"Get going! Get going!" Thoron's voice shouts from nearby.

"Get him in the wagon! Quick!" Pedregal orders. "I'll grab the reins."

In the blink of an eye, I am in the back of a covered wagon. It lurches forward. My breath catches in my throat.

Elysa's face appears above mine, pale as a ghost's. She glances down at the wound. "He is bleeding out!" she yells. "Oh, Eodain!" The desperate look in her eyes alarms me more than anything.

"Move over," Thoron orders, pushing her aside

and kneeling beside me. "I will get that arrow out."

"No!" Elysa warns. "You will tear the wound. We have to apply pressure on it. Hold on!" She disappears from sight, and I want to call her back, but everything dances before my eyes and every lurch of the wagon is agonizing.

The sound of the helicopter bursts through the night as the metallic beast lifts into the air.

"Wraith Lord..." I moan.

It flies over us several times, a bright searchlight piercing through the dust. Its shadow cuts against the night sky as lightning strikes. The storm has caught up with us.

Thoron's face swings like a pendulum. "Pedregal, get us out of here!" he yells.

"What do you think I am doing?" I hear the reply.

I am not going to make it. Something tells me this is the end of the road. And if that is so, then there is something I have to tell Thoron. Something important.

"Thoron..." I breathe. But now it is Elysa hovering over me.

"What is it?" Thoron's voice says in my ear, and I blink in confusion. I cannot make out who is there and who isn't.

"Do not fall asleep, Eodain." That is Elysa.

I sway between darkness and consciousness. I turn my head and find Thoron sitting next to me, but he looks ghostly. I grab his arm to make sure he is real. "Uncle Denesius... he lives. We must go back... to the Atheneum. Save Uncle..."

Elysa's face swings above my own, eclipsing Thoron's. Was he even there? "Do not fall asleep, Eodain. Do not fall asleep."

She turns into the Wraith Lord, sword raised to end my life.

I scream inwardly.

You are dead. You are supposed to be dead!

CHAPTER 26 *The Killing of the Lord*

For the first time in my ten years of life, the Roarim have succeeded in breaching the fortified wall surrounding the city of Eliadys. I huddle with the orphans in the dormitory. We hold on to each other and whimper. The women carers speak in hushed tones, the fear in their voices difficult to ignore.

We can hear the fighting outside, the urgency in our soldiers' cries as they try to push back the enemy.

The doors to the dormitory fly open. Women shriek. We children burst into tears.

A group of Knowledge Seekers enters, yelling, "Hurry, women! Gather the children. Head to the vault. NOW!"

The women burst into action, urging us to stand and follow them. "Have they reached the Atheneum, then?" one of the carers asks, her voice trembling.

My stomach lurches at the prospect.

The Seeker glances at her and does not reply.

Instead, he claps his hands. "Come on!" he barks, "Get on with it!"

We scramble out of the dormitory, but someone grabs me by the arm and stops me. "Not you!" a voice says. I look up at Thoron. "You are coming with me."

"But..." I watch my companions rushing off without me.

"Come, quickly!" Thoron urges. He pulls me in the direction of the Atheneum, and we weave our way through fighting soldiers. My breath quickens, and I would be lost in the chaos were it not for Thoron's guiding hand. The main doors to the Atheneum are well guarded, but the fighting has already reached the inner courtyard.

Thoron and I slip through the soldiers and the open door. Now we are running over the marble floor in the direction of the Library.

"Open up!" Thoron orders the next row of soldiers. They move aside at once and let us in.

I find myself in the massive room beneath the main dome, blinking as my eyes adjust to the gloom.

Uncle Denesius is standing there, tall and forbidding, surrounded by a group of the bravest Knowledge Seekers. All have their swords drawn, ready to make a last stand. He glances at me, his eyes hard. Then he looks at Thoron and says, "You know what to do."

"Yes, Master," Thoron replies.

An explosive sound tells us the main doors have been breached.

"Uncle..." I breathe in terror.

"Go!" the Grand Protector yells.

Thoron pulls me away to a side corridor within the Library. It leads to a room where the Knowledge Seekers have spent countless hours restoring the Books.

There is a less visible door at the back that leads down rickety stairs into a dark storage room. Thoron pulls me down these stairs, and we hide between boxes and piles of parchment paper, and leather book jackets.

"Thoron..." I whimper as I think of Uncle Denesius out there, facing the enemy. I struggle to get out of his arms.

"Shh!" he urges, pinning me down. He holds his sword in front of me.

I obey, but only because I hear the Roarim crashing into the Library.

We listen to the violent battle taking place not far from us. It seems to go on forever. I hunker against Thoron, terrified. Minutes turn into hours. Finally, the screams die down, and we hear loud footsteps and shouts erupting into the room beside us.

Thoron lifts his sword higher and squeezes me so hard I forget to breathe.

The door crashes open. Men appear in the doorway. "Thoron!" someone yells.

Thoron releases his grip somewhat.

"Thoron?" the man calls again, coming down a few steps. He is wearing a Seeker cape. "You can come out now. We won!"

Those few words fall like a blessing in my ears.

We won!

Does that mean the Roarim are on the run? Is Uncle Denesius safe?

We emerge into the larger room and find a group of our Seekers and soldiers there. Thoron briefly forgets about me. I do not wait. I burst into a run. I sprint down the corridor, heart pounding, afraid of what I will find.

"Termite!" Thoron bellows from the back room.

I burst into the Library, and what I discover there

chills me to the bone.

Shafts of light drop from the dome, causing dust to fly around, creating a ghostly mist. Bodies litter the floor. Uncle Denesius's dark form stands with his back to me, his bloody sword at his side. Half-a-dozen Seekers stand with him in a circle. They look like they are performing some kind of twisted ritual.

Uncle Denesius turns towards me, revealing the object of their attention. A man in heavy, shiny armor lies sprawled in their midst. Nasty, metal spikes jut out of his thick helmet.

Lord Erawan!

Even now, the dreaded Roarim Lord looks formidable and dangerous.

But it is the atmosphere that makes the hairs on the back of my neck stand up. The air that hangs around the group is thick, as if I were attending a dark, forbidden ceremony, one where men have turned into beasts, and I am witnessing the aftermath of their insanity.

Uncle Denesius lays his eyes on me. His pupils are so dilated he looks like the demon he must have summoned up from within to defeat the enemy. I am struck by what a powerful, terrifying opponent he is. Only he could have defeated the Roarim Lord. Only he could have saved us.

Thoron's thudding boots come up behind me. He grabs my arm to pull me away. As he does so, my gaze falls on Lord Erawan. The Lord drops his arm to his side as if pointing at me, and through the fearsome helmet, his grey eyes stare. With his dying breath, it is me he sees.

My knees buckle.

Thoron holds me up and pulls me across the room.

My uncle-turned-demon faces the circle again,

hiding the Lord from me, and he raises his sword.

I do not see him slay the Lord, but I hear the unmistakable fall of the blade as it digs into the flesh, and the final gasp of air.

I retch.

Thoron rushes out of the Library with me in tow. We stumble into the main hall and watch Roarim soldiers being chased from the building. "This way," he urges, shoving me into another corridor. I swallow the bile in my throat, turn a corner and slam headfirst into a Roarim soldier.

I collapse to the floor, dazed. Through the ringing in my ears, I hear Thoron yell. Black Roarim boots thud around me. Swords clash. Just as I fall into unconsciousness, a razor-sharp pain travels from my left hand up my arm, and somewhere far away, I hear myself scream.

* * *

That scream has haunted me through the years and finally catches up with me as I fight for my life. The image of the Wraith Lord grows stronger in my mind as I grow weaker. Lord Erawan, setting his dying eyes on me. The Wraith Lord, observing me through slits in his evil helmet. Lord Erawan lived and died. The Wraith Lord is dead, yet lives. They are one and the same.

There are no such things as wraiths, Uncle Denesius says in my mind, but he says it with fear. He feared the revenge of the Wraith Lord. And now I fear it, too—he knows I was there, on that fateful day of his defeat. He found me once, and he will find me again. He no longer cares for Talismans and Books. He will not rest until his wrath is complete.

"Eodain," the voice of the dead Lord booms

through the helmet.

I flinch.

"Eodain!" My cheek stings as someone slaps it. "Wake up! Eodain!" Elysa's voice is loud in my ear.

I blink.

Elysa's face is contorted in anguish. "I told you not to fall asleep! Stay with me!"

I try to stay with her, if only to escape the nightmare that waits to pull me back into darkness.

"Eodain!" Her voice snaps me to attention. I was drifting off again. "We are going to remove the arrow now."

The arrow?

As if on cue, pain explodes through my side. I groan.

"Lie still," she says. "I know it is hard, but you have to try."

What she is asking for is impossible. My body shakes. Sweat rolls off my forehead and dampens my back. I take in the cave walls, the fire, and the men sitting around it: Thoron, Pedregal, and Draxis.

Draxis grabs his hair with both hands and turns away. Thoron and Pedregal look like they are at a funeral.

"Are you ready?" Elysa says.

I nod. I am not ready, but there is nothing left for me to do. Once the arrow is out, it will be like pulling a plug.

Elysa reaches behind her towards the fire, never taking her eyes off me.

"Hey!" Thoron yells. "What do you think you are doing?"

I am upset that he shouts at her, but when I see her pull my sword out of the fire. I wince involuntarily. The tip of it is red from accumulated heat.

Thoron grabs her wrist to take the weapon from her.

"Wait!" she protests.

"Do you truly think I will stand by and watch you kill him with that?"

"You do not understand!" she insists. "I need the heat collected in the blade to cauterize his wound. It will stop the bleeding once the arrow is out."

Cauterize...

Strange. Even in my weakest state, that part of my mind that is always alert is still in optimal form.

"To cauterize: verb, to burn the flesh of a wound with a heated instrument, to stop bleeding and prevent the wound from becoming infected."
Medical Encyclopedia, p. 367, Tome III, 2029.

"Thoron," I manage to mumble.

He glances at me. He seems to understand because he lets go of Elysa. "Are you sure?" he asks me.

I nod.

"Here," Elysa says, lifting my empty scabbard to my mouth. "Bite on this."

I frown but obey.

"It will hurt," she warns, her voice dull, as if she has surrendered to the inevitable. She lifts the burning blade, fire reflecting in her eyes.

I remember nothing after that, but I find deep teeth marks in the leather of my scabbard when I awaken.

CHAPTER 27 *A Futile Trip*

I know I will live when I open my eyes and am confident I am not in a nightmare.

Sun beats down on the canvas covering the wagon, and a breeze lifts torn parts of the material. I listen, but all is peaceful. For the first time in a while, I am not drenched in sweat, the Wraith Lord is not hanging over my head like a bad omen, and my right side does not feel like a hundred knives pierced it. My head is clear. I know who I am, who my companions are, and what my mission is.

The canvas opens at the back, and Elysa appears, carrying a bowl. She smiles when she sees me awake.

I smile back, and it feels good.

She climbs up and sits next to me. "Are you done napping yet?" she teases gently.

My smile widens. "I am not sure. What does my healer recommend?"

The flap opens again before she can answer, and Pedregal leaps up, making the wagon lurch a little.

"Whoa!" I say, wincing. "Not so fast, big guy!"

"For Spirits' sake, lad!" he grins. "It is so good to see you awake! You had us worried sick."

"You? Worried?" I taunt him, spotting the bandage around his forearm. "I could say the same for you."

He shrugs. "Ah, that is nothing. Just another scar to add to my collection. And proof that the great swordmaster lacks practice."

My stomach tightens at the thought that I could have lost him in the fight, but I decide to focus on the fact that we are alive, together, and free.

Elysa lifts a corner of my shirt and gently removes the bandage covering my wound.

My stomach tightens some more. "Should I look?" I venture.

"Ugh!" Pedregal exclaims, glancing at the wound. "Nah, lad, I would not look. What a mess!"

I stare at him in alarm.

He bursts out laughing. "Ha! I am kidding. You have gotten yourself the mightiest scar of us all."

I glare at him, feigning offense.

He winks at me and says in a more serious tone, "You got lucky, Eodain." He points at Elysa. "This girl knows what she is doing."

Elysa blushes but keeps on cleaning the wound.

I think Pedregal is getting emotional because he clears his throat. "Well... have to get back to preparing my rabbits. Do not be late for dinner, kids!" He winks and, with that, jumps out of the wagon.

Elysa and I grin at each other.

"And Draxis?" I ask, remembering his look of dread at my plight. "Is he all right?"

"He is fine—I think," Elysa replies. "He keeps to himself, mostly. Between us, I think he was pretty shaken by what happened to you. He has not been in to see you once. I do not think he could handle it."

I consider her words. Poor Draxis. Ever since the fire at the Atheneum, he has not been himself. I really will need to press him about how he is doing. I should have done so before, when I had the chance. It makes me anxious to get better soon.

I lift myself on my elbows so I can look at the wound. It is clean and healing. Elysa has sown the gash made by the arrow, and she is applying a soothing ointment on the burn mark left by the hot blade.

"Wow!" I say, impressed.

Her face droops. "The burn mark may never completely disappear. I do not have the necessary medicine at hand. I am sorry, but this is the best I could do."

I place a hand on her arm, and she stops applying the ointment. "You saved my life!" I say. "Don't you dare apologize!"

She tears up. "I had my doubts there for a moment—serious doubts." She bites her lip, then adds, "I thought I was going to lose you, too, like I did my brother." The last word is almost inaudible.

I lie down again, staring at her. "Do not ever doubt your ability, Elysa. You will be a great healer. I do not know why the Spirits allowed me to live, but not your brother. Do not put that burden on your shoulders. All you can do is try the best you can, and I know that you do."

"Thank you," she breathes. She sniffles and wipes the tears away with the back of her arm so she can concentrate on placing a clean bandage on the wound.

Thinking back on how bad things were, I stare at her in awe. She truly performed a miracle. "I will take you home," I vow. "So you can continue with your studies."

She looks at me with a sad smile. "Even if it means I must end up doing bad things for the greater good?"

I frown. "What a strange thing to say. What bad things? Do you mean like burning my flesh with a sword to save my life? I think the question answers itself. As a healer, sometimes you will need to hurt someone. However, if the outcome is to save them, then I am sure they would understand."

She seems shaken by my words because she bends down until our noses almost touch. Her hair tickles my cheek. "I should hate you," she murmurs, looking straight at me.

I suppress a smile. "I should hate you, too," I whisper.

I think she will kiss me, but Thoron bursts into the wagon. He climbs up, looks at me, then at Elysa. She is pretending to straighten a makeshift pillow behind my head. "Good," he says, nodding in satisfaction. "Good, good." Then he turns and leaps off the cart again.

"Huh!" I snort. "Yes, Thoron. It was a pleasure to see you, too!"

Elysa stifles a giggle.

I shake my head. "Well, here is someone whose temper we can always count on."

I am hoping Elysa will stay, but she gathers up the bowl and used bandage. "I had better make some more ointment," she says vaguely. "I suspect Thoron will want to head into Roarim City tomorrow."

It takes me a second to absorb what she just said. Goosebumps rise on my skin. "What?" I sit up, wincing at the pain in my side. "What did you just say?"

"Hey!" she warns, turning towards me again. "Gentle with that."

"What do you mean, Roarim City?" My voice raises louder than I meant for it to.

"Shh!" she says, waving a hand at me so I will lie down again. But it is too late; the brief joy I experienced at having healed is gone.

"I am sorry!" Elysa says hurriedly. "I should not have broken the news to you like that. But I thought it would make you happy."

I have stopped listening to her. Blood rushes through my ears, and I stand, pressing my left hand against my wound, making it more manageable for me to get out of the wagon. I lower myself to the ground, and my legs struggle to accept the weight of my body.

"Eodain, wait! You are not ready!" Elysa calls after me.

I blink to get used to the daylight. We are hidden away in a nook of a mountain. It resembles all of the mountains we have traveled through since the burning of the Atheneum: dry and rocky.

"Thoron?" I call out.

I find Pedregal sitting by a fire pit. He stands, dropping a lifeless rabbit to the ground.

I ignore him and turn the other way, striding away from our hiding place. "Thoron!" I yell again, reaching a ledge.

I stop in my tracks.

Roarim City spreads out before me. The city clings to a hill and is surrounded by a moat. The water in the moat comes in from the ocean, which spreads out into the horizon to my left. A wide bridge crosses over the moat and connects the city to the mainland below me.

I ball my fists and rush back to the wagon. I spotted my satchel in a corner just now, when I woke up. I pull out Uncle Densius's spyglass and hurry back to the mountain ledge to get a better look. I place the spyglass in front of one eye and stare out at the ocean. Small fishing boats sail on it. I blink at the sight because I have never seen the sea before. The pictures in the Books do not do it justice.

Then, I direct the spyglass towards the mainland. In the valley below my feet, thousands of tents are set up. Countless Roarim soldiers occupy them and many others line up on the bridge to enter the city. A massive, fortified wall surrounds the city and, in the center of it, at the top of the hill, is a large palace structure made of three overhanging decks. Beside this palace stands the NASA Ground Station. I would recognize the thick stem carrying a huge, parabolic dish anywhere.

Roarim City! What are we doing here?

"Piece of cake, huh?" Pedregal says to me, making me jump. He rests his hands on his hips as he scrutinizes our enemy's lair.

"Where is Thoron?" I insist, just as the guardsman appears and scrambles down the side of the mountain to our location. I fold up the spyglass.

"What is going on?" he pants, rushing towards us.

Waves of anger and disappointment wash over me, almost impeding me from speaking. "*What* are we doing here?" I force the words out of my mouth.

Thoron's face is a blank.

I yell, unable to contain my anguish, "What are we doing here?" I step towards him menacingly, and he backs away.

"Keep it down!" he rumbles.

"The Atheneum!" I shout, in spite of his warning. "We were supposed to go back to the Atheneum!"

He stares at me, bewildered.

I cover my face with my hands, trying to calm down. When I lower them, Thoron, Pedregal, and Elysa have gathered around me. "Thoron, I told you to go back to the Atheneum!" I say with as much calmness as I can muster.

Thoron lifts an eyebrow and scratches his beard.

I groan. So, I never told him, after all. I must have been hallucinating in the back of the covered wagon, and it would seem the words never made it out of my mouth. "Uncle Denesius..." I explain. "He is alive. He is under the rubble of the Atheneum, deep in the vault. He cannot get out."

The three of them stare at me, probably expecting that I am making a bad joke.

"Thoron, I told you to go back to the Atheneum! Or, at least, I thought I did."

Thoron shakes his head. "No, Eodain. You said nothing of the sort. And in any case, how would you know that the Grand Protector is still alive?" He pauses, then adds more cautiously. "Do not tell me that the pirates told you this."

I bite my lip. "They did."

Thoron snorts. "Oh, come on, Eodain. You know better than tha..."

"I *do* know!" I snap. "I know for a fact. Trust me!" I stare at them in turn and repeat, "Uncle Denesius is alive!"

Silence falls among them as they glance at each other.

Thoron wipes his face with his hands and steps back. He starts pacing. After a while, he rejoins us, saying, "All right, then. Let us suppose that what you say is true: the Grand Protector survived the inferno. There is nothing we can do about that now." He stabs a finger at Roarim City. "But we can do something about *that*."

The blood drains from my face. He means the NASA Ground Station. He means that I should use the Talisman to spread the Knowledge.

I drop down into a crouch, grasping my hair with both hands, focusing on the pain from the wound. How shall I tell them? How many days have they been traveling and avoiding detection to get me to my original destination?

"What now?" Thoron yells. "What are you not telling us, Eodain?"

I look at the ground, then straighten again because there is nothing I can do except face the consequences. "There is a problem with the Talisman," I begin.

Thoron places his hands on his hips. "A problem? What kind of a problem?"

I pull the chain from around my neck and hold up the Talisman for them to see. I stare at the dismal thing, the one that has caused so much suffering. "It is empty," I say blandly.

They do not seem to understand because there is no reaction.

Thoron glances at the others, still with his hands on his hips. "What is that supposed to mean: it is empty?"

I keep my eyes glued to the Talisman and set my jaw. "It is empty. There is not a single Book from the Library scanned into it. It is corrupt."

Pedregal whistles.

Thoron looks from me to the swordmaster, then back at me. "This is no time for pleasantries, Termite," he seethes.

"It is empty!" I yell. "It was all for nothing! Everything we did, all those days of walking and danger, it was all for nothing! Something happened to the Talisman, something Uncle Denesius did. Maybe he was in a hurry. Maybe he miscalculated. I don't know. All I know is that it is all gone; all the Knowledge from the Library is gone!"

"The Grand Protector does not miscalculate!" Thoron shouts angrily. "It is you who is wrong! You did

containing my excitement. Uncle Denesius found a way to awaken the internet data servers across the globe by way of the satellites!

My brain scans through an impossible array of Books on how the internet worked, what it was used for, how the Enlightened People accessed it to download infinite Knowledge.

My mind whirls, and I lean into our little gathering. "Listen," I say. "Originally, the internet used miles and miles of fiber optic cables spread out over the land and under the oceans, linking continents together. But warring superpowers spliced these cables, cutting off the world from the internet. Not indefinitely, though. At the time of the Final Wars, the internet no longer relied solely on these fiber optic cables. At the height of their civilization, the Enlightened People used thousands upon thousands of tiny satellites to connect to the internet. Unfortunately, most of these fell back to Earth over the centuries, but bigger ones, belonging to important corporations, organizations and governments, would have survived through the ages. Their thermonuclear cells and their titanium-erzats envelope would allow them to orbit the planet indefinitely.

"So, technically, as long as there are satellites in the sky and functional data storage centers sprinkled across the Earth, this program in the Talisman could potentially revive the greatest invention in the history of humankind!"

I am so thrilled that the pages of the Books related to the history of the internet mingle in my mind. *Uncle Denesius did it! He actually did it!*

Thoron and Pedregal are staring at me blankly. I do not think they quite understood what I told them. But Elysa's mouth widens in an unrestrained smile.

"I wonder why he didn't say anything," I say, more than a little disappointed that Uncle Denesius did not confide in me.

"I am not sure, Eodain," Thoron admits. "I guess he knew you would follow his orders, no matter what."

My throat closes up with emotion. *Oh, Uncle!* Once again, my path is crystal-clear. My life's purpose is set out before me. "My friends," I say, full of awe, "We are going to the NASA Ground Station. It is time we woke up the cloud and gave the Knowledge back to the world, where it belongs."

I look at each in turn, and it takes me a moment before the question hits me. "How long have I been unconscious?"

* * *

"Five days!" I exclaim for the hundredth time. "I have been out for five days?"

Pedregal nods. "You missed a captivating trip across desert and mountain trails, then more desert and more mountain trails."

I search through the contents of my satchel, pushing aside the National Geographic, the spyglass, a rotten apple, and my empty water bottle. Finally, I pull out the folded papers that I had torn out of the West Tower Logbook. I spread out the crumpled pages, and flatten them on the ground to get a better look.

"What are those?" Pedregal asks.

"I need to double-check the last records of satellites that passed over the Atheneum," I explain. "I have to be certain." I point at an inscription. "8:17 pm," I say. "I must be at the Ground Station today at 8:17 pm." I look up at the others.

"Today?" Pedregal repeats. "I do not think that is

wise, lad. You are still recovering."

I close up the satchel and stand firmly. "Today, Pedregal. The quicker we get this done, the quicker we will get to Uncle Denesius."

Pedregal nods, rubbing his golden beard, which has grown considerably since we left Eliadys. "And how do you propose we enter Roarim City?" he asks.

"Oh, that part is easy," Elysa speaks up. She has remained quiet until now. "Eodain and I can enter as brother and sister."

We all stare at her.

She shrugs. "What? I lost my brother, remember? But no one except you knows that."

I offer her a grateful smile.

"That is out of the question," Thoron interjects. "Eodain, there is no way you are entering the enemy stronghold on your own with a Roarim soldier."

Elysa stomps her foot. "I am *not* a soldier!"

"Oh, really?" Thoron snorts. "And what is that armor you are wearing?"

She turns red in the face.

"Will you get off her back already?" I argue. "Elysa has saved me countless times."

"Saved you?" he cuts in. "Or saved the Talisman?"

I glare at him. I vividly remember Elysa insisting I save myself from the pirates without the Talisman. For some reason, I do not picture Thoron doing the same for me had he been in her shoes that day. "That is enough," I say. "I have decided. Elysa will take me to the city's main gates, and I will pretend to be her brother. It makes total sense."

Thoron turns to Pedregal. "Come on, swordmaster! Talk some sense into the boy."

Pedregal shifts uncomfortably and glances at Elysa. "Begging your pardon, Elysa..." he looks at me, "...but

Thoron is right. It is madness to do this on your own."

Thoron nods in satisfaction. "Pedregal, you go with the two young ones. I am sure Elysa has an uncle or distant relative you could impersonate. Draxis and I will swim across the moat and find another way in. Though Draxis does not speak, he is good at making noise. We will cause a distraction to give you a chance to enter the Ground Station."

Thoron annoys me, but I have to admit he has his moments.

"You mention Draxis," I say. "I have not seen him. I would like to know what he thinks of all this."

"He will follow the plan, Eodain," Thoron says. "He is the least of our concerns."

I sigh. "We are all set, then."

"Not quite," Elysa says. Her voice is devoid of emotion, and I wonder if she is nervous about heading home in such strange company. "You cannot go into Roarim dressed like this. Eodain, your clothes are torn and bloodied, and your Seeker cape would stand out like a sore thumb. You all look like dangerous villains from the heart of Eliadys," she adds.

Pedregal jumps to his feet. "Leave that to me. I am sure those soldiers will have something decent for us to wear."

Elysa's eyes widen.

I say quickly, "Er... Pedregal, be gentle with them."

Pedregal glances sideways at me and winks as he heads away. "Who do you take me for, lad? Under these scars hides the tenderest of lambs."

I grin and watch him begin to climb down the rocky mountain. Pedregal is right: a gentle soul *does* sleep under that thick skin of his.

Thoron kicks the dying embers of the fire. "We have a few hours to rest," he says. "We leave after the noon hour." He lies on the ground and rolls to his side with his back to me.

I consider resting in the wagon, but it would be unfair to the others. They, too, have suffered and are tired. We have shared this journey together and will end it together.

I worry for Draxis, but Elysa has had her eyes on me for some time. We have not had a chance to talk about the latest developments. She approaches and lies down beside me. "Eodain," she whispers, "About this afternoon..."

I catch my breath. *Yes, about that...*

It is strange. Just this morning, I was promising her that I would bring her home safely. And here we are, at the doorstep of Roarim City. I did not expect we would have to part so soon. I try to sound strong. "This afternoon, once we enter the city, we go our separate ways. You will go back to your family, and I will do what I have to do. There is no need for you to go any further with us. Whether we succeed or not, we will remain outlaws in the eyes of your people. There is no place for me in Roarim." Those last words hit me hard. I had not thought that far ahead. *There is no place for me, anywhere.*

She lowers her eyes. "What about the Wraith Lord?" she whispers.

I shudder. "What about him? You are not going to suggest I surrender to him again, are you?" I tease her gently but mean it.

"Oh, no, no! Of course not. I just wanted to make sure you understand that this is his home you are breaking into."

"Just like he broke into mine," I cut in. I do not know why she keeps bringing up that monster. "I do not know how you can stand living under the rule of this tyrant," I say.

Her eyes harden. "And I do not know why you keep defending your Grand Protector!"

I open my mouth to retort, but it is useless. The hostility of our people has seeped into our relationship. It was bound to happen at some point.

"Are you really going to save your uncle from the vault of the Atheneum?" she asks.

I stare at her. "Of course! That goes without saying!"

Her eyes shine a little too brightly. "Then our people will continue to fight each other," she murmurs. She takes in a shaky breath and says, "I hate war."

I take her hand in mine. "So do I." I hold her gaze, thinking of what might have been.

She looks at me for a long moment, then leans over and pecks me on the lips. She jumps to her feet before I can hold her back and disappears into the covered wagon.

I cannot sleep after that. What seemed like a solid plan suddenly feels insane. I wish there were some way Elysa and I could be together. But the doors of her city have reminded us of our people's hatred for each other. Elysa is the enemy. She belongs here, with her family. I have nothing to offer her. I have no home, nothing to look forward to. I will save Uncle Denesius, and we will live the lives of outcasts, always trying to stay one step ahead of the Wraith Lord. If I get out of Roarim alive, that is.

If I pull this off, if the Talisman truly unlocks the internet, then maybe, just maybe, life on this planet will improve. It will not be for me to enjoy, but for future generations who will benefit from the Knowledge they learn to absorb again.

That is a lot of ifs... Roddrick's words seep into my

mind.

I roll over, my mind filled with questions. Where did the pirates find the program? What did Uncle Denesius offer the pirate overlord in exchange for it? How can I be sure the program will work? I wish there were a way to test it before entering the Wraith Lord's lair. But that is impossible. I only get one chance. Could this plan fail? *Yes, drastically.* Should I still do this? *Yes, there is no doubt about it.* What if future generations make the same mistakes as the Enlightened People?

I pause to think on that point. Is it irresponsible of me to unleash every bit of Knowledge into the world? What if we use the Knowledge for evil again? What if we destroy ourselves for a second time?

I cannot find peace as I lay there on the ground. I sound like a God, deciding the fate of its subjects. I stare up at the cloudy sky, wishing I were not alone in this decision.

Uncle Denesius, I pray. *I wish you were here...*

CHAPTER 29 *Fractioned*

I must have fallen asleep at some point because Thoron is not there when I wake up. I glance around and find Pedregal in a deep sleep next to a pile of Roarim armor and helmets. The noon sun beats down on the mountain.

I struggle to stand. My muscles scream at me, and the scar from the burn mark tugs painfully. I hesitate to get some of that soothing balm from the wagon, but that would mean seeing Elysa, and I cannot handle that right now. She has already cut me off. There is no point in dragging out the inevitable.

I turn towards the mountain instead and start climbing. I want another good look at the Wraith Lord's city. Only, I don't make it far. I round a tall boulder and stumble into Draxis and Thoron sitting side-by-side. I back away. They seem to be in a heated discussion. I glance from behind the boulder and watch the odd pair. They are arguing, all right. I cannot read what Draxis is saying with his hands, however, because he has his back turned to me, but his jerking movements tell me that my giant friend is not happy.

Thoron gets to his feet. "That is the plan, Draxis!" he snaps, tense and dark. "You will do your part. End of discussion!"

I back further away, heart rate quickening. *What is going on?* I hear Thoron's footsteps as he comes my way, and I slip behind the boulder to hide. I snuggle into a nook just as Thoron storms by. Then he is gone, no doubt, heading back to our camp.

I stand there for a moment, cold sweat forming on my forehead. Is Thoron forcing Draxis to go along with the plan? It troubles me to see the two of them together like that. They have never liked each other, and now they are on disagreeable terms almost as if they had had many discussions like this.

I realize I have been out of the game for some time. I have not seen Draxis since Roddrick kidnapped me two weeks ago. The others spent a lot of time together, hiding and planning my release. It would be logical for them to have created deeper bonds during this time.

Yet, things seem to have taken a wrong turn, and I need to set things right before we leave.

I emerge from my hiding spot and approach Draxis, who is still sitting in the same place. My footsteps alert him, and his head snaps around. When he sees me, he jumps to his feet and stomps away.

"Wha—?" I stare after him, baffled. "Draxis! What are you doing?" I hurry after him.

I would have trouble catching up with his giant strides, but fortunately, he slows down, stops, and slumps into a sitting position again.

"Draxis?" I call, wincing at the burning in my side. I reach out and touch his shoulder. "What is the matter?"

He ignores me, so I step around him. Before him lies a pile of flat rocks as high as my waist. The pyramid rests on a ledge with a stunning view over the ocean and the mighty city. Dark, grey clouds paint the sky above us. Draxis has placed white flowers in the gaps between the flat rocks and his daughter's hairpin lies on top of the pyramid. The purple decorative flower flickers in the breeze. Draxis's hammer rests against the structure. My heart sinks as I begin to understand. "You think you will not survive to see your daughter," I state, coming around to sit beside him.

He does not answer, so I say, "Draxis, I told you before, you do not have to come. You are free to go. I can take care of myself." I stop there and clear my throat. That sounded absurd, considering what I just went through.

He looks at me finally, his small, brown eyes unreadable. He gestures with his hands. *You almost died.*

"But I did not," I reply.

You must not die.

My heart flutters. "I... I will not, Draxis. And neither will you!"

He looks me up and down. Maybe he expected me to be torn into tiny pieces, and he realizes that I am doing well for the first time. Elysa had said he could not bear to see me in pain.

"Hey," I insist. "Something is bugging you; I can see it. You have been distant ever since we left Eliadys. What is the matter?"

He flinches and looks away.

"Draxis?" I am really starting to worry. Something has been nagging at him for weeks. "What is it?"

Leave me alone, he gestures.

"I do not think so. Something is the matter, and I

want you to tell me!"

Nobody tells me to do anything! He speaks harshly with his hands. *Go away.*

I jump to my feet, surprised by his animosity. "Draxis!"

His head snaps my way, revealing big square teeth in a nasty snarl. *GO AWAY!*

I stumble back and stare at him without moving.

He turns his back on me.

"Draxis," I breathe, certain that I offended him in some way. If only he would tell me so I could help him, but my giant friend has become closed off and sits like a stone.

I continue to stare at him, wishing I could do something, but the giant makes it clear that he wants to be left alone. "I miss you, Draxis," I say. "You are my best friend. You know that, right?"

Draxis hunches in on himself.

I sigh and stumble away, deeply wounded by his reaction. Something bad has happened to him, something he thinks he must face on his own. It bothers me that he has not managed to resolve whatever it is in all the time we have traveled together.

The day ahead feels a lot gloomier. Pedregal and I put on the Roarim armor and helmet. We decide to leave the covered wagon behind and we all set off together with Pedregal leading our two horses. We make our way down the mountain, treading with care so the horses can follow. As we descend, we begin to hear the clatter of armor and the voices of the Roarim army below.

I struggle not to give in to the waning spirit of our group.

Elysa stays away from me. She is no longer one of us. She must have decided to take on her previous role as a Roarim prisoner captured by the soldiers of Eliadys. I know it is no use trying to dissuade her.

Draxis trudges behind us, avoiding us altogether. Thoron walks purposefully, caught up in his own, dark thoughts. Only Pedregal remains steady. Our group feels fractured, and I wonder if the others are having second thoughts about our endeavor. I cannot blame them. There is little for us to look forward to. Even if we make it into the Ground Station undetected, I doubt we will have the same luck on the way out. Perhaps they feel they are taking unnecessary risks for something that is most likely going to fail.

It hits me that my companions do not understand the stakes as well as I do. They have not read the Books. They did not learn about the Enlightened People and their awe-inspiring inventions. Aside from Elysa, my companions are illiterate. All they know are the superstitions the townsfolk talked about: that the spirits of the Enlightened People still roam the land, killing the crops and poisoning the water. They fear the past. They have not seen the images of the wonders of the world, as I have. They do not understand the power of the internet. In short, they do not fully understand what they are fighting for.

It is up to me, then, to keep the mission alive, except it is hard to do so when I am already assailed by so much self-doubt myself. One thing, in particular, hangs over my head that I have not allowed myself to think about: the Wraith Lord lurks within these walls. There is a great possibility I will run into him before the end of the day, and I would very much like to avoid that.

"What are those?" Pedregal asks, pointing across the water. He is focused on the ocean that expands into the horizon.

I see it, too.

"Wind turbines!" I exclaim. Propeller-like blades placed high on top of poles turn lazily, indicating that the turbines are probably functional and creating wind-generated electricity. There must be hundreds of them.

It is becoming more and more apparent that the Wraith Lord is knowledgeable in the ways of the Enlightened People and their inventions. That makes him a dangerous man. If he were to get his hands on the Talisman, he would be able to exert enormous power over others. I slow down and come to a complete halt, almost overwhelmed with crippling fear.

"Eodain?" Pedregal comes up beside me. "Are you all right?"

The others stop and glance at me.

"Yes, yes," I say, pressing my side and puffing air out of my cheeks. "Just catching my breath." I make a huge effort to keep walking, trusting that my feet will take me forward without breaking into a hysterical run.

"Hold it, lad," Pedregal says. "We are far enough down the mountain. Might as well make good use of the horses. You and Elysa take this one. I will ride the other one."

I take the reins of one of the horses and glance at Elysa. She looks away, but gets on the horse anyway. I heave myself up behind her, the wound digging at my side as I do so.

Pedregal gets on his horse.

"I am counting on you, swordmaster," Thoron says. "Make sure our bookbug reaches the Ground Station in one piece."

Pedregal nods once, then Thoron and Draxis take their leave without a single word.

My stomach lurches. This may be the last time I see them.

"Draxis," I hiss, but the giant, his heavy hammer at his side, slips away without looking at me. I bite my lip, pushing down a wave of disappointment.

Alea iacta est. The die has been cast. There is no turning back.

Shortly after, we approach a dusty road filled with Roarim soldiers. I glance back, and it is like looking at a river of men, all of them heading towards Roarim City at a slow, tired pace.

So, the Roarim army is still arriving home after their attack on Eliadys. The hairs on the back of my neck prickle. I hate them and fear them. They destroyed my home and my people; there is nothing I can do to defeat them, and yet, here I am, having to ride among them.

My heart thuds harder, and the spot where my finger was cut starts to itch. We make our way across the plains, traveling right through the Roarim camp, then cross the bridge that stretches over the moat and is packed with enemy soldiers. We approach the fortified wall of Roarim City, which is made of thick concrete, not cut stone like in Eliadys. This requires some knowledge from the past, and I am curious what other tools the Roarim still implement from the Enlightened Era. They have a helicopter, wind electricity, and access to the NASA Ground Station. I do not know of any other people who are knowledgeable about this type of advanced technology.

We join a line waiting to enter the city. Pedregal glances at me, then spurs on his horse by clicking his tongue. I calculate that it is late afternoon, but it is hard to tell because the grey clouds have darkened to the point where I cannot see the sun.

"Let me deal with them," Elysa says, referring to the soldiers barring the gate and checking the identity of travelers. "Lean against me, Eodain. Look unwell," she tells me.

Half-a-dozen, heavily armed Roarim soldiers surround us. They tell us to remove our helmets so they can check our faces. A taller one advances towards us and barks, "Names?" His eyebrow raises as he looks at me.

"Officer!" Elysa pleads. "Please give us passage. My brother is unwell. He was wounded at the Siege of Eliadys, and we have just returned home after much hardship. Please, be merciful!"

The Officer eyes us sternly. "What are your names?" he asks again.

"Elysa Dundurn. And this is Simon Dundurn." Then, she turns and looks meaningfully at Pedregal.

Pedregal clears his throat and states the name she gave him. "Joseph Martinez," he says.

The Officer turns, and I watch him discuss us with a couple of other soldiers standing by a table set in the shade of the gateway. One of the soldiers examines a box with what looks like thousands of little cards, while another dips a feather pen in a pot of ink and writes something down—our names, presumably.

"What are they doing?" I whisper.

"Searching for our names," Elysa replies.

I am stumped. These soldiers can read and write!

The Officer returns with a couple of cards in his hand. "Well, Ms. Elysa, Mr. Simon, you were listed as missing a month ago. You may enter the City. Head for the military infirmary to your right, after the gates. The General will want to debrief you." He turns to Pedregal. "As for you, Sir Joseph, we have no record of you having left the City. You will have to step asi—"

Elysa digs her elbow so hard into my side that I groan and slide off the horse in shock.

Pedregal catches me just in time.

What the...!

"Oh, please!" Elysa begs. "Allow Joseph to take us inside. My brother needs medical attention! Please!"

The Officer backs away. "Quickly then! Make way, make way!" he yells, gesturing to the soldiers to give us passage. "No helmets allowed within the city!" he yells after us. "And, you! Sir Joseph, you will wait by the infirmary, is that clear?"

"Yes, Officer," Pedregal calls back at him as he spurs on his horse, still holding on to my arm, so I do not slide off.

"For Spirits' sake, Elysa!" I seethe under my breath, as we pass beneath the massive gateway.

"Sorry!" she says hurriedly. "Pedregal, we will leave the horses beside the infirmary, there." She points.

We stop at the furthest end of the tents and slide off our horses. I almost keel over as I land on the ground, a spasm traveling through my side.

"Are you okay, lad?" Pedregal asks, clutching me under the armpit so I can steady myself.

I nod and wave my hand at him to let me go.

The soldiers who were with the Officer are already heading our way.

"Quickly!" Elysa urges.

We dive on to a side street.

"Hey!" The shout comes from behind us.

"Hurry!" Elysa shouts.

We do not need further urging. We thrust our helmets aside and follow Elysa into a bustling street to get lost among the crowds. We seem to be in the main street of Roarim City. Rows of tables adorn both sides of the street and are filled with market produce. Vegetables, fruits, grains, meat, and fish; everything one could want for a well laid-out table is available here.

The Roarim truly are rich. No wonder they were able to gather such a mighty army. We pretend to look at trinkets when troops of soldiers march down the street. I wish we could have kept on our helmets, but it would have looked odd since no one else is wearing them.

A thick raindrop falls on my head, and I stop, bewildered. I lift my hand, watching the drops of water trickle down my palm.

Rain! Real rain!

Pedregal glances up, blinking. Merchants rush to pack up their produce. People cover their heads and hurry to finish their transactions. If this rain continues, soon we will be the only ones around.

"Let's go!" I urge the others, but when I turn, Elysa has not moved.

"Elysa?" I ask worriedly.

She rests her hazel eyes on mine, and then I know. "You are leaving, aren't you?" I say, my stomach squeezing. Everything is happening so fast. There is no time to say goodbye: not to Draxis, not to Thoron, and not even to Elysa.

"I understand," I say.

She turns and points up the bustling street. "Follow this road. When you see a three-story tower with a red, pointed roof, turn left. Follow that street. It will take you to the Ground Station."

I stare at her. That's it. There is nothing left to say. Yet we stand there as if time has stopped, our eyes saying all the things we are not allowed to utter.

Pedregal breaks the spell. "Thank you, girl. You have done more than enough. Now go and find your family, and may you live a long and happy life." He hugs her quickly, then backs away, sniffling.

A thousand things spin around my mind as I take in her hazel eyes one last time. I resist the urge to stroke away the wet hair stuck to her cheek. *Thank you for saving my life. Thank you for guiding me. I wish you well, and I love y—.*

"Come on, lad," Pedregal says, nudging me.

"Goodbye," I say, stepping away from Elysa—the lamest, weakest form of farewell. Not even a hug, not even a kiss, nothing.

Her face tears up. She turns and runs, plunging into the crowds.

As I follow her with my eyes, I spot a troop of soldiers turning into the street.

Pedregal sees them, too, and urges me on.

I follow him reluctantly, a painful lump forming in my throat.

Goodbye, Elysa. I love you.

CHAPTER 30 *The Ground Station*

Pedregal and I wind our way through the crowds, making our way up the hill. The cobblestones of the main street are becoming slippery as the drizzle turns to real showers. Word of our escape at the city gates does not seem to have reached higher up yet, and the NASA Ground Station looms taller above us, shrouded in dark clouds.

After some time, though, we become worried. We have not yet spotted the tower with a pointed red roof that Elysa mentioned.

"What if we continue straight up until the end?" Pedregal shouts over the drumming rain, his face streaming with rivulets of water. The Ground Station seems to be in a direct line up the street, but a high wall wraps around the hill below the Station. There are stairs cut in the side, but I cannot tell where they start.

I shake my head. "No, that does not look right. We need to follow Elysa's instructions. We need to find the tower." I take a big risk and stop a passerby, who is rushing by with his coat over his head to protect himself from the downpour. "We are looking for a three-story tower. One with a round, pointed roof. Do you know where it is?"

The man looks at me as if I have lost a screw. "You mean the grain tower?" he says. He points to his right, back where we came, then rushes off.

I see it. The pointy roof sticks out from what seems to be a parallel street. Pedregal and I are already on our way. "We missed it!" I gasp, trying to ignore the burning sensation in my side. We have to retrace our steps for about four blocks, then we turn and rush towards the street. "Elysa must have forgotten a turn," I pant and stop before the building she referred us to.

"This way," I say, hurrying to the left of the grain tower. We end up in a narrow alley littered with garbage and a couple of screeching cats. There is no one in sight. I shudder because I am reminded of that time in Eliadys when thieves ambushed me. Still, we run on and are relieved to enter a small, square marketplace. We rush to the middle, searching for the next alley, but find none.

I groan. "Wrong turn, again!"

Pedregal grasps my arm. "No, lad!" he yells, glancing all around. "A trap! It is a trap!"

Spiders crawl up my spine. "What?"

Shouts bounce off the walls of the houses.

"Your sword!" Pedregal yells. "Get your sword!"

I grab my satchel and search for my blade wrapped up in my Seeker cape, just as doors swing open on all sides, and Roarim soldiers spill out. I unsheathe my sword, the scabbard dropping to the ground.

"She tricked us!" Pedregal yells.

No!

"Get behind me!" Pedregal pulls me, so we are

back-to-back. The enemy surrounds us, their swords raised.

No! Not Elysa!

We take a defensive position, ready to block any incoming attack.

"Eodain!" Elysa's voice carries over the rain.

My blood turns cold. I spot her in the doorway of one of the houses.

Not Elysa!

Pedregal urges me on, "Get ready, Eodain—to your left." He is letting me know that we are going to break through the way we came.

"Drop your weapons!" a soldier barks.

Elysa's voice cuts from the side, "Eodain! Do not resist them!"

"You say when," I tell Pedregal, seething.

"Eodain!" Elysa insists. "Listen to me! Sometimes you have to do bad things..." she breaks off.

My heart drops. *How dare she! "Sometimes, you have to do bad things for the greater good."* That is what she said. *For the greater good of whom? Of the Roarim?*

"NOW!" Pedregal shouts. My sword-fighting teacher's order triggers me into action.

I roll to the ground in the direction of the soldiers, taking them by surprise. As they lower their swords to attack me, Pedregal leaps at them from above. We expertly divert the blows. Our window of escape is small.

I thrust my blade at the knee of an approaching soldier, maiming him through the joints of his armor, then at another's wrist—the last ones to bar our way into the alley—while Pedregal takes care of the ones attacking us, from behind.

"Clear!" I yell at Pedregal, diving into the alley, but my steps sound hollow. I spin around.

"What are you waiting for?" Pedregal roars, pushing back at a wave of steel.

I freeze.

"Get out of here!" he shouts.

I stumble backward and fall.

"The Talisman!" Pedregal yells, swinging his sword at the enemy. "Think of the Talisman!"

My stomach lifts to my throat. I pick myself up and plunge into the streets or Roarim City, leaving Pedregal behind.

It is not fair.

Pedregal's life is worth a thousand times more than the Talisman. But this is not about us. It has never been about us. Humanity does not care about a swordmaster or a Knowledge Seeker who will be lost in the flow of history. It only cares about how it will rise from the ashes of these Dark Ages.

But still, it is not fair.

I hide behind a pile of crates and lean against the wall, gasping for air, angry shouts and thudding boots passing me by. Rain enters the slits in the armor, drenching my body. My missing finger throbs painfully.

Elysa!

She betrayed us! She has picked her side, and it was not mine. She healed me from one arrow, only to plant a new one deep into my heart. I thought... I really thought we had bonded. *This is the home of the Wraith Lord you are breaking into*, she warned me. I shudder. She wanted me to hand over the Talisman to the tyrant from the very beginning. It always boils back to the Talisman. The pirate overlord, the Wraith Lord... and now Elysa. All they care about is the Talisman.

I bend forward with my head between my knees to fend off waves of bitterness. It is all I can do not to grab the Talisman and break it. I have had enough!

"I am counting on you," Uncle Denesius whispers in my mind.

I cannot do it! I grasp my hair with both hands, swinging back and forth.

"Eodain *is* the Atheneum," Pedregal's voice echoes through my brain.

But, I do not want to be...

"You are the Atheneum." The words bounce around in my head, over and over.

I am the Atheneum.

I release my hair.

I am the Atheneum.

Tremors travel through my body. I cannot allow Elysa to take the Talisman. Nor the Wraith Lord, nor the pirates. Not anyone!

I remove my satchel from my shoulder and drop it to the ground. I tear off the Roarim armor. I cannot bear to wear this enemy attire another second. I hate it!

I pull out my Seeker cape and attach it in a swift movement so it hangs down my back. I am a Knowledge Seeker. That is all I know how to be. What happens to me now is of no importance. Either I connect the Talisman to the Ground Station before I am slaughtered, or I carry out the Sacred Pledge.

By now, half the city is searching for the Seeker from Eliadys. The one who has broken into their city and is seeking revenge. Well, let them come. I will show them what I am made of. This last Seeker will not go down without a fight.

I glance around the street corner and, this time, spot the start of the stairs to the Ground Station. There is only one way to go, and that is up. I leap into the street and throw myself at a couple of soldiers who are searching for me. They are down before they can utter a cry. I bolt up the street, sounds of boots and cries of alarm erupting behind me, rage and heartache spurting me on.

I have to fight my way through a handful of soldiers who have accumulated at the bottom of the stairs, but I make it through, swinging my blade without a second thought. I climb up, two steps at a time, slipping twice on the wet slabs. The second time, my fall saves me from arrows that collide into the wall just above me.

A large troop of soldiers makes its way down the stairs from the top of the hill. My hope fizzles.

Just then, a massive *bang* rattles the ground. I lie flat and watch a portion of the city's fortified wall blow up behind me, leaving a gaping hole to the lands beyond it.

Draxis!

My heart leaps. Whatever it is that Draxis and Thoron did, the distraction worked. Half of the troop above me takes off, disappearing from the stairs and across the top of the hill. The other handful continues down towards me. I fight my way through them, rage over what Elysa did, fueling my onslaughts. When the final soldier collapses, I climb the last steps to the top of the hill.

I burst on to a wide, open area. In the middle soars the Ground Station with its parabolic antenna poised on top of a two-story tower. It reaches up, high above me, seeming to touch the black clouds. Its base is easily twice the size of the grain tower in the city, and the antenna stretches on all sides, massive and dark.

My heart lurches. I have lost track of time. Elysa's confusing directions, the battle in the small marketplace, and the arduous climb up the hill must have taken a large chunk of precious time. I pray the satellite has not yet passed overhead.

Half-a-dozen soldiers arrive from the right.

I leap forward. If I can make it to the Station before they do, I might have a chance. If only my throat weren't on fire and my side didn't scream at me. I crash into the door of the Station before the others arrive. I push it inward, but it does not open!

The soldiers are a few steps from me. I dash away, rounding the base of the structure, and almost slam into another door that opens outward right before me. I freeze, not only because two soldiers are heading out, but because, for the first time, I can see the opposite side of the Ground Station. A gaping chasm ends in the moat below, and I can hear the sound of ocean-waves crashing against the rock at the bottom.

This is no time for sightseeing. I hurl myself at the soldiers and knock them aside. I leap over them and shut the door. There is a latch. I close it. I am inside. My boots echo across the corridor that follows the circular base of the tower.

Soldiers swarm through the door in front of me, and I rush towards them, intent on shutting them out, but there are too many of them. I am going to have to backtrack. But then a roar echoes through the corridor, making my blood turn cold. A large shadow paints itself on the wall, and Draxis appears, looking fearsome and deadly.

The soldiers yelp and fall over each other in their haste to get out. Soon, that door is secured, as well.

"Draxis!" I cry, almost bursting into tears.

"No time for hugs. We must go." Thoron appears from behind the giant.

"Thoron!" I exclaim. "You made it!"

"Been here a while, cleaning the way for you."

"But the city wall...?"

He shrugs. "Nothing a handful of timed explosives could not handle."

I stare at him, surprised that he would have access to something like that. But now I notice that his backpack looks much lighter.

"Where is Pedregal?" Thoron asks.

I shake my head. "He got swamped." I cannot get myself to say *because Elysa betrayed us*. My throat closes up.

"Let's go," Thoron says. "Those doors will not hold forever."

I nod, following Thoron and Draxis down the corridor, my clothes dripping with rain. A faded, blue circle is painted on the wall, containing the remains of white letters which I can barely read: A S A.

NASA! The hairs on the back of my neck raise. So it is true. This is truly the NASA Ground Station!

The Station is clean and complete, yet there are cracks in the steel structure and, although it seems to have been well taken care of, there is no denying how ancient the building is. It is a miracle that the parabolic dish is still attached to the summit of the Station.

We reach a door leading further into the center of the station, and I gasp in awe. Three sets of desks, set out in half-circles, are filled with computers. They are all facing the opposite side, where several screens hang against a straight wall with the biggest one in the middle.

"The command center!" I breathe.

"Whatever it is, you had better get on with it," Thoron warns.

Two doors lead into this central space: the one we came through, which Draxis guards, and one directly opposite it, where Thoron places himself. A set of winding, metal stairs climbs up to two superimposed galleries that go all the way around the inside of the tower and from which one could observe the command center. The stairs continue into the gloom above, where I suspect one could access the dish at the top. The stairs must be from recent times, as I do not think the original ones would have stood the test of time this long. Windows placed near the middle of the tower do little to illuminate my surroundings. All I see are swirling black clouds outside while rain drums on the window panes. I notice an unusual smell in the air, but the source of it eludes me.

"Eodain!" Thoron hisses.

"Sorry," I say, unable to stop gawking. I head down one row of computers. They are in excellent shape. Come to think of it, everything looks in perfect working order as if the Enlightened People had left yesterday. I ponder on this, imagining the effort it must have taken the Roarim to maintain this place in its original aspect. Clearly, the Roarim are aware of the importance of the Station. I wonder how many times they have tried to use it and if they ever succeeded.

With that in mind, I select a computer and press the ON button. I hold my breath. The computer flickers. My heartbeat quickens. *The wind turbines are providing the Roarim with electricity!*

As the computer comes to life, so does the giant screen at the front of the room. I watch in awe as it fills with horizontal and vertical lines. There are also scribbles that would look random to anyone who has not read the Books. I catch my breath. That is the outline of the Earth's continents, as they were five hundred years ago. So much has changed since then! Spots of light appear on the screen, and they advance from right to left.

East to West.

I am looking at satellites. Those elusive Sky Spirits that float through space, disconnected from their source, lost in the emptiness.

"Eodain! Get on with it!" Thoron urges. We can hear a distant thudding as the Roarim try to force their way in. All Thoron sees are random lines and dots on a screen. He does not appreciate their awe-inspiring meaning.

I am dismayed, though, when I estimate there are only fifty satellites left up there. Have things become this bad? I watch the spots move slowly over the screen. One of them is almost on top of the jutting piece of land previously called Florida.

"Tungsten X-173!" I read aloud. "These satellites have a name!"

A red circle has appeared with the location of Roarim City in its center, and I can tell that Tungsten X-173 is not going to pass through it.

"The Ground Station isn't aligned!" I exclaim.

On the right, there are several columns with a jumble of information. The left column always starts with TUNGSTEN.

"That is the list of active satellites," I murmur to myself.

Each satellite is followed by a string of words such as altazimuth, VHF, GhZ, and numbers that I do not understand.

"Here goes nothing," I breathe. I click on the name Tungsten X-173. At first, nothing happens, then there is a loud bang followed by a booming sound that resonates through the room.

"What is happening?" Thoron shouts.

I duck, half expecting the roof to come crashing in. But the rumbling sound continues, then dies all of a sudden.

I straighten up again. "The parabolic dish!" I breathe. "I just made it move!" My skin tingles. *It works! It actually works!*

The red circle has moved upward, in range of the satellite, which is heading straight for it.

"This is it!" I gasp, watching the dot move into the circle. Smaller screens burst into life, and rows of information scroll down them. The outline of a satellite appears with fully expanded solar panels. The name TUNGSTEN X-173 appears on top.

The thumping outside has died down for now, and I picture the Roarim having fled in terror when the parabolic dish activated. But now, the dull sounds resume, and I know there is not much time before the enemy breaches the doors.

"Is it done?" Thoron yells.

"Almost," I breathe to myself when a new screen appears on the computer that says:

JUNE 27, 2021, 20:17:04

DOWNLINK:
TUNGSTEN X-173
STATUS: CONNECTED

UPLINK:
SIGNAL: _ _ _ _ _ _
[or upload HERE]

I pull out the Talisman and plug it into the computer. I click on HERE and am taken to the folder containing Uncle Denesius's program. A small, grey screen opens, and I type in the password TERMITE. The document containing the program appears. I click once on that, and a button appears:

UPLOAD.

I catch my breath. Could it be that simple? If all is set, then all I have to do is press UPLOAD. This one command taunts me, and I slide the arrow of the mouse on top of it. *Just one click!*

Terrifying doubt seeps into my mind. What do I know about satellites? Will this program unlock the Cloud?

I make sure everything is in order. There can be no mistake. I only get one chance. My eyes scan Uncle Denesius's program and fall on a single word embedded in the code: MASA.

My hand freezes over the mouse. I scroll down the program from beginning to end, and the word flashes out at me: MASA, MASA, MASA... Suddenly, the acronym is everywhere, repeated in one section after another among the incomprehensible string of text.

MASA...

Something nudges at the back of my mind, something sinister.

There is a loud crash down the corridor, and we hear soldiers piling through the first door. Draxis rushes out to push them back.

"Eodain!" Thoron roars. "Do it already!"

But I cannot. My mind is a jumble. Cold sweat drenches my back.

MASA...

That is what was written on the side of the pole I found next to the fallen satellite. But it was not a mere pole. It was a rod of God, a weapon of mass destruction.

My hand starts shaking. "Wait a minute!" I tell Thoron, who is pacing behind me. "Something is wrong."

MASA... What in Spirit's sake is MASA?

I crouch and search for the National Geographic in my backpack. Even though it is rolled up in a protective cloth, the whole magazine is wet from the rain. I slide my finger down the titles on the cover and read the last one: *The Fall of NASA.* I unstick the pages until I reach the article and read it.

"The end of the National Aeronautics and Space Administration (NASA) as an independent agency of the U.S. federal government is a blow to human endeavor,' NASA Director Peter Horgan stated last week.

The U.S. Secretary of Defence defended the move, saying that the new name for the organization showed a willingness to uphold NASA's spirit. "We have no choice," the Defence Minister declared. "Our society is on the brink of World War III. We must use every available resource at hand."

Peter Horgan, who was dismissed from his NASA post by the President of the United States on September 9, 2093, feels the new name is a mockery..."

I reach the end of the page. The rest has been torn out of the magazine. I turn over my satchel, its contents clattering to the ground. I search feverishly until my hand falls on the missing pages.

"Eodain, I swear..." Thoron seethes, and I know he is struggling to contain himself. "This is not a time to be reading Books!"

My finger slides over the end of the article.

"'MASA,' Peter Horgan scoffs. 'stands for Military Aeronautics and Space Agency. M-I-L-I-T-A-R-Y! Where is NASA's spirit in that?'"

I stare at the word.

Military.

MASA stands for *Military Aeronautics and Space Agency.*

I stand. Suddenly, the name is everywhere: at the corner of the big screens, on the side of the computers, in faded letters on the doors...

I stare numbly at the UPLOAD button on the computer screen. This program is not a program to wake the internet. It is a program to wake and guide military satellites—MASA satellites, laden with rods of God. Those terrifying kinetic weapons changed the face of the Earth, and this program would lead them straight here, to Roarim City. This Ground Station does not belong to NASA, but MASA.

I have been duped.

Shocked, I let the pages of the National Geographic slide out of my hand and feel something on my shoulder.

"Termite," Thoron's voice is so close to my ear that I flinch. His sword slides beside my neck. "Release the program."

I become numb. "Thoron?"

His voice is ice-cold. "I said, release the program."

"N-no!" I protest. "Thoron! You don't understand. We have been tricked." As I speak, I reach for my sword, which I left on top of the desk.

Thoron reaches out from behind me and thrusts it aside. "Oh, but I do understand!" he says. He grabs my right arm and pins it painfully behind my back, making me wince. "I know exactly what it does!" His sword slides under my chin. "Release the program! Now!"

"No!" I gasp, my mind in turmoil. *Thoron!* "What do you think you are doing? Did you know about this? Let me go!" I protest.

"Of course, I know. I have known from the beginning. Activate the program!"

"I will not! This is suicide!"

"Now, now," a voice speaks from one of the

galleries above. I freeze. The voice is all-too-familiar. Footsteps descend the winding stairs and stop at the bottom; the smell that eluded me earlier now filling the room... tobacco!

Something clicks, and bright light from neon bulbs flood the command center. Uncle Denesius looks at me from across the room. "Is our bookbug giving you trouble, Thoron?"

CHAPTER 31 *The Hammer Strikes*

"Master!" Thoron exclaims. "It is good to see you."

"It is good to see you, too, Thoron. I take it you found the secret tunnel into the Ground Station?"

"Yes, Master. It was right where you said it would be."

"Good," Uncle Denesius inspects the large screens. "I was about to give up on you. I have been holed up in this place for days, waiting."

My mind explodes. Is that really Uncle Denesius? How did he escape the vault under the Atheneum? What is going on? "Uncle!" I warn. "Be careful!" Does he not see Thoron's blade?

"I am sorry, Master," Thoron says, ignoring me. "The bug almost gave up on the mission. He wanted to return to the Atheneum to save you. I had to convince him to carry on, using the cloud story."

A smile creeps up on Uncle Denesius's face. "And he believed you, no doubt? I told you he would. He is so gullible."

"Wha...?"

Thoron snorts. "He came running, Master, but that is not the reason we are late. The pirate overlord delayed us. He did not respect the agreement and kept Termite for days. I suspect he had no intention of releasing him."

"Hmm," Uncle Denesius says, walking towards us. "He got greedy, did he? Why am I not surprised? No wonder his men took their time pulling me out of the rubble at the Atheneum." He looks around. "What of Roddrick? Where is he?"

"He did not make it, Master. He ran into some pirates who did not recognize him as a Seeker. They killed him before John McNeil could do anything about it."

"Ah." Uncle Denesius walks around the row of desks with his hands behind his back, the way I have seen him do many times when he is thinking. "What a shame. I liked that boy. I sent him after you, in the hopes he would come to Roarim City with you. But deep down, I knew he might scamper to the pirates. Not that it matters. I killed two birds with one stone: I fulfilled my side of the agreement with the pirates, and our bookbug is right where I need him." He comes around to the other side of the desk and looks at me with dark, cold eyes.

"Uncle?" I breathe. Cold sweat pearls on my forehead. I cannot understand how it is possible to feel joy and dread at the same time. Why is he talking like this? Why is Thoron not letting me go?

"Surprised, Termite?" Uncle Denesius smirks.

"What agreement with the pirates?" My gut clenches.

"Why, Termite, the agreement between me and my friend, John McNeil. He required payment to pull

307

me out from under the Atheneum and for the program. He is an expensive one, that McNeil. I was hoping to avoid having to lend you to him. It delayed my plans, but, ah well, at least my debts are cleared, and here we are in the end."

"Uncl—" I start, aghast, and struggle against Thoron's grip.

Thoron thrusts me down so hard against the desk that dark spots swim before my eyes. He still has my right arm pinned high behind my back, and his blade scrapes my head as he presses me down.

Uncle Denesius leans over and speaks in my ear, "I would have liked to see your face when you opened the Talisman. What did you think when you saw it was empty?" He smirks, and I shudder. "What did you do, bookbug? Did you manage to pull those wonderful memories from your brain? Did you use your photographic memory? Did you toy with the pirate overlord and provide him with incomplete snippets of Knowledge? Did you, now?" He straightens and chuckles. "Truly, I hope you did!"

I shut my eyes. My head is spinning. Who is this man? What is he saying? It is like the demon has burst out of him—the one I caught a glimpse of when he killed Lord Erawan. And the price for the program? It was me! I feel sick to my stomach.

"Master," Thoron says. "The pirate overlord is dead. The Wraith Lord killed him!"

Uncle Denesius slams the desk right next to my face, making me jump out of my skin. "Enough, already! I have been cooped up in Roarim City and have seen no such thing as a Wraith Lord!"

Thoron shuffles on his feet, but he insists, "That is because he has been searching for us ever since we left Eliadys. I swear it, Master. I saw him with my own eyes.

He almost killed Termite."

"Believe what you will," Uncle Denesius snaps, backing away. "It does not matter—not once Termite launches the program. Then, Wraith Lord or not, not a hair of him will remain."

Thoron leans over me. "Hear that, bookbug? Time to do your thing."

"No!" I gasp in horror. "Why me? I will no... Aah!" Thoron pulls up my arm until I think it will snap. "I... will not... You cannot retaliate against the Roarim for destroying the Atheneum. Not like this!"

Uncle Denesius looks down at me. "Termite, you are so naïve. Don't you understand yet? The Roarim did not destroy the Atheneum." He leans in closer. "I did!"

It takes a few seconds to sink in. But then, it does, and reality blasts through my mind. "No!" I wail. "No! I do not believe you! It... it cannot be! Uncle... please... No!" I struggle, but Thoron is too strong. "The Seekers!" I pant. "All the Seekers! And the Books! And... and..." I catch my breath, "...the orphans. You wouldn't..."

"Oh, but I would," Uncle Denesius whispers. "I obtained vats of explosives from the pirates in exchange for some of our solar panels. You see, I would never allow the Roarim to get their hands on the Books. I would rather see the Atheneum destroyed than have it fall back into their miserable hands. And now we will be rid of them, once and for all. You will help me, Termite. It has to be you. It has to be you who releases the rods of God. Do it now!"

"No! Why?" I yell, twisting and fighting against waves of nausea.

Thoron presses his elbow into my back and grabs one of my fingers. "Shall I remove another finger, Master?" he asks.

I tense up. I fall into the dark pit of my memory. I

recall how, just after I slammed into a Roarim soldier and was losing consciousness, I saw black Roarim boots running away from my ten-year-old face, followed by Thoron's brown boots. Thoron's voice echoes in my head, *another finger... another finger...*

"*You* cut off my finger!" I choke.

Uncle Denesius sighs loudly. "Yes, yes. Do it, then, Thoron. But hurry up. We are going to lose the satellite."

Thoron sneers, "Hear that, bookbug? Release the program, or I start with your thumb." I feel the blade cut the skin.

"All right, all right!" I yell. My left hand is free, and the computer and keyboard are in arm's reach. I stretch out and see the UPLOAD command. All I have to do is press the RETURN button on the keyboard. My hand shakes as it hovers over the command.

Why does it have to be me? Why do I have to be the one to bring the ire of the Gods upon the Roarim? One thing is clear in my mind: there is no way I am going to press that button.

In one swift movement, I extract the Talisman from the computer and sling it away from me as hard as possible.

"No!" Uncle Denesius roars, rushing after it.

I hear a thud behind me, and Thoron's weight falls off me. We both topple to the ground.

"Eodain!" someone yells.

I roll off Thoron and look back. Pedregal is leaning against the doorway behind us, looking haggard and bloody. He must have thrown something at Thoron because the guardsman groans before getting to his feet with his hand to his head.

"Thoron! Get him!" Uncle Denesius orders. "I will deal with Termite."

"I can help you with that, Master." Thoron kicks me in the side on the way out, and my wound bursts open again.

I roll up into a ball in pain.

"Eodain!" Pedregal yells, but the guardsman is already leaping towards him, forcing him into the corridor.

Through the ringing in my ears, I hear swords clashing. I press my hand against my side, and blood oozes through my fingers. All that effort to save me and now Elysa's care falls to nothing.

Uncle Denesius is searching for the Talisman. He picks it up, then heads to the door that Thoron and Pedregal just crashed through. He closes and locks it from the inside. His face is contorted with rage. He rushes to the computer, inserts the Talisman, then yanks me up and thrusts my finger on the RETURN button before I can react. I catch my breath.

A message appears on the screen.

STATUS: DISCONNECTED

The satellite has passed and is no longer in range. TUNGSTEN X-173 disappears from the screens.

Uncle Denesius roars. I slip out of his grasp as he thrusts the computer to the ground and kicks over the desks.

I scramble away, leaving a trail of blood as I go. I get to my feet and stumble towards the other door, but Draxis enters, dragging his hammer behind him.

"Draxis!" I yell. "Get out of here!"

My giant friend takes in the room, sees Uncle Denesius, and locks this door behind him.

I freeze and gape at him. "Draxis?"

Uncle Denesius's laugh chills my bones. "Save your

breath, Termite. I have a little agreement with Draxis as well. Don't I, Draxis?"

Draxis grunts, showing his big teeth to me.

"It is so easy to control a giant once you know how," Uncle Denesius says. "Things have always been clear between us: as long as he does what he is told, I have promised not to touch a hair on his lovely daughter's head. She is staying with some friends of mine, up North, a short flight away for a messenger pigeon."

I sag to my knees. "Draxis!" I breathe. "Your daughter!"

"Draxis!" Uncle Denesius's voice booms across the room. "Kill him."

My eyes widen in horror. I shake my head in disbelief. "No! Draxis! You wouldn't..."

Draxis takes hold of his giant hammer with both hands.

I scramble back but end up against the wall.

The giant lifts the hammer, the muscles in his arms tensing as he swings it over his shoulder. It bears down on me, and I brace myself, but then it pivots and flies through the air.

Uncle Denesius ducks at the last second, and the massive object crashes through the wall, then into the next one, leaving a gaping hole to the outside. At once, the ancient structure gives way. Thick slabs of steel drop from the ceiling and I raise my good arm above my head in a weak attempt to protect myself.

Draxis is already there, closing his big hand on my arm and pulling me under him. He curves his back to create a protective roof over me, and I hear heavy thuds against his body as the Station collapses down on him.

"Draxis!" I scream.

Outside, the metal of the parabolic dish crunches,

and an ear-splitting crash tells me it has fallen to the ground. It seems like the world is coming to an end.

"Draxis!" I sob, praying for the devastation to be over. When it finally ends, silence falls over the Ground Station. I am safe beneath the giant, surrounded by debris. Draxis does not move. "Draxis!" I beg, crying freely because I know his body is broken.

He lifts an arm, just enough for me to drag myself through. I cling to a slab of steel and begin to pull myself out into what remains of the dark, dusty room, but just then, his arm slumps, pinning my feet under it.

"Draxis!" I cry. "Wake up. Please, Draxis!" I tug and push at his arm.

His eyelids open a crack, and he looks at me without moving.

"Draxis!" I sob. "We will save your family. I promised you that! You will see your daughter again and return to your home. Just... stay with me!"

I see his hand move, and he signals, *My daughter is dead. A giant knows in his heart.*

I shake my head. "You cannot know that. You will get better, and we will look for her! Together!"

Draxis smiles sadly. *Long ago, I decided to stay to save you and bring you home.*

I shake my head, confused. "What?"

You became my family, he says. *I fulfilled my duty. I saved my family.* He smiles, then closes his eyes for the last time.

"No!" I cry. "Draxis! Wake up! Draxis!"

CHAPTER 32 *Clash of Foes*

Dust seeps out through the gaping hole caused by Draxis's hammer. Electricity crackles through broken wires and a single neon bulb dangles from the fractured wall. The roof of the Ground Station snapped off when the parabolic dish collapsed and a drizzle from the receding storm falls on me. I push and shove at Draxis's arm, trying to wake him because I cannot accept that he is gone.

Something topples to the side and crashes in a heap. Uncle Denesius struggles to his feet, his shadow stretching against the wall. He stands warily, his greatsword gleaming at his side. He turns to search the dancing shadows with his eyes but freezes when a rumbling cuts through the air. The sound passes above the Station.

I stiffen.

The dragon-helicopter!

Grasped by fear, I manage to release one foot from under Draxis's arm. Except that only increases the pressure on the other foot. And the effort is taxing. Groaning, I press my hand against my side, only to find my shirt is sticky with blood.

Uncle Denesius stands in front of the gaping hole of the Station, rooted to the spot as he watches the helicopter land. Roarim soldiers erupt from the side of the metal beast, followed by the Wraith Lord. Uncle Denesius staggers back, no doubt in shock. The soldiers swarm him, yet he is much stronger than them and single-handedly fights them off. They topple in a heap, one after the other, until only the Wraith Lord remains.

The Roarim Lord's thick armor gleams, and the spikes on his massive helmet look like sharpened knives. His chest armor still has the dent in it from Draxis's hammer. He holds a sword that looks more like a saw with sharp teeth and a hook at the end. He stands outside, outlined by the red headlights from the helicopter, and faces Uncle Denesius as if toying with his terror.

Uncle Denesius backs into the room, stumbling over debris. I have never seen him this shaken before. Then, realizing he has no way out, he readies himself to face his foe.

"So it is true!" he gasps, his voice thick with fear. "You are alive!" He hesitates. "Or... are you?"

The Wraith Lord marches into the Ground Station and stands before him, colossal and terrifying, like a specter from the underworld. His silence turns my blood cold, and I cringe at the sight.

"Whatever you are..." Uncle Denesius pants, taking a position to defend himself, "...I have vanquished you once, and I will vanquish you again!" He holds up his sword in front of his face, readying himself.

I dare not make a sound.

The Wraith Lord makes his move, swings his saw-sword in an arc at Uncle Denesius, who slams his blade upwards to stop the impact. The weapons clash, sparks fly, and both men are thrust backward from the power of their blows. They lunge at each other again, the force of the Wraith Lord undeniable, yet Uncle Denesius stands his ground.

I am paralyzed, forgetting what I am supposed to do as I watch these two forces of nature battle.

They move outside.

The rain has stopped and a ghostly moon makes its way from behind the clouds.

The helicopter blades are still turning, lifting dust in all directions. I squint through the hazy cloud, lit by the machine's red headlights, and realize no one is flying the beast.

As the Wraith Lord and the Grand Protector battle for their lives, it is not clear who will win. The Wraith Lord slams Uncle Denesius's sword to the ground, making him groan at the force of the blow. The Wraith Lord lifts his sword high, intent on handing out the deadly blow. But he makes a fatal mistake. The helicopter blade catches the tip of the weapon, sending the fearsome sword spinning through the air and over the edge of the chasm.

Uncle Denesius sees his opportunity. He delivers a fierce kick to the Wraith Lord's stomach, causing him to fly backward. He rolls over and is up again, yet a second too late. Uncle Denesius kicks him again, and the Wraith Lord teeters at the edge of the ravine. I catch my breath, then watch the monster topple over the side into the deep moat below.

My jaw drops. Uncle Denesius has defeated the Wraith Lord—again!

The Grand Protector tightens his grip on his greatsword, waiting, but the Wraith Lord does not reappear. His Seeker cape billows in the dust lifted by the helicopter's blades. Then, he turns and heads my way, back into the Ground Station.

My heart skips a beat. I heave Draxis's arm with both hands, almost releasing my foot, but the giant is too heavy. Uncle Denesius is entering the Station and stops by the hole in the wall.

I lift Draxis's arm again, but this time, I wiggle my foot from within my boot out of desperation. My foot slips out, and I am free. I flip up and stumble backward, rolling down a heap of rubble, making a racket.

"Termite," Uncle Denesius says. "Come out now. You have seen it. Not even the spirit of Lord Erawan can defeat me. And if he cannot defeat me, what chance do you think you have? Come out. It is time for us to end this."

Why does he hate me so?

Was the Uncle Denesius that I loved a mask he always wore to hide the demon that lived within him? Where is the man I admired? I glance around, breathing hard, looking for an escape. The only way out is through Uncle Denesius. Something shines to my left, and I crawl towards it. I reach for the gleaming thing and discover my curved sword. Now at least I have something to defend myself with, though it feels small and meaningless after the battle I have just witnessed.

I freeze when Uncle Denesius makes it up the pile of rubble to Draxis's body. He snorts. "Come now, Termite. You are leaving a trail of blood that even a blind man could follow."

"Stop!" I yell in dread. "Just, stop it! What do you want with me? What did I ever do to you? Why did you give me your Talisman? Why didn't you bring it here yourself?"

"Why?" he says. "I planted a seed in you, Termite. I

raised you to be the boy who dreamed of pulling humanity from darkness."

The demon is making his way down the pile of rubble, and I squat backward into a nook.

"I sent you on a painful quest of self-discovery. You followed your noble heart and let your irritating optimism guide you here. You came to Roarim City, thinking you could save Mankind from the misery it brought upon itself. But Mankind is not deserving of Knowledge, Termite. I hope you realize that by now."

"You are wrong!" I retort. I know I should not say anything. My voice keeps attracting him to my hiding spot. But I cannot help it. "There are those who are worthy, but you ruined it all. The Knowledge is gone, the Ground Station is gone." I pause, then add, "MASA is gone. It is over, Uncle!"

He hops further down the pile of rubble, and I slip through two overturned desks, trying to hide in the shadows. The wound in my side screams at me.

"Uncle..." Uncle Denesius repeats after me. "To think you should have called me *father*. Because I *should* have been your father, Termite. But life decided otherwise. I should have ended your miserable life years ago, but I could not get myself to do it. You see, Termite," his voice softens, "I grew to love the part of you that looks like your mother..." He pauses. "You have her face..." He kicks aside one of the desks, but I am already sheltering behind a section of the shattered metal stairs. "And I hate you because you look so much like *him*!"

I stiffen, a paralyzing feeling gripping my stomach.

Uncle Denesius moves forward, and I have a chance to slip by him. Unfortunately, my body will not obey my mind and, instead, I find myself numbed into inaction.

"I promised her the world," he says. "I was charming. I was kind. I restored the Ground Station for her. But she would not listen. The witch chose *him* over me. They were wed, she became Lady, and, together, they conspired to send me away. They filled their words with honey. They covered me in praise and gave me the noble task of running the Atheneum in their name. But I knew that, deep down, they hated me. They wanted me far away from them. So I obeyed, but I took with me the one thing they loved more than they loved each other."

A gaping black hole opens up beneath me. I stumble and fall.

Uncle Denesius rounds the metal stairs. "I took you—their only child. I threatened to kill you should he try to come after you. And try, he did. Over and over, year after year. He attacked Eliadys; he sent his armies against the fortified wall. The fool! He never accepted my strength, my superiority. He would not give up!" He pauses. "Until I finally killed him."

Dread crushes me to the ground. I try to stand, but the floor is spinning under me.

I am thrust back in time to that day in the Library. Uncle Denesius, looming over the fallen Lord. Lord Erawan, dropping his arm to his side as if pointing at me. And his grey eyes, staring at me through the helmet. Grey eyes, like mine.

Uncle Denesius's footsteps stop beside me. "That is right, Termite," he says, his voice low, and I wish with all my heart that he would not say the next words. "Lord Erawan was your father."

I clench my fist, letting shards of dirt dig into my skin.

"You were my Trojan Horse, Termite," the monster says softly. "What better way to obtain revenge against the Roarim Lady than to send her own son to destroy her home? Had she only been here to see this!"

The fake efforts to make me like him: teaching me the ways of the Seekers, teaching me to read and write, showing me the satellites, coaxing me to love the Atheneum and defend it, making me believe in the Ground Station... Deceit! All of it! Even my name: Termite... All of them, twisted jokes at my expense.

And now I know why he hates women!

"It is not your fault that she did not love me, Termite," the demon murmurs, placing the tip of his greatsword on my neck as I hunker in a ball, shaking. "But it is your fault that I was not able to fulfill my revenge on your city."

My hand closes on my sword, lying beneath me.

"Get up," he says.

It is all I need. I roll to face him and smash my sword into his. He staggers back, eyes widening. I only have seconds to act. I jump to my feet, swing around and the tip of my sword slices through his thigh. He cries out, his greatsword jerking upwards clumsily. I knock it aside with my own blade but my head is spinning and I have to fall back. I have lost a lot of blood and each lunge makes me weaker. Uncle Denesius's words have triggered an inner earthquake that I cannot control.

Uncle Denesius eyes me with disdain. Now he knows I have been trained against his will. Unfortunately, all I have achieved thus far, is to make him angrier.

He bares his teeth, gathers momentum and swings his greatsword at me.

I am not ready. I leap back just in time, barely deflecting his blow, but the force of it splits my curved sword in two.

He leaps forward and slaps the useless pommel out of my hand, then grabs me by the shirt and places his blade under my neck.

I think this is the end of me. I shut my eyes.

But nothing happens.

I open them again.

The demon's grasp loosens slightly. "Look at me, hesitating to finish you off, yet again." He pauses as if thinking. "I wonder..." he begins, studying me. "I wonder.... That condition of yours, that ability to remember everything. Did you read the program? Do you remember it, line-by-line? Is it all there, in your head?" He nods to himself. "It is, isn't it? You will give it to me—the program, the Books, the Knowledge. All of it, so you may repay me for what I have lost. I will build a Ground Station, piece by piece, and gather an army so I can strike at the Roarim again. Come to think of it; it seems the pirates are in need of a new overlord..." he trails off, then nods. "It seems I may have use of you yet."

He lowers his greatsword, turns me around and pushes me out of the Station. The blades of the dragon-helicopter are still spinning, causing my hair to thrust in all directions. The dust glows from the blood-red headlights.

"Look at that, Termite!" the demon murmurs in wonder. "Wouldn't you love to disassemble that engine and figure out how it works, like we would in the good old days?" He shoves me inside the cockpit of the dragon-helicopter and shuts the door. I slump over, drained and shocked, but just conscious enough to know I have to get out of here. I glance down the hill and, in the moonlight, notice fresh Roarim troops making their way up the city streets. I remain still to make him think I have passed out.

The demon slides into the pilot's seat. "This can't be too difficult, can it?" He pulls a lever, and the helicopter lurches up.

I fumble around, my fingers latching on to a handle. I pull, and the door swings open. He yanks me back in and the wind slams the door shut again. We wrestle, and I bite his wrist. He cries out. I kick the lever, and the helicopter swerves dangerously to the right. The door swings open again, and I tumble out of the craft, landing hard on the ground.

The helicopter flies the other way and before the demon can right it, it dips over the chasm.

I pick myself up and look toward the ravine, my heart beating fast. I can still hear it, the muffled sound, like a giant hornet. Then the helicopter surfaces over the edge, its red dragon-eyes glowing at me through the dust, and hovers right before me.

Frantic, I look around and find Draxis's hammer a few paces to the right. In seconds, I pick it up. It is the heaviest thing I have ever carried in my life, yet adrenaline from my rage gives me superhuman strength, and I fling it, straight at the helicopter. I feel my wound tearing, but the hammer crashes into the window, making the aircraft dip to the side.

"THAT is for Draxis," I sob.

The blades catch the edge of the cliff, propelling dirt and pebbles in all directions. I hurl myself to the ground, covering my eyes, but not before seeing the terror in the demon's eyes as the craft falls to its end.

It is hard to breathe. I crawl on my stomach and glance over the edge just as the helicopter crashes into a ball of fire next to the dark, churning waters of the moat. But it is not Uncle Denesius's demise that catches my attention.

It is the Wraith Lord.

The Wraith Lord clings to the cliff wall, climbing up, one inch at a time. He sees me and stops. I stare in fascination and dread at the slits in his helmet, where I cannot see his eyes.

He pauses, then removes his metal gloves, followed by his helmet. Long, blonde hair is released from the protective armor and waves in the wind. The helmet tumbles into the void. A woman stares at me, the moonlight catching her piercing blue eyes. The impressive armor is loose about her, even though she looks tall.

Her face is smooth, and her cheekbones are firm, yet the soft lines on her forehead and the creases in the corner of her eyes tell me she must be in her early forties. Her face is pale as she struggles to reach the top. She looks at me and thrusts her hand in my direction.

Even though she is the Wraith Lord, I am mesmerized and baffled at the same time. I reach out my hand. At this point, nothing makes sense anymore, and I do not think I have much longer to live, anyway. Pulling her up the final part of the cliff drains the last of my energy, and I flop onto my back, staring up at the settling dust. Blood flows from my side through the fingers that press against the wound. The periphery of my sight becomes dark.

The Wraith Lord—or should I say Lady—hunches over, gasping, then crawls to my side. Her lip is split, and an ugly lump is forming on her forehead. Her long hair flows down her back, and her eyes are deep pools of grief.

My body trembles, and there is only pain, inside and out, but I still see her.

She places a hand on my cheek. "Eodain!" she says, her voice floating into my brain from far away. "My son!"

CHAPTER 33 *Home Again*

The Wraith Lord stands before me in the darkness. I can see the outline of his armor, and I know he is looking at me. I want to flee, but I cannot seem to find my feet.

The Wraith Lord reaches up and takes off his helmet. I squirm because I do not want to see the head of a rotting corpse. But instead, it is something much, much worse. It is Uncle Denesius who is inside the armor. I gape at him. Uncle Denesius! He cannot be the Wraith Lord! I moan and wish to get away from this suffocating nightmare.

Uncle Denesius smiles a dark smile and lifts his deadly sword. I do not register it falling, but he must have hit me because my side bursts in pain, and I scream.

Water splashes on my face. A soft hand holds mine. It is enough to send me from one twisted dream to the next.

Clear white light shines through thin drapes,

blowing gently in the breeze. Birds chirp, and wind chimes clatter softly by the window. The drapes part, and grey eyes look down at me, creasing in laughter-lines at the corners. "Eodain," the man whispers, smiling. He bends down, and his thick beard tickles my cheek. I giggle. He places a kiss on my temple. "You are free at last," he says.

I want him to stay, but he is already backing away.

"Sleep, now, my little one," he smiles as the drapes fall into place again.

"Wait!" I cry.

"Eodain!"

I struggle, and a strong hand clasps my own. "Eodain!" the voice says firmly, and my eyes flutter open. A man with a beard is sitting beside me, but this man's beard is blonde.

"Pedregal?" I frown.

Pedregal nods. His eyes are moist.

"Pedregal!" I gasp. Everything comes back to me at once. "Draxis..." I break off.

"I know," he says.

"And Uncle Denesius, he..."

He nods. "I know, lad." He taps my hand. "I am sorry."

"Thoron?"

"He will not be bothering you anymore." He sniffles.

I stare at him, then look around, feeling lost. The room I am in is comfortable, and the bed is soft and clean. There is an open door leading outside and a window to my right. There are white drapes on these windows, too.

"Where are we?" I ask.

"Ah," Pedregal begins, taking in a deep breath. "We are in Roarim City. This is the home of the former Lord

Erawan and his lovely Lady Isobel." He pauses to clear his throat, then adds, "It is also *your* home."

"Eodain!"

I glance towards the door at someone standing there.

A girl rushes to my side, kneels, and takes my hand in both of hers.

I stare into Elysa's wonderful hazel eyes.

"I am so sorry," she says, holding back tears. "I never wanted to see you get hurt!"

Pedregal lets go of my hand and coughs, "I had better inform the Lady."

The Lady... Something tugs at my brain, but all I can think of is Elysa. I stare at her and say, "Sometimes you have to do something bad for the greater good..."

She blushes. "Yes, Eodain. For the greater good of *you.* I had hoped you would understand. I wanted to help you! I knew your companions were up to something; I just could not figure out what it was. And I knew the Lady would have approved of your mission, but I did not know how to get you to her. You were in such denial, and rightly so. There was no way you could have known the Lady was the Wraith Lord."

"And you did not tell me, because...?" I ask, thrilled yet cautious at seeing her again.

She shakes her head. "You do not know the Roarim, Eodain. We have the greatest respect for our Lady. We all knew who was hiding beneath that armor. We all knew she was our best weapon against the Grand Protector and his army. We are loyal to her to the death. I could not tell anyone, not even you." She looks down. "That said, things would have been different had I known who you were," she breaks off.

"Who, I am?" I repeat, feeling the chasm opening up beneath me again.

"The Roarim all know the story of the Lady's stolen child," she continues. "It repulsed us. How could a man be so cruel as to take away someone's baby? If he could do such a terrible deed, then what else was he capable of? When he built a wall to keep the Knowledge away from us, we knew we needed to defeat him before he could become an all-powerful tyrant. Men signed up to follow Lord Erawan into battle for years..." she swallows, "...until we lost him, too."

Lord Erawan, lying in the middle of the Library, reaching out for me; and Uncle Denesius, raising his sword...

The inner agony is so intense I roll towards her, groaning.

Uncle Denesius killed my father!

The fiery pit opens below me, threatening to consume me, and I grasp her hand in my panic.

Elysa places her other hand on my cheek and keeps her forehead against mine. She stays close as waves of anguish tear me apart from the inside.

Vivid memories clash into my mind: Uncle Denesius, playing hide-and-seek with me in the Library; Uncle Denesius, slapping my cheek at the West Tower; Uncle Denesius, talking excitedly about a piece of hardware we put together; Uncle Denesius, smirking when he gives me my nickname...

Termite.

I moan and clutch harder. Elysa holds on to me.

Uncle Denesius... I loathe him, and I love him, but where does that leave me? I cannot find myself in these clashing emotions.

"He ruined everything!" I choke.

"No!" Elysa says. "Not everything! We would not have met otherwise. Do not let him take everything away from you. I am still here. I am not going anywhere. I love you, Eodain. And your mother loves you, too. The people of Roarim have been waiting for you for sixteen years."

My mother! I let Elysa go and sink further into the bed. I blink at the ceiling. *My mother!* The word sounds foreign in my ears.

As if in answer, a shadow passes before the doorway. A woman with long, blonde hair and a long purple dress stands there looking at me. She is like a specter from my childhood when I would lie for hours in the dark of the Atheneum dormitory, imagining what it would be like to have a mother.

The woman wavers at the doorway as if she were too afraid to enter. She raises her hand to her heart, then turns and flees.

I open my mouth, but she is already gone.

Pedregal stands outside, shrugging at me.

"Eodain," Elysa says. "Your mother has been by your side for entire nights, watching over you. But I think, to see you awake like this, is too much for her. She has hoped for this moment for so long that it must come as a shock for her. You must understand."

I draw away the bedsheets, then realize I am half-naked. Elysa blushes scarlet and turns her head. I pull the bedsheets back in a hurry. "My clothes!" I blurt out. "I need my clothes!"

Elysa places a hand to her mouth to stifle a giggle. "All right, all right. Hold on a minute." She hurries to a cupboard and pulls out a shirt and trousers as well as socks and boots. Then she turns her back to me so I can dress quickly. "Eodain, maybe you should wait. You are far from having recovered."

"I have waited for sixteen years," I say, buttoning up my trousers. Then, I pull Elysa towards me and kiss her forehead. "Don't go anywhere!" I whisper.

Her smile reaches all the way to her eyes.

I head out, barefoot and struggling to put on my shirt. I come to a halt at the end of the open corridor. Before me stretches the ocean, shimmering in the sunlight, and to my right lies Roarim City. I am standing on one of the three decks that hug the side of the hill where the Ground Station stood. Leaning over, I see the Lady heading to a ledge further down. I take these same stairs, panting a little as the wound in my side strains under the bandage. I make it down and approach my mother, who has stopped in front of a stretch of trimmed grass and a cascade of giant orchids overlooking the ocean.

She stands with her back to me, motionless, and I catch my breath as I spot a grave... the grave of a lord.

I come up beside her, and we take in the moment, together.

"He never stopped trying, Eodain," she says. "He tried to get you away from that demon. It tore him apart to know that you were right there, beyond the fortified wall of Eliadys and that he could not get to you. Only once did he manage to send a rescue team into Eliadys to try and get you out. You must have been eight at the time. We never heard of our soldiers again. Your father was left with no choice but to continue putting together entire armies and lead them to attack Eliadys. Two years later, he managed to breach the wall and make his way up to the Atheneum..." She breaks off.

It takes a while before she continues. "When Denesius sent Erawan's broken body back to me, I fell into despair. I stopped living and, for years, I was a shadow of myself. But something prevented me from letting go." She points to the left of the grave. There is another tiny grave there, though it looks way too small to contain a human—let alone an animal. I lean in to take a closer look.

"Your finger," she says, and I leap back, shocked.

"Yes," she confirms. "Your finger. Denesius sent it to me as a warning. I was not to approach Eliadys or to try and save you. But it gave me hope because I knew you were still alive, and I could not stand knowing that you were living with that monster. I grew obsessed with finding a way to get you out, and that is how it hit me: I needed to strike Denesius with strength and fear. I needed to become the Wraith Lord."

I stare in awe at my mother.

"I trained for three years. I had the armor made from titanium-erzats so that it was light and manageable for me, yet also strong as steel. Around that time, our engineers patched together a functional helicopter. I thought of the dragon tales my mother would tell me when I was a child, and that is how it all came together. I would be a wraith, riding a dragon, come back to avenge my death.

"When my army invaded the Atheneum a short month ago, I had everyone checked. My men looked for the boy with a four-fingered hand, but he was not found. No one knew what Denesius had done with you."

He sent me away!

"I knew he was a monster," the Lady continues, "but I never thought he would take his wrath this far. When he destroyed the Atheneum, I feared I had lost you forever. But then rumors spread of a Knowledge Seeker—the last to remain. He was seen at the West Tower. Then, later, my spies reported he was being held captive at the pirate stronghold. I needed to get to this Seeker to find out what had happened to the Atheneum, to Denesius, and you. And that is when I found you at the hands of John McNeil, in the middle of a tumult of wagons and pirates. You lifted your hand, and I saw..."

"...my missing finger!" I exclaim.

She nods. "Yes. I could not believe it. Could the last Knowledge Seeker be my son? Was it really you? But fate took you away from me again. I flew over the mountains for days, fearing the worst because I knew an arrow had wounded you. It is only when I returned home and met Elysa Dundurn that I found out you were in Roarim City."

I stare at her, trying to take all of this in. What a cruel twist of fate! I look away because the weight of so many years of despair emanating from her is difficult to witness. I do not know this person, but I want to. Right now, we are barely coming to terms with each other's existence. There will be time for hugs and tears later.

She sets her eyes on me for the first time, as if finally daring to accept that I am here in the flesh. "Look at you. You are almost a grown man," she says softly. "The demon opened a chasm between us that can never be filled. One that is as deep as the chasm that took his life. Never will we have a chance to recover those lost years and share the moments unique to a mother and a child: the uttering of the first word, the growth of the first tooth, the healing of scraped knees, and the soothing of tears. He took that from us—all of it!"

I close my eyes and feel the ground sway beneath me. The dark pit is there, waiting. "You are right," I say, fighting to remain strong for her and to find a way forward through this mess. "We will never get those years back. They are lost in an endless abyss." I reach out my hand, and my fingers touch hers. "But we can build a bridge over it. It will be frail at first, but we can make it stronger with time until we forget that there is emptiness beneath it. There is a saying in the ancient Books—that time heals all wounds."

Her blue eyes well up with tears. Her hand closes around mine, and she murmurs, "Then may that time be swift."

EPILOGUE

I glance up at the starry night as Elysa and I sit on a bench on the highest deck of the palace. The Moon reflects on the ocean. A dot high above makes its way across the sky.

"Isn't it pretty?" Elysa says.

I wrap my arm around her without answering, and she leans her head into the cradle of my neck. I do not look at satellites the same way anymore. Some Sky Spirits are good, others are evil, and I have no way of telling them apart.

I have not told Elysa about the MASA satellites. In fact, I have not told anyone about them. I have been meaning to, but I always pull back; what point is there in making everyone aware of a deadly threat when there is nothing we can do about it? It would be unnecessarily cruel. But I know that the MASA satellites will fall back to Earth one day and whether they land or crash will determine our fate. The Enlightened People, who I had admired so much, have left us a deadly legacy.

For now, peace reigns over Roarim City. Things are going well. I have gotten to know my mother, attended city meetings, and understand how things are run here. People seem to appreciate my take on things, even though I am young, by their standards. Elysa is continuing her healer studies, and we are closer than ever, which is a problem considering that I am leaving.

A shadow detaches itself from the end of the deck.

"Oh," Elysa says, disappointed. "Is it time already?"

It is one of Elysa's older brothers. Though she lost one brother, she has four other living siblings. Ever since her return to Roarim City, her parents have had a hard time letting her out of their sight. One of her brothers is sent as a chaperone every time we meet.

This brother sends us a quick gesture of greeting. It is clear he does not want to be here. I watch as he leans into the wall, making himself barely visible while he waits.

Elysa sighs. "If I could stay longer, I bet I could pull you away from your Books for a while."

I smile and squeeze her shoulder. "You know you can pull me away from my Books anytime." I catch myself and immediately feel badly for saying that. It is cruel of me to make her believe we are fine when soon I will be gone.

She does not seem to catch on because her voice is low when she says, "Eodain, did you hear the rumors?"

My smile fades.

She does not wait for me to answer. "They want to make you Lord of Roarim City. I have heard the townsfolk talk about it. You will be eighteen soon. They think it is a good age for you and that you are ready."

I wish she had not gone there. "I know," I say. "My mother has mentioned it."

She straightens in surprise. "She has already asked you to become Lord of Roarim?"

I shake my head. "No. Not directly. But she has mentioned the idea of abdicating in my favor, and I can tell she is hoping I will say, 'Yes'."

Elysa's eyes fill with tears. One rolls down her cheek. That is when I know she is on to me.

I wipe the tear away.

"I did not know things were this far along," she says. "I know you. You will say, 'No.' You have other things on your mind, things you will not tell anyone, not even me."

My stomach squeezes. *Am I that obvious?*

"...and when you say, 'No,'" she continues, "...it will be impossible for you to stay." She sits there and glares at me. "When were you going to tell me?"

I drop my hand from her shoulder. There it is, that inner conflict that will nag me for the rest of my life.

On the one hand, I would stay in Roarim City and marry Elysa if I could. For Spirit's sake, I would even consider becoming Lord one day, when I felt ready. *I could reinstate democracy*, I think to myself.

On the other hand, fifty MASA satellites are circling above our heads, carrying their deadly cargo. I need to find a way to deactivate them. I need to find a new Ground Station, and I have a hunch that the Newarkers could help me.

Uncle Denesius's program scrolls over and over in my head, never letting me rest. I have thought about it countless times. If I put my mind to it, I could come to understand the code. I could change it so it would shut down the MASA satellites. It would just take a very long time.

You are your very own Talisman, Uncle Denesius told me once. He said it was a blessing. I think it is a curse because it is never about me or what I want.

"Eodain?" Elysa calls, pulling me out of my thoughts.

"I don't want you to wait for me," I whisper. There is no point in denying the obvious.

She glares at me. "You cannot tell me what to do."

We look at each other.

She leans forward and kisses me on the lips. "Whatever it is you have to do," she whispers, "do it, then come back to me." She releases me, stands, then sprints away. When she reaches her brother, she turns and shouts, "I will wait!"

I sit there, feeling numb, watching her disappear from my life.

Gathering courage, I stand and head to the small, makeshift library that I set up. It is filled with stacks of paper and half-finished Books that I have pulled from my memory. I glance around, feeling slightly panicked that I will never finish the task of writing down all the Knowledge that I carry in my head. The amount that remains to be written would last me a lifetime. I hope these Books will still be here when I return.

If I return.

I pick up a Book called *Medical Encyclopedia, Tome III*, and place it visibly on the table so it will be found after I have left. I wrote it for Elysa. Perhaps, if I am lucky, I will find *Tomes I and II* along my journeys.

I place the letter I have written to my mother beside Elysa's Book, then I pull out my Seeker cape. I have not worn it in eighteen months, yet it still feels familiar on my shoulders, like a warm blanket I had misplaced. I know then, for certain. I am a Knowledge Seeker. And Knowledge is out there, waiting to be found—even though the truth it brings with it may hurt sometimes.

I pick up my satchel and my new greatsword, close the door and make my way out of the palace, but I am distracted by a light in my mother's apartment. She and Pedregal have found solace in each other's arms. They have a baby boy, my half-brother. Many happy years lie ahead of them.

But it is not the light that catches my attention. It is the lullaby, I hear. I close my eyes for a moment, then let my mother's voice accompany me as I walk away:

> *"Twinkle, twinkle little star,*
> *How I wonder what you are.*
> *Up above the world so high,*
> *Like a diamond in the sky.*
> *Twinkle, twinkle little star,*
> *How I wonder what you are.*

LEAVE A REVIEW:
If you enjoyed this book, please leave a review in the 'Write a customer review' section:
https://www.amazon.com/dp/1989605311

The Alien Skill Series

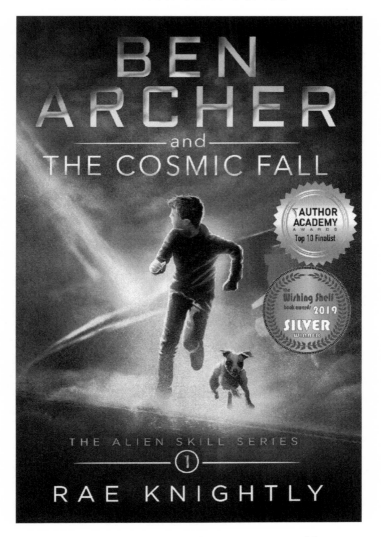

Turn the page and start reading…

CHAPTER 1 *Missing*

Ben Archer knew that something bad had happened to him on the night of *The Cosmic Fall*. He knew this because, precisely one month after the event, he was still waking up every morning from the same nightmare. He would sit up straight on his bed, a scream stuck at the back of his throat. It was always the same. One minute he would be reliving that fateful night behind his closed eyelids, the next he would be wide awake, sweat pearling his forehead, his mind grasping for the fading images.

Wednesday morning, September 27th, was no different. The alarm clock yanked the boy out of his turbulent slumber, sending the dark threads of his nightmare scattering to the back of his mind where he could no longer reach them.

A Jack Russell Terrier jumped onto Ben's bed to check on his master.

"'Morning, Tike," Ben mumbled, patting his faithful dog before sinking back into the bed. Gathering his thoughts, he searched his mind for the smallest hint of a memory. But it was too late; whatever he had been dreaming about was already lost to his conscious mind.

The family doctor had explained that it was normal to experience temporary amnesia after having been bedridden for almost three weeks. High fever could distort one's memory and provoke terrible nightmares. Seven days ago, when the doctor declared Ben healthy again, he recommended the boy take it slow but try to get back to his normal life as soon as possible.

Whatever normal means...

Tike wagged his tail, then nudged Ben in the neck with his wet nose.

"Okay, okay, I'm up already!" Ben grumbled.

He dragged himself out of bed, and pulled on the jeans and t-shirt that lay in a heap on the floor of his messy room. He headed for the bathroom where he checked his reflection in the mirror. His cheeks hadn't fully recovered their colour, and there were dark pockets under his brown eyes. His auburn hair stuck out all over the place, as though someone had tried to vacuum it during the night. He gave his head a quick brush but had to abandon a mesh of hair that poked out from the back of his head.

Tike waited impatiently by the front door.

Ben opened it. "Hurry up, Tike. I gotta go in fifteen minutes."

The white-and-brown dog scurried down the stairs of the apartment block, then headed to the yard to do his morning business.

In the meantime, Ben filled Tike's bowls with crackers and fresh water. He poured out his cereal and milk before sinking into the couch to gulp down his breakfast in front of the TV. He flipped through the channels as he munched on the crispy cereal. 8:00 a.m. meant the morning news came on.

"...tensions between China and the US have once again escalated due to the event social media has dubbed *The Cosmic Fall*," a news anchor with a serious air reported on Channel 2. "A source from the US Defense Ministry has claimed off-the-record that the American satellite which was destroyed in space four weeks ago, was in fact, designed to spy on Chinese territory. The head of the FBI has denied these allegations and continues to accuse China of destroying its communications satellite. On a more reconciliatory note, the President of the United States has once again urged the Canadian government to grant access to the crash site to both Chinese and US investigators to help them determine the exact cause of..."

Ben switched channels.

A morning talk show came on, showing a cheerful man who held up a palm-sized rock. "...it is so compact it weighs six pounds! But wait until you hear its price tag! One pound of this meteor debris is worth over a million dollars!"

The show host squealed while the audience

watching the live show gasped.

"I can picture folks frantically overturning their yards to find meteor nuggets!" the show host laughed.

Ben pressed the control again.

This time an old black-and-white image of hills covered in torn-up pine trees appeared on the screen while a soothing voice explained in the background, "Thousands of hectares of trees were crushed to the ground like toothpicks by the shockwave of the exploding meteorite in Siberia in the 1970's..."

Ben turned off the TV in a hurry. His hand shook over the control.

I should know by now not to watch the news!

He jumped when he heard a scratching on the door, his cereal spilling over the edge of the bowl.

"Darn!" he muttered.

He opened the door to let Tike in, leaving a trail of milk all the way from the living room to the kitchen. Having lost his appetite, Ben placed the half-eaten bowl of cereal in the kitchen sink. He tore off a paper towel, then roughly soaked up the milk drops on the carpet. Tike watched him curiously with his head cocked.

"Think it's funny, huh?" Ben uttered, as he scrubbed the floor.

Not a sound left the dog's throat. Ben observed the terrier sitting patiently in front of him.

How come you never bark anymore?

Ben picked himself up from the ground and threw the paper towel away. He put on his jacket, then flung a water bottle, banana, energy bar, and a wrapped-up ham sandwich loosely into his backpack before heaving it onto his right shoulder. While struggling to zip his jacket, he headed down the hall to his mother's room, his backpack scraping against the wall. The door stood ajar so he peeked inside.

Tike joined him and peered through the crack below him.

Laura Archer lay on her bed, fast asleep. She had recently begun working night shifts at restaurants and bars after losing her day job. Her former boss had not appreciated her spending week after week watching over her ailing son.

Ben hesitated to leave his sleeping mother, half hoping she would open her eyes. He wanted to tell her he'd had another nightmare. But when she didn't stir, he whispered, "Bye, Mom," before tiptoeing away.

He put on his runners. "I'm outta here, Tike. I'll see you in a bit." His eyes fell on his dog. Tike gave him a forlorn look that dug deep into the boy's heart.

Ben bit his lip. "Oh, come on, Tike! Don't do this to me again! I have to go to school. You know that!" He knelt to hug his four-legged friend. As he rubbed Tike's back, he felt the warmth of the fur and the beating heart inside the dog's chest.

We share the same fear.

Ben stood hastily, bothered by that thought.

Out loud, he said, "Take care of Mom, okay?" He quickly closed the door to avoid glimpsing Tike's eyes again.

* * *

At the doctor's recommendation, the twelve-year-old had reluctantly gone back to school, which was a drag because he had missed the first two introductory weeks of September. One of Ben's closest pals had been placed in another classroom where he had already made firm friends with a new boy. Ben's other classmates had formed tight-knit groups; they had prepared their first homework assignments and knew which teacher taught what. Ben felt like an outsider disrupting a well-established order.

It didn't help that he spent the first week in a daze. He had a hard time concentrating on the lessons and felt exhausted by the time he got home. His mother told him to be patient, his body had experienced a great shock and was still pulling itself together. Young people recover quickly, she would say. You will be fine in no time.

I don't think so...

As he let himself out of the three-story building, Ben took out a plastic bag to pick up his dog's poop before the downstairs neighbour could complain. He threw the waste in a public garbage can, then jogged down the street towards school.

Not so long ago, he would have run down the three blocks of houses without a second thought. Yet although four weeks had passed since Ben fell ill, he ran out of breath as soon as he reached the first pedestrian crossing. He slowed to a fast pace as he hugged the walls of the houses, hunching over to fend off a sprinkling rain, and made it in time for the school bell. He weaved his way through the groups of students, intent on reaching the main door so he could get away from the outdoors and the crowds.

Something ripped. The weight of his backpack fell away from his shoulder. Catching his breath, he glanced down to find the strap had torn off. In his haste that morning, he had neglected to zip the backpack all the way. Its contents spilled onto the ground, his pens rolling over the playground, his notebook falling into a patch of mud, and his water bottle emptying itself on a library book.

Students burst into laughter around him while others pushed past in their haste to get inside. No one offered to help. Ben was left to fend for himself as he painstakingly recovered the pieces strewn around him. By the time he was done, the last couple of giggling students ran by, their shoes thumping on the asphalt.

Ben lifted his backpack with both arms to avoid any further embarrassing fabric tears. But as soon as he stood, he became fully aware of the empty playground and the immense sky above. He was alone, at the complete mercy of the emptiness, unprotected and vulnerable. His head swam dizzyingly and his vision blurred. Ben clung to his backpack for dear life. His heart raced, and his breath came in gasps as he experienced the burden of a full panic attack. As soon as he shut his eyes, the nightmare erupted without pity: a dark mass falling from the night sky, his Grampa shouting in warning, twisted eyes, the shadow of a man with white hair reflected in the fire, a whisper...

Mesmo.

Tike's snout on his cheek.

"Ben!" someone shouted, shaking him by the shoulders. "Wake up! Ben!"

He opened his eyes. Tike's paws were on his chest, the dog's face close to his own. Above him, his mother called to him anxiously. He blinked and found himself lying in the middle of the playground, surrounded by Tike, Laura, and a couple of teachers.

A school assistant ran up to them, a cellphone in her hand. "I'm calling an ambulance," she announced, holding the phone to her ear.

"No!" Laura objected. "Please don't! I'll take Ben to our family doctor. He's familiar with Ben's condition."

The assistant hesitated, then put the phone away.

"Are you okay?" Laura asked Ben, eyebrows knitted.

Ben nodded to reassure her.

She helped him up carefully. "The school called me and said you were standing by yourself in the middle of the playground. I hurried over with Tike. You were completely paralyzed." She accepted Ben's backpack from one of the teachers.

Ben became excruciatingly aware of the adults staring at him strangely. From inside the school, students pressed their noses against the windows, pointing in his direction.

Oh, great! Nice way to blend in...

Continue reading:
Ben Archer and the Cosmic Fall (The Alien Skill Series, Book 1)
https://www.amazon.com/dp/1989605192

PREQUEL:
Read the prequel to The Alien Skill Series,
The Great War of the Kins:
www.raeknightly.com

About the Author

Rae Knightly invites the young reader on a journey into the imagination, where science fiction and fantasy blend into the real world. Young heroes are taken on gripping adventures full of discovery and story twists.

Rae Knightly lives in Vancouver with her husband and two children. The breathtaking landscapes of British Columbia have inspired her to write The Alien Skill Series.

Follow Rae Knightly on social media:
Facebook/Instagram/Twitter/Pinterest
E-mail: raeknightly@gmail.com

Acknowledgments

Special thanks to Peter Vogel, who brought the "science" to the "fiction". The knowledge he has shared on satellites, ground stations and the future of the internet has been eye-opening.
Special thanks to Cristy Watson for helping me elevate the story, as well as Giselle Schneider, John Smiff, Mystee Pulcine, Jane Ballard and Frank Muellersman. To Shlayne Harms for invaluable feedback on photographic memory.

To you, reader, for taking the time to read *The Knowledge Seeker.*

Thank you!
Rae Knightly

Made in the USA
Middletown, DE
09 December 2021

54875392R00208